CHRISTMAS AT FERNDEAN MANOR

JANE EYRE CHRONICLES BOOK THREE

JOANNA CAMPBELL SLAN

Joanna Campbell Slan

Spot On Publishing

9307 SE Olympus Street

Hobe Sound FL 33455 USA

http://www.SpotOnPublishing.org

Covers by Dar Albert, Wicked Smart Designs

http://www.WickedSmartDesigns.com

Christmas at Ferndean Manor: Book #3 in the Jane Eyre Chronicles

Joanna Campbell Slan

Revised May 22, 2021

CONTENTS

PRAISE FOR DEATH OF A SCHOOLGIRL — WINNER DAPHNE DU MAURIER AWARD OF LITERARY EXCELLENCE

A MYSTERY GUILD ALTERNATE SELECTION

"Everyone's favorite character, Jane Eyre, returns in a marvelous new adventure. Joanna Campbell Slan's *Death of a Schoolgirl* is a must for all her many fans as Jane Eyre searches for an elusive killer who has Rochester's young ward in his—or her —sights."

—Charles Todd, *New York Times* bestselling author

"Charming, winning, mannered, and so genuine it seems like a long-lost Brontë original. . . . The Jane Eyre we know and love is revealed as a nifty detective, just as resolute, clever, and independent as her fans always knew she was."

—Hank Phillippi Ryan, Agatha, Anthony and Macavity-award winning author

"*Jane Eyre* was always one of my favorite books and I'm delighted to be able to peek at her life as Mrs. Rochester. I always knew she'd make an excellent sleuth."

—Rhys Bowen, Agatha and Anthony Award-winning author of the Molly Murphy and Royal Spyness mysteries

"A terrific beginning to a new series. In *Death of a Schoolgirl,* author Joanna Campbell Slan has given us a fully fleshed sequel to *Jane Eyre,* as darkly gothic as the original, only this time Jane uses her insatiable curiosity to solve a murder. An intriguing new sleuth!"

—Jeri Westerson, author of the Crispin Guest Medieval Noir series

"A wonderful book. It's the best sort of historical mystery— richly detailed, cleverly plotted, and filled with characters you'll not want to leave behind."

—Stefanie Pintoff, Edgar® Award-winning author

"This tasty blend of well-drawn characters and unexpected plot twists has all the rich flavor of England in the early 1820s. One nibble and you won't be able to stop until the very last morsel is nothing but a memory. Thank goodness there are more Jane Eyre Chronicles to come!"

—Kathy Lynn Emerson, author of *How to Write Killer Historical Mysteries. The Art and Adventure of Sleuthing through the Past*

"A delightful chance for Brontë fans to expand their acquaintance with Jane Eyre, who continues her modest but strong-willed ways in an ingeniously contrived return to teaching . . . and sleuthing."

—Charlaine Harris, #1 *New York Times* bestselling author

"Layered with compound mysteries that unfold in a manner true to Brontë's style . .

. A faithful and ultimately satisfying continuation of an English classic."

—*Ellery Queen Mystery Magazine*

"Captures the essences of Jane and Rochester . . . The mystery is entertaining fun, but it is what happened to Jane and Rochester since the classic ended that subgenre fans will enjoy."

—*The Mystery Gazette*

"Slan has woven in some nice bits of real history and knitted her new story almost seamlessly onto the end of the Brontë novel. If you have read the original, your enjoyment will be enhanced, but if you haven't you will still enjoy this involving tale."

—*New Mystery Reader*

"Slan has produced the perfect sequel to Charlotte Brontë's classic . . . It flows effortlessly, as if Brontë herself were doing the writing, and it rings absolutely true. . . . It is a joy for lovers of the original novel, as well as those who savor a good mystery.

—*Mystery Scene*

"A beautifully written story . . . Slan has marked *Death of a Schoolgirl* with her own indelible brand of suspense and intrigue while adhering to the cadence and restrained emotional atmosphere of the original Brontë novel. Anyone who has ever read and loved *Jane Eyre* will be captivated."

—*Criminal Element*

"A nicely constructed plot . . . An interesting mystery in period style."

—*San Francisco Book Review*

"Refashions a beloved heroine as a surprisingly canny detective.

—*Kirkus Reviews*

"A very entertaining, believable extension of *Jane Eyre* . . . [Slan] has done an impressive job using rich historical details to transport readers back in time."

—*RT Book Reviews*

"A promising competitor in the popular field of historical mysteries.

—*Florida Weekly*

"A charming read . . . Smart, sexy, and delightfully fun . . . A well-plotted little mystery, one fans of the genre (and also those of the Victorian novel) are certain to enjoy."

—*Life in Naples,* WGCU

"Who would have thought Jane Eyre was such an excellent detective? . . . A great new series in the making and an incredibly fresh story."

—*Killer Nashville*

"It's like Jane Eyre walked directly off the pages of Brontë's *Jane Eyre* and into this book. The transition was flawless."

—*Girl Lost in a Book*

"Jane Eyre is back! . . . Slan faithfully re-creates the Gothic world of *Jane Eyre* with every bit of the dramatic, intense emotions which made the first story popular . . . If you're a fan of Gothic and *Jane Eyre, Death of a Schoolgirl* will not disappoint."

—*Fresh Fiction*

"[A] wonderful mystery. Slan beautifully captures the characters and the atmosphere, the tone of *Jane Eyre* . . . A compelling, fascinating mystery."

—*Lesa's Book Critiques*

"[An] enjoyable continuation of the *Jane Eyre* story."

—*Stop, You're Killing Me!*

"An extraordinary read! . . . A great way to introduce a new generation to Jane Eyre."

—*Escape with Dollycas into a Good Book*

"Would that all sagas which left readers wanting more could be continued as skillfully!"

—Molly Weston *(Meritorious Mysteries)*, winner of 2012 MWA Raven Award

ACKNOWLEDGMENTS

I want to thank the many wonderful book clubs that have chosen to read *Death of a Schoolgirl,* the first book in the Jane Eyre Chronicles. Your emails to me are a source of great joy and encouragement. I am very pleased that this new series has sent many of you back to read or re-read Charlotte Brontë's classic *Jane Eyre.* It certainly remains my favorite book of all time. For book club questions or more information about my other work, please visit my website at www.JoannaSlan.com.

Last but not least, my sister, Jane Campbell, provided wonderful insight along the way. She's a fantastic plot-buddy who never lets me down. If you are lucky enough to write books for a living, better hope you have a sister as wonderful as Jane.

It is madness in all women to let a secret love kindle within them.

—*Charlotte Brontë, Jane Eyre: An Autobiography*

There is abundant evidence to prove that despite the wrong he did her in after years, she was always in his heart of hearts his "only real and true wife."

—*William Henry Wilkins, Mrs. Fitzherbert and George IV*

CHRISTMAS AT FERNDEAN MANOR

BY JOANNA CAMPBELL SLAN

He settles the childless woman in her home as a happy mother of children. Praise the Lord.— Psalm 113:9

Therefore, whoever takes the lowly position of this child is the greatest in the kingdom of heaven. And whoever welcomes one such child in my name welcomes me.— Matthew 18:2-6

And without faith it is impossible to please God, because anyone who comes to him must believe that he exists and that he rewards those who earnestly seek him. —Hebrews 11:6

CHAPTER 1

There are compensations. Always, there are compensations. Although one might have to look hard to find them, they exist. For example, when my beloved husband, Edward Fairfax Rochester, moved into Ferndean Manor, the walls were damp, the roof leaked, and mice danced their way along the floorboards nightly. The exterior was equally distressing. Iron gates and stone barriers forced visitors to climb down from their conveyances and navigate their way through harsh foliage, by parting the overgrown shrubs and young trees that block the path to our front door. No one felt welcome here at Ferndean. My husband's great-grandfather bought the disreputable hunting lodge as a lark, ignoring the fact the place was haphazardly constructed of materials filled with an intense longing to return to their natural origins.

And yet…

We have come to love this place. With the help of our housekeeper, Mrs. Fairfax, Edward's distant cousin, my husband and I have slowly transformed this ugly castoff into a welcoming home. Under the shelter of this roof, Edward and I were blessed with a son, Ned. A year and six months after his birth, Ned has started to crawl his way around Ferndean. It is his very own playground.

At first, Edward and I made adjustments to the old lodge reluctantly. One crisis after another impinged upon us, forcing us to make necessary improvements. As we did, the Manor gradually gave over its stern objections to our occupancy. Indeed, I cannot say with certitude when the change came to fruition, but I can vouch for the fact the realization came upon me rather suddenly, the sense that Ferndean is our home. My home! How pleasant those words are! The walls I once scorned now seem to enfold me and my little family in a welcoming embrace.

If Ferndean had not been so disheveled, if the

lodge had not suffered from such deleterious neglect, I doubt that we would have ever grown so fond of each other. But I have since observed, and I hold it to be a truism, that whatever we care for, whatever demands our attention forcefully, whatever loudly begs for our notice, ultimately conquers our heart. When we give of ourselves or our time or our coin to another, we must overcome our innate selfishness. We must act with empathy. We are forced to consider the plight of the other. Thus, we burst out of our hardened shells and meld with the object of our notice.

Thus Ferndean, broken down as it once was, has laid claim to our hearts. The unkempt nature of the place assures me that I shall never explore for long, without stumbling over a fresh delight. Each of my walks affords me with a sense of wonder, as new aspects of nature are revealed to me. Thus, I am invited to partake of an endless banquet of glimpses into nature, a world that had been chiefly hidden from my view. And, so, I have come to cherish my long walks.

The changing of the seasons reminds me that life is fleeting, and yet each period is rich with wonder, even if some days are more harsh than others. This October has proved no different. The month dawned mild and temperate, extending to me an invitation to spend hours exploring the wooded surrounds. A path trampled by deer led me to a stand of thistle gone to seed. The contrast, between the green of the spiked leaves and the brown of the sepal caressing the fluffy white head gone to seed, was pleasing to behold. The arrival of a red-throated goldfinch balancing delicately on the green stalk proved irresistible. Pulling my sketch book from its tattered muslin bag and digging for a stub of charcoal, I hurried to capture in my notebook the essence of the scene, thinking it aptly illustrated what poet Alexander Smith called these "thoughtful days." When I felt confident I'd managed a rough rendering, I returned my supplies to the bag. As I did, I noticed the loose stitches along the hem of the drawstring. Needs must, I would see to the repair in the evening.

After the bird flew away, I resumed my stroll. The rustle of a stray oak leaf warned me that a passenger was clinging to the hem of my skirt. Rather than toss the leaf away, I gently removed the pilgrim and held it up for inspection. The deep shades of maroon, crimson, and brown were mixed by the Master's hand, and I admired the divine artistry of the colors. The dying foliage warned me that winter would come all too soon. As much as I relished autumn, the thought of cold weather brought back memories I would rather cast aside.

Rather than discard the leaf, I stuffed it in my tattered bag. I would take this treasure back to the house, create a still life setting, and use it to practice working with watercolors. But a single leaf would be but a paltry remembrance. Surely, I could add other subjects to my tableau. Weak sunlight sketched out shadows wrought by the overhead boughs of two trees, one walnut and one horse chestnut. Their fruit had fallen under foot. I filled my pockets with walnuts and then turned my attention to gathering conkers, those shiny seeds from the horse chestnut tree. The balmy air turned cool, as the sun sank slowly in the sky. Satisfied that my walk had been well-rewarded, I headed for home.

On my way back, I spied a bush of bilberries, that small rough shrub that only grows wild. The globe-shaped berries were not ripe yet, and their dark skin lacked the silver blush indicative of their peak. The bush was partly hidden. If I hoped to visit it again when the berries were ripe, I would need to mark the spot. Thinking quickly, I happened upon the idea of using my handkerchief as a flag. I tied that humble square of muslin from the highest portion of the bush. In doing so, I uncovered a handful of ripe berries. These I also tucked into my bag. No doubt, Cook would find good use for them.

As I wandered back to my home, a delegation of swallows soared overhead. I could almost feel the wind under their wings. On an old tree stump, I spotted a dazzling redstart, a male. He was as fascinated by me as I was with him, as he pecked at the fruit of the wild Guelder Rose. The bird and I studied each other for what seemed like a long time. Not wishing to disturb him, I stood still and closed my eyes, breathing in the heady fragrance of fallen leaves crushed beneath my boots. For one brief moment, there was naught but me and the untamed world around me. I reveled in the caress of the breeze against my skin. I basked in the fading warmth of the sun.

A song from the redstart may have served to warn away his mate, but I let every note soak into my soul. It was as uplifting as any church hymn ever sung and ever so much more praiseworthy. When the bird flew off, the sun turned a definite cold shoulder to me, suggesting the time had come for me to go directly home. So, I did.

I approached the lodge from the back, skirting the low brick wall that borders a kitchen garden, brimming over with herbs and edibles supplementary to our meals. No one was waiting for me on any of the three benches we have built under grape arbors. Often Edward and I take our tea out here. Mrs. Fairfax frowns upon the practice, but my husband has told me that dining *al fresco* is a common practice in Italy. He has vowed, "Someday, darling girl, we shall go traveling, and I shall introduce you to the wonders of the wider world." I admit the prospect sounds intriguing, if for no reason other than the sights I long to see and commit to paper.

As I walked through the kitchen door, I happened upon Cook, as she expertly chopped a handful of herbs. The sharp tang of chives filled the air. "To serve with eggs for Mr. Rochester?" I asked. Cook has only come to work for us lately. Early on, she took note of our favorite foods and carefully arranged her pantry, so these are served more often than not.

"Aye," she turned to me, "that and with potatoes, Missus."

Cook's real name is Susan Clabber, but she

much prefers Cook, explaining honestly, "Took me years to learn what I needed to know to be a proper cook. My given name came to me by chance, but the title of 'Cook' I earned myself, and I feel a wee bit chuffed whenever anyone calls me Cook. If that's all right with you, that is."

Calling Mrs. Clabber by her job title suits all of us, even though Edward occasionally slips and calls the good woman Susan. 'Tis natural, considering that he and she practically grew up together. For generations, Susan's family have lived on the Rochester estate. Her father was a blacksmith, who did much work for the Rochesters, shoeing horses and making whatever metal implements the estate required. Susan is two years older than my husband, and she wasn't a part of his social circle, but she met young Edward when he accompanied his father whilst bringing horses to be shod. Cook has confessed that a youthful game or two of hide-and-seek might have been shared along the way. After all, children know naught of class divisions until so instructed by adults.

Cook has been wise enough to downplay this youthful shared history, lest it embarrass Edward. Even so, I have done my best to prise stories from her a little at a time. Hearing about my husband as a lad delights me, as I often wonder what he was like before life dealt with him so cruelly. In seeking more information, I've learned that Cook is likely to be chatty, when her hands are busy preparing food.

Today she concentrated on exactly where to cut the chives, so they would yield their most desirable flavors. Her thick hands are criss-crossed with thick scars, white, red, and pink. Badges of honor, she told me. She said, "These scars, they're marks of service. Like a general after his campaign, I expect. I know I can rightly tell ye where each of them came from. Mile-stones along the way toward mastering my trade."

I must admit that she handles a cleaver with the sort of confidence I show when working on paper with a nub of charcoal. Each of us has a hard-won skill, I guess. Looking up from her work, she asked, "Did ye enjoy your walk, Missus?"

"I did indeed," I said.

"Good. Winter'll be on us sooner than ex-pected. This one will be a hardship, if the signs are true to form, and they've always been so thus far."

"What do you watch for?" I tugged my bonnet

strings, until they were untied, and then went and stood next to her.

"Ain't any one thing. There's lots of signs, if ye know what to look for. The birds I've plucked have been extra generous with their feathers. I've seen squirrels hiding more nuts than usual. That old oak tree at the far end of the pasture has produced more acorns than I can ever recall."

This made sense, as Mother Nature has a way of caring for her children and preparing them for the unkind days to come. I shivered, as I thought about the miserable dark days that lay ahead of us.

"Are ye all right, Missus?" Cook cocked an eyebrow at me.

"Yes," I said slowly. "Yes, I am."

Although my response was not a half-truth, my reply lacked complete candor. The coming of winter manifests melancholy in me, a sadness that I struggle to tame. Winter's miserable days had made life perilous for me, during my eight years at Lowood Academy. The charity school had proved both a godsend and a misery. There I had accumulated the skills necessary to earn a living wage; there I had suffered deprivation. My life has lacked warmth on a variety of levels, emotional, spiritual, and physical. When reminded of those bleak circumstances, I cannot help but grow pensive.

In an attempt to hide my innermost thoughts, I turned my gaze away from Cook.

"Is anything wrong, Missus?" She repeated, adding emphasis to her query.

The remark was couched in formality, even though Cook was treading perilously close to a line that servants dare not cross. In a small household such as this, familiarity happens easily, but Mrs. Fairfax has often warned me that I shall lose the respect of our staff if I blur these lines.

"Nothing is wrong," was my quick rejoinder. As a diversion, I plunged a hand into the muslin bag. "This was a glorious autumn day. The leaves are colorful, and the horse chestnuts are plentiful. I brought back a dozen conkers for the horses."

"Lord above, Missus. Ye can't feed those to the horses, or any other animal, unless ye be planning to poison them."

"Oh, no!" This unexpected news caused me to drop what I was holding. The conkers rolled across the slate floor.

The good woman smothered her laughter behind her hand. "Aye, and ye were raised in town, were ye not? I should not be surprised. That name of theirs, horse chestnut, threw you off, I wager. Not to worry, Missus. I won't tell anyone what ye said. Certain animals can eat conkers with no ill effects, but most of them cannot feast on those seeds without suffering."

I stooped to retrieve my bounty. Picking up a horse chestnut, I examined the nut once more, as if looking for signs that it was ill begotten. But the conker was so lovely! Its smooth brown shell framed a small oval of creamy beige.

"You are right, Cook. I was raised in towns, and all I've known of conkers is that children prized them for playing games. I am not even acquainted with the rules that govern such engagements. I assume that when my son is older, he will undoubtedly find these nuts valuable, but toward what end I cannot say."

Her eyes turned soft with kindness. Cook explained, "No doubt, he'll want to gather them as ye did. Then he'll try various ways of hardening the shells. My own brothers liked boiling theirs in vinegar, but my uncle swore by boiling the conkers in salt water. My uncle was then fond of coating them with wax from candles, and my grandfather swore by baking them in the oven. I've had the best luck by leaving them to cure for a year."

"And then?" I prompted.

"Once ye're satisfied the nut is battle-hardened, ye pierce it with a skewer. That done, ye thread a string through it and knot it off. Holding on to the string, the players bash their conkers against each other. The loser is the one whose shell splits first."

"I see." I marveled at the idea of such elaborate preparations. Yet, hadn't I seen the serious way folks took the competition? This time of year, the town square would fill with children happily swinging their conkers and bashing them together. I had seen as much, although I was not sure exactly how the game was played. All I knew was that I hoped one day my own son, Ned, would be out there with other children. Of course, that was years away, and yet I imagine it will be so. Every evening when I kiss him good night, I pray that my child will have the sort of carefree, happy childhood that I was denied.

"I collected a few walnuts as well," I said, trying to regain my dignity. "There were not many ripe ones, but I marked the spot and hope to go back. I do hope you can put these to good use?" I fumbled whilst opening my muslin bag. The walnuts took that as an opportunity for escape and spilled out of my makeshift purse. With a clatter, my harvest fell to the floor, rolling in every direction and joining the conkers on the floor.

"Oh, dear!" I dropped to my knees and hastily retrieved as many as I could. My peregrinations brought me nose-to-nose with Mephisto, the black cat I had adopted after his mistress died. Usually, Mephisto would have chased the rolling orbs all over the place, but today he hopped nimbly out of his bed. Instead of turning those lemon-yellow eyes on me and ignoring my presence, he rubbed against my boots and pressed his back into my hand. The cat set up a loud yowling, the likes of which I've never heard from him before. I stroked his head. "Cook? Mephisto appears to be out of sorts."

The cat continued to meow loudly and rub his face against my skirt.

"Aye," Cook agreed, coming closer to where I remained in a kneeling position. She leaned over to watch the feline more carefully. "I noticed that, too."

"I wonder if he's unwell." My fingers slid under his chin to rub the v-shaped spot under the cat's throat. Mephisto rewarded me with a noisy purr of satisfaction.

"No," said Cook. "I'd say your cat is perfectly

well. Happy. Doing exactly as nature intended that beast to do."

My concerns were interrupted by the sound of Edward's heavy boots in the hallway. My husband, tall and dark, with a stormy face that hid a loving nature, said, "Jane? May I have a word with you, when you are finished speaking to Cook? I shall be in my study."

"Of course," I said. With a nod, Edward left us.

I removed my bonnet and spencer, so I could hang them on the hook by the door. Unconsciously, I reached down to smooth the skirt of my dress and noticed that I had managed to dirty my pockets considerably. "Oh, no," I mumbled.

Cook came over to examine the damage. "When you change for dinner, have Amelia bring me your frock. I'll see what I can do about those walnut stains."

Since I have refused to hire a lady's maid, the daily care of my wardrobe has been parceled out to Cook and Amelia, the nursemaid. A woman from nearby Millcote comes every fortnight, but minor repairs and stains cannot wait. So, the two women step into the breach when necessary.

Holding the dress in her rough hands, Cook sighed over the poor state of my muslin walking dress. "Perhaps I can get most of this stain out before the laundress comes. If I may be so bold, you need to stop putting things in your pockets, Missus."

"Initially, I used my bag," I said, holding up the sorry fabric sack.

"Begging your pardon, that bag of yours ain't good for much, Missus. Not as it is."

"I know. I plan to sew it up," I said. Five years ago, I'd crafted it by hand, using an old nightdress of mine, one destined for the rag pile at Lowood Academy. Even then, the material had been thin and fragile. Now, of course, the piece had gone threadbare.

"Sew it up? I think ye need to replace it. What do ye keep in there typically? Looks nigh onto bursting."

"My sketching materials. A large notepad. A pencil. An eraser. Cakes of watercolor paint. A couple of brushes and a rag."

"Hmm," Cook said. "Mrs. McClellan, the lady I worked for before, had a leather portfolio. I suspect you need suchlike."

"Probably," I agreed.

"I've seen some of your work." Cook's eyes grew wide with wonder. "Mrs. Fairfax showed me. I ain't never seen anything so beautiful."

A warm sense of embarrassment crept up my

neck. So, Mrs. Fairfax showed my art to the Cook? That was an invasion of my privacy, to be sure! Anger replaced my chagrin. Alice Fairfax had no right to share my artwork. Increasingly, Mrs. Fairfax and I seemed to be at cross purposes. In many ways, Mrs. Fairfax treats me as she might a granddaughter or goddaughter, if she had one. Early on, she warned me against my growing feelings about Edward, saying, "I am sorry to grieve you, but you are so young, and so little acquainted with men, I wish to put you on your guard. It is an old saying that 'all is not gold that glitters'; and in this case, I do fear there will be something found to be different to what either you or I expect."

To this day, I wonder exactly how much Mrs. Fairfax knew about Bertha Mason, Edward's first wife, a woman who eventually burned down Thornfield Hall, nearly killing Edward. But on balance, I have decided that I do not wish to plumb the depths of Mrs. Fairfax's knowledge. Some secrets are best buried deep, never to see the light of day.

By nature, Mrs. Fairfax is a kindly person, and I owe her thanks for hiring me as Adèle's governess, else I was never to have met my husband. I appreciate her efficient manner of running our home. Certainly, I have no training in the intricacies of housekeeping, nor do I wish to be burdened by the responsibility of overseeing our household expenditures. Mrs. Fairfax harbors firm ideas about her role, my role, and what she perceives as the Rochester family's role in the community. I owe it to her to get along with her as best I can, even when she irks me. However, there are times when Mrs. Fairfax oversteps.

Like she has now. She showed my work to the Cook! That means she opened my folder where I keep my pieces. From now on, I shall take care to secure the folder in a locked drawer. Thank heavens I've never indulged in my desire to capture my husband in any pose but his most public self.

Cook stared at me curiously, wondering why I'd taken so long to respond to her appreciation of my skills.

"Your compliments are most gratifying, but I am only a novice," I said, swallowing down my jumble of emotions. "I very much enjoy drawing and painting."

Cook clasped her hands to her bosom in a gesture long associated with pure rapture. She said, "Novice or not, I've never seen such. It was a rare treat for the eyes, Missus, I'll tell you plainly."

"Thank you," I said, "if you'll excuse me, I need to attend to my husband. When I have finished, I'll change my frock."

As is often the case, Edward sat behind his large oak desk, which we'd recently repositioned to take advantage of the sunlight streaming through a nearby window. He sat with a magnifying glass in one hand and attempted to read a document that required his attention. The fire at Thornfield Hall has caused Edward to fight against blindness for years.

For the second time in a matter of minutes, I was forced to consider the sad plight of Bertha Mason, Edward's first wife. She had gone mad, shortly after their marriage. To keep her safe, my husband confined her in a suite of rooms. Grace Poole was hired to be Bertha's caregiver, but over time, the tedium and the drama wore Grace down. Her affection for strong spirits provided her a welcome escape from life with Bertha. That proclivity proved her downfall, as Bertha learned to keep an eye out for those times when Grace overindulged. One night, when Grace was in a stupor, Bertha escaped from her quarters and set the house ablaze.

I was far away, when the conflagration spread through Thornfield Hall. Once I learned that Edward was not free to marry, I ran away, in order to remove myself from the temptations of the flesh. Despite the fact he'd been tricked into marrying Bertha and that he, too, had suffered because of her insanity, Edward tried to save her life. Once he smelled smoke, he raced to the upper floors of the house, searching for her. The burning beams of oak belched thick smoke. Yet Edward continued to call out to Bertha. In the midst of such destruction, a miracle occurred.

"Had Bertha not wailed like a banshee, I would have been lost," he has told me. "My eyes streamed with tears that precluded me from seeing my way to her. At one point, I despaired of rescuing her and of saving myself. But Bertha's screams guided me, showing me the way. The sound of her shrieks led me to her side. I tried to stop her from climbing onto the roof, but she was determined and escaped my grasp. I followed her in a vain attempt to keep her safe. Even as I grabbed at her, she launched herself from the rooftop. Despite that tortured decision to do herself harm, she did me a good service before she died. Had I not followed her as I did, I would have been crushed to death by the crumbling structure. Instead, I was felled by just one beam."

Indeed, it is a miracle that he survived. One

eye was destroyed, and the vision in its twin was severely damaged. A beam crushed his left hand, mangling it beyond all repair. Mr. Carter, the surgeon called to the scene, severed the crushed portion before Edward even regained his senses. In addition, the fire melted my husband's skin in various places, leaving shiny pink skin that is stretched tight. The result is a man who sees himself as a monster but to me is more impressive than before, because this man is a survivor. Whilst it is true that my husband's visage is far removed from the delicate looks cultivated and praised by today's society, I see Edward through the lens of love. I am thankful that he is my husband.

Today, I interrupted him while he squinted at a receipt, trying to make out the words. "I am in the midst of placing an order with a furniture maker, Mr. Foster-Davies."

"To what purpose?" I pulled a chair close to the desk.

He pushed back in his seat and crossed his boots at the ankle. The soft leather showed much wear, and the footwear would soon need to be replaced. "As you are aware, Thornfield Hall will take a long time to rebuild."

Thornfield Hall had been destroyed in the

blaze that Bertha had set. Shortly thereafter, Edward moved here to Ferndean Manor, and this is where we were reunited. After much debate, we decided that Thornfield Hall should be rebuilt, not for us but for Ned. The location of Thornfield Hall is more congenial than that of Ferndean Manor. Thornfield Hall is not only closer to Millcote, the next town, but also an easy ride for Mr. Carter, our surgeon. Furthermore, Thornfield Hall is more conducive to socializing than is Ferndean Manor. As Ned grows older, he'll be desirous of playmates, so there's that. Also, at some point in the future, our son might wish to take his place in society, as the scion of a local squire. Should Ned desire to live as the lord of the manor, Thornfield Hall will be ready for him. Once we'd discussed the various benefits, Edward directed much of the Rochester family fortune toward rebuilding Thornfield Hall. Immediately, we realized the process would take years.

"Yes," I agreed. "Rebuilding Thornfield Hall will take a long time. Especially if we are to make improvements to the original structure. There is no way of knowing how long the new construction will take."

"With that in mind," Edward said, "we should make ourselves comfortable here at Ferndean."

"I concur."

"Toward that end, I have made a list of furnishings I think we need." He pushed a sheet of paper my way. I picked it up and studied his scraw,l as he continued, "I hope you'll approve of these choices, and I trust you'll feel free to make any adjustments as you see fit. You ask for so little, my Janet. You have shown a great willingness to make do here in this old hunting lodge, but there is no reason for us to do without. Nor should we impose our rough living on any guests who might join us."

"Guests," I repeated, as I ran my fingertips over the surface of the paper. Edward's heavy hand had engraved the words into the note. I believe this is a natural response to the problems with his eyesight. By pressing down as he writes, he creates an embossed message his fingers can read.

I wondered, *Who would want to visit us?*

"Lucy," Edward amended, by way of reminding me. "In fact, Lucy supplied me the name of the furniture maker."

"Yes, of course," I said, feeling delighted, once I knew the provenance of the craftsman.

Lucy Douglas Brayton is the wife of Edward's dear friend, Captain Augustus Brayton. Not too long ago, I visited Lucy in London after learning that Adèle, Edward's ward, was miserable at her boarding school, Alderton House.

Initially, I was intimidated by the thought of meeting Lucy. After all, she had been described to me as a woman totally at home in London society. Those concerns were quickly discarded. In a short time, dear Lucy became the sister I have never had. She was kind and gracious. After I discovered the cause for the disastrous events at Alderton House, Lucy did her best to help me soothe Adèle. The little girl came back with me to Ferndean, but Adèle is a will-o'-the-wisp at heart, and this hunting lodge could not provide the sorts of amusements the child craved. Once again, Lucy stepped forward to offer assistance. She was enchanted by Adèle, and moreover, she felt badly about the problems Adèle had endured at Alderton House, a place Lucy had recommended, based on the approval of other members of society.

"Let Adèle stay with me until the holidays," Lucy had pleaded with us. "Give her a little time to put the trials of the past months behind her. Seeing the gaiety London can offer will encourage her to adopt those habits expected of a proper lady."

Of course, Lucy did not make this offer in Adèle's presence. If she had, we would have been doomed to an excess of exuberance, and making a sensible decision would have been impossible. Instead, our friend wisely made the proposal in private, giving Edward and me the chance to mull over our decision.

"Jane and I are much obliged to you, Lucy, for both the offer and the manner in which you proffered your invitation," said Edward. "Are you positive that this would suit you? You have only just gathered little Evans to your bosom, and a guest, no matter how well loved, might be a terrible inconvenience."

Evans is the infant son of Augustus Brayton and his paramour, a woman who recently passed away. Despite this, a situation that many women would have found intolerable, Lucy bears no ill will toward the baby. No, Lucy is nothing if not surprising. She was thrilled to welcome the little boy into her home, as Lucy has always longed to be a mother. It is a testament to her charitable nature that she has been able to forgive Augie and open her heart to a child some would see as a daily reminder of his infidelity. But Lucy is nothing if not remarkable in a myriad of ways.

"I forgave Augie his indiscretion many

months ago," she had told me. "The responsibility for our estrangement was mine as much as his. I shunned him, and he succumbed to another woman's charms. I should have known better!"

"But do you see the baby as your penance?" I worried that she did, and that taking the boy into her home would one day lead to resentment. Having been the object of such misplaced emotion, I wouldn't wish that on any child.

"You misunderstand me, Jane." Lucy smiled through her tears. "I have always wanted to be a mother, although sadly, I've been told that will never happen. Bringing Evans into our house is a dream come true for me. A son! And one who might look like my beloved Augie? I am over the moon with happiness!"

As it turned out, Evans duplicated Augie's coloring in such a manner that there could be no doubt that he was his father's child. Adèle and I had been guests in Lucy's home when Evans first arrived, and thus, I was able to record in my diary that this little baby had been received with extreme pleasure. I do not think that Lucy set him down once in the next ten days. At length, his nurse, Mrs. Wallander, pointed out that the infant needed a chance to explore his surroundings, and such an opportunity had been extremely limited, because his new mother was holding him prisoner in her arms.

"Alas," Lucy had confessed to me with a wry smile, "I have been warned by Mrs. Wallander that, if I keep interfering with Evans's naps and feedings to coddle him, I shall ruin the lad. Thus, I have yet another reason to request Adèle. Her presence will offer me a welcome distraction, another direction to point my interests. Oh, Jane, please let her stay with me through the fall! She and I will have such a jolly time. Season ends in September and does not begin again until after Christmas. London can be very dull in the winter, indeed."

When I presented the idea to Edward, he said, "Then why don't you ask Lucy to stay with us for a while, when she brings Adèle to Ferndean?"

I thought this was pure perfection. When I took it to Lucy, she said, "The idea has great appeal to me, but I have much to do to get ready for Season. I have to make multiple visits to my mantua-maker in October, or else my gowns won't be ready in time. However, once my fittings are over and I've selected my fabric and trimmings, I should be free to spend the winter months with you and Edward at Ferndean. I'm assuming that

Evans and Mrs. Wallander will be welcome as well?"

"Of course!" I hurried to confirm. "Your lady's maid, Polly, too."

But Lucy's expression did not relax at the confirmation I'd quickly put forth. There was the slightest touch of hesitation in her. "Jane, dearest? You should be forewarned. Please know that I detest cold weather. After our mother died and my brother Bruce and I were turned out onto the streets, we passed many a miserable night huddled in the architraves of churches and other vast buildings. I swore to myself that, one day, I would spend all the rest of the winters allotted to me sitting in front of blazing fires with rugs over my legs and a heated brick or two under my feet. If you can supply me with such at Ferndean, and if I can make the trip without

suffering too much misery, I shall be happy as a butterfly on a fine spring day."

Bit by bit, Lucy had shared her sad story with me. This explanation regarding her hatred of foul weather further illuminated another page from her past. Whilst I felt keen sorrow for her, I must confess that my heart gladdened to realize that she was entrusting her history to me. As such, she was making a solemn commitment to our friendship.

"Dear Lucy, as long as I walk this earth, you'll never fear being cold again," I said. "You have my word upon it."

All of this flooded back to me, as I sat here in Edward's comfortable office. The fire in his hearth provided a steady source of warm air. Our manifold improvements to Ferndean had greatly helped to create a wholly pleasant atmosphere.

Edward reclaimed my attention. "Augie has told me, repeatedly, that Lucy abhors cold weather. Therefore, we must do all we can to tempt Lucy and induce her to visit. When she does, we shall want our friend to have all the proper amenities. She deserves to be pampered."

I heartily agreed.

"Mrs. Fairfax reckoned that the guest bedroom lacks an armoire or clothes presses, a proper bed, bedside tables, and a comfortable chair. Of course, a washstand must be considered, too." Edward gave a nod toward the list I held in my hand. I turned my attention to the paper.

"Pray don't forget that Mrs. Wallander, Evans's nurse, will come along with Lucy," I added. "And Lucy might also wish to bring her lady's maid, Polly."

"I did not forget. For Evans's nanny, I propose that we purchase a truckle bed, as Amelia's current bed is barely sufficient. The ropes have all gone slack. The new furnishings should improve the upstairs room for both the older woman and for Amelia."

Amelia, our son's nursemaid, is a placid young woman only two years younger than I am. Although she would never complain about her accommodations, as she feels we treat her very well, a new bed would please her greatly. She's terribly proud of her position in our household, and she spends all her free time planning improvements for her room. Recently, she lashed together twigs to form a frame and asked me shyly if she could have a drawing I had tossed away. Of course, I said she could, and the girl was immensely pleased.

"Adèle and Lucy arriving together," I said, savoring the news. "I do hope Lucy will stay a while."

"I'm hoping she'll be our guest over the holidays," said Edward.

"Oh! That will be delightful."

Edward smiled at me. "I want my little Janet to be happy. Do not assume that Mrs. Fairfax's list is the end of the discussion. It is merely a jumping off spot. You might wish to compose another list, detailing whatever linens and curtains you think we should provision. A room with naught but bare furniture will not be pleasant enough for Lucy."

"Yes," I said, feeling a surge of happiness. "I would be pleased to do just that."

CHAPTER 2

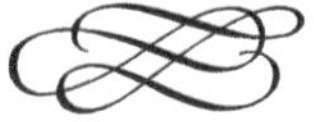

After our evening meal, we—Edward and I—adjourned to the parlor. Edward's sight, although much improved since a visit to the ocular specialist in London, is still not good enough for him to read small type. Therefore, on most nights, we have invited Mrs. Fairfax to join us, so that she can read out loud to him and to me whilst I do various handicrafts. On this particular night, we sat in a row, with Edward nearest the windows, I next to him, and Mrs. Fairfax taking the chair to my right. As the logs in the fireplace glowed a blood-red and dark gold, Pilot, Edward's Newfoundland, rested near his Master's feet. The old dog sighed in his sleep. To one side of the fireplace was an old crate provided with scraps of fabric. This was the bed for Mephisto. The black cat opened a sleepy eye to glance at the dreaming dog. Convinced the dog was not plotting to be a bother, the cat drifted off to sleep.

On this particular night, Mrs. Fairfax read to us an article about a proposal for enclosing land. According to the piece, there was a rising interest among the members of Parliament, the objective of which was said to be a way to promote better stewardship of all farmland. Whilst that might be a goal, the truth was more unsettling. Enclosures would make it nearly impossible for commoners to herd their livestock to good grazing areas. Thus, enclosures would force them into deeper poverty. I wondered, what would be enough? When would the wealthy landowners quit nibbling at the few rights the poor still had?

There was a frown on my face, when Mrs. Fairfax set the paper aside. Glancing my way, she asked, "What are you working on, Jane?"

Turning the wick up on the oil lamp on the table between the housekeeper and me, I was using the meager light to repair the hole in my muslin bag. To answer Mrs. Fairfax's question, I raised the bag, so she could examine it. "I am sewing up the sack I use to carry my sketching supplies."

"Did you enjoy your walk today, darling Janet?" Edward asked, calling me by his favorite nickname.

I explained how my walk and the harvesting of nuts had increased a small tear in my muslin bag. I also mentioned that I used my handkerchief to mark unripe bilberries.

"Bilberries? How unusual for this time of year," said Mrs. Fairfax. "I would have expected them to all be gone by now. I do hope you will be able to pick them when they are ripe. A bread-and-butter pudding with them would be a delicious pudding."

"I should be able to find them easily enough, thanks to the white flag I tied onto the uppermost branch. The bilberry bush was not far from a walnut tree and a horse chestnut. I gathered leaves and nuts, because I so admired their coloring and their shape." I struggled to thread my needle in the weak light. "I even found some conkers."

A smile flickered on Edward's face. "Ned is too young to do battle with conkers, but someday he will be ready. Or are you proposing a duel between the two of us? Tell me, dear wife, did you hope to vanquish me in a game of conkers? If so, I give you fair warning: I am a champion conkers man. My brother Rowland and I often battled each other. We would spend days seeking out the fruit of the horse chestnut tree and examining each fallen nut with an eye toward its usefulness. Ordinarily, Rowland and I were at odds with each other, but we did enjoy a good game."

"Sir," I addressed him with pride, "I have never played conkers, so you would have the advantage of me. Therefore, I suggest that you be my teacher in that art of warfare. I shall expect you to share your recipe for strengthening and fortifying the seeds. As I understand it, one cannot hope to win unless the hull is toughened up considerably. And then you thread a string through the nut. Is that right?"

"Yes, but you forgot the most important part of the game. You try with all your might to bash your opponent's conker and break the shell. If you are the first to destroy your foe, you win."

"My, that sounds very rumbustious," I said.

"It can be, and I intend to teach our son every trick I know. Or did you suppose, Janet, that I would raise our child without passing on the requisite formula for toughening up a conker? Or without passing on my battle tactics?" Edward reached over and took my hand in a mild caress, as he stared into my eyes. "Of course, I shall teach him everything I know. For naught and for no one would I ever shirk my duties as a father. You can count on that."

His promise melted my heart. My husband loves our son with a passion that is only exceeded by Edward's love for me. This amplifies my love for Edward a hundred times over. Hot tears gathered behind my lids. Raising one hand to my face, I brushed away the moisture.

"By the way, I asked James to take the letter with the order in it for our furniture down to the post-bag in the lane," said my husband. "I must confess to an ulterior motive, however. James was able to ride Mesrour for me. The trip was not long enough to properly exercise my horse, but at least the animal was able to stretch his legs."

Mesrour is Edward's beautiful black stallion. Edward was riding the horse, when we first met. Since the fire at Thornfield Hall, Edward has had problems managing the high-strung animal. The loss of one eye has complicated Edward's perception of depth. The loss of Edward's left hand has further complicated his efforts to control the horse. Staunchly, I have rebuffed any effort by Edward to call himself a cripple, but this is how he sees himself. I do not think he fears Mesrour, but he doubts his ability to control such a spirited mount. If the horse would sense Edward's lack of confidence, he might injure himself as well as his rider.

"James Harrigan had time to do that? Exercising your horse for you?" asked Mrs. Fairfax.

James is our man of all work. A strapping fellow, he's the grandson of John and Mary Harrigan, my husband's lifelong retainers. I cringed at the way that Mrs. Fairfax asked her question of my husband. Her bald assertion seemed to blame Edward for his inability to do such a menial chore.

Regrettably, she persisted in her line of inquiry, "Does that mean James's grandfather is getting better at last? Is that why James has so much time to spare?"

"No," said Edward in a brusque tone. "John Harrigan is still unwell. As for exercising my horse, James is always short on time, but we both knew that Mesrour needed to be ridden, so he saddled the steed and rode him down the lane. The ride was brief but better than no ride at all. Would that I could ride my horse the way I once did!"

A bitter silence followed. Sadly, my husband's mood had taken a turn for the melancholy, and mine with it. Mrs. Fairfax did not seem to notice.

Soon after, Edward and I bid Mrs. Fairfax good-night and went to bed.

When I first moved into Ferndean, John and Mary Harrigan helped us set the lodge right. We began by cleaning the master bedroom, the nursery, the parlor, the dining room, the kitchen, an attic bedroom, and an office for Edward. The old couple and I worked side-by-side. On occasion, Mrs. Fairfax also lent a hand. Once the rooms were cleaned and thoroughly scrubbed, John set about doing repair work. After those six spots were deemed inhabitable, the other six previously abandoned bedrooms had slowly been cleaned and restored, although two were still in need of furnishings. At first, Edward and I had seen this place as a very temporary roof over our heads. Sadly, we had underestimated the amount of time rebuilding Thornfield Hall would take. Once it became clear to us that rebuilding the burned-out shell of the family home from the ground up would be a huge undertaking, our priorities necessarily shifted. We put a higher priority on refurbishing this lodge, even as the work on Thornfield Hall continued.

With the prospect of Lucy coming to visit, there was much to be done. Edward was right: Ferndean lacked some of the material comforts that would make our life here more enjoyable and that would make this place more welcoming for visitors. The next morning, I set about to correct our deficiencies. Measurements were taken, furnishings were described and occasionally sketched by me. The final step was ordering soft goods—pull-up window coverings with matching pelmets, bed hangings, bedclothes, and a variety of cushions and small pillows. In addition to my drawings, I went so far as to include scraps of watercolor paper on which I'd painted the shades that pleased me. These I hoped would indicate the colors I had in mind. Mrs. Fairfax thought my insistence on such details foolish, and she said as much. "The shopkeeper will select whatever is fashionable and send it along. You do not need to bother about such trivialities."

"Color is important to me," I said in a rejoinder, "and by sending samples, the likelihood is much increased that the final product will be more to my taste."

"Perhaps," she said with a tiny shrug, "but if you wish to have those items before winter, you had best make sure your letter is in the mail."

She was right about that, and I had another request that needed posting. This was a special letter I'd written in German, a language I'd learned from my Rivers cousins. If my foreign letter made it to Seesen, Germany, in time, Edward might enjoy yet another holiday surprise. But heeding the housekeeper's warning, I needed to make sure the mail made it to Millcote, the closest village for collection of the Royal Post. When John Harrigan served as our manservant, the mail went out regularly. These days, getting the post collected has become much less predictable. Several days might pass before James took our correspondence into Millcote, where a mail coach would pick it up on the way to London.

Left to their own devices, the letter to Lucy and the list for the soft goods merchant might remain here or in the post-bag in the lane for the better part of a week. That would never do. There was a much better chance of the mail making it to other locales, if I walked the correspondence to the Harrigans' cottage. That would alert James to the need to carry it to Millcote.

I hesitated. Yes, I wanted to grab my spencer and my hat and hurry to the Harrigans' home, but prudence overcame impulsivity. I owed Lucy a response to her most recent note. Perhaps this would be a good time to encourage her once again to visit us. After all, if she did not decide to stay a while, all our preparations would be for naught. I took pen in hand and crafted a message:

Mrs. Captain Augustus Brayton

24 Grosvenor Square,

London

Dear Lucy,

I write in haste so that I might get this missive out and into the post-bag. As always, I am thankful that you have opened your home and your heart to Adèle. No doubt, she is delighted beyond words to be staying with you! She writes the happiest notes, with cunning commentary praising little Evans. You are so good to Adèle. I trust she is on her best behavior, and I know she benefits from spending time with you.

We spoke before about you joining us for the holiday season. I trust you've been able to meet with your mantua-maker, and I hope all is well in that regard. However, it would be unfair of me to assume your plans have not changed. I know how very popular you are in London.

Regarding Adèle's homecoming, I am of two minds. If she is intent on staying with you, I would not ruin her winter vacation by forcing her to come here. That said, I believe Edward misses her—as I do. He mentions her frequently. If you have tired of Adèle's company, of course, we would want you to send her to Ferndean Manor at your earliest convenience. Or I can come and fetch her, if necessary. If she is still pleasant company, there is no hurry. Your choice will be the deciding factor in this matter, as Edward and I would never want to impose upon your hospitality. You are far too dear to us to run that risk.

With those options in mind, I shall remind you of our invitation: Please come and spend the winter holidays with us here at Ferndean Manor. Of course, Mrs. Wallander and your lady's maid, Polly, are welcome as well. I recognize that we shan't be able to offer you all the amenities of a Christmas in London, but we would try to make up for any deficiencies with our deepest affection. With high hopes that you'll grace us with your presence, we're making every effort to freshen up your room, so it will delight and pamper you! As you know, you are ever dear to me, my adopted sister. I will do everything in my power to make your visit enjoyable. But I shall also be the first to understand if your desire to stay in London trumps my invitation.

Much love,

Jane

P.S. I look forward to seeing how Evans has grown. Ned has gotten so big!

Grabbing my bonnet and spencer and giving a quick goodbye to Amelia lest I be missed, I set off to visit the Harrigans.

CHAPTER 3

John Harrigan and his wife, Mary, have taken care of my husband for most of their working lives. Indeed, John had planned to be in service to Edward as long as God allowed that good man to walk this good earth. However, an untimely accident has changed all of our plans—and not for the better.

My husband held himself responsible for the fall that John took last spring. The heavy rains had caused a multitude of leaks in the roof. Despite Edward's protestations, John insisted on climbing onto the roof and examining the damage. Alas, he lost his footing and rolled off the roof. At the time, we feared for his life. As it happened, the damage to his bones was slow to heal, but the blow to his head left longer lasting problems for the old man. Over the summer, we thought that John might regain his health. Instead, we have seen a precipitous decline in his well-being. These days, the old man spends most of his time sleeping, and rarely does he venture forth from his bed. Mary is lost without John, and initially she acted as his constant nursemaid. When it became clear to all that John was unlikely to recover his former vigor, Mary asked their grandson, James, and his wife, Leah, to move in and help out. Rather than make it clear to John that we do not expect him to recover, Edward has respected the older man's pride, which is his last remaining possession. Edward has eased James into the various jobs his grandfather once handled, and the younger man has proven himself to be adept. Hence, all of us have accepted that the young couple, James and Leah, will live permanently in the older Harrigans' cottage, a small house located at the end of a path, a few minutes' walk away from Ferndean Manor.

The granddaughter-in-law, Leah, is a plain woman, taller than I, with a gap between her front teeth and a head full of coppery red hair. Her form has been shaped by years of hard labor, making her lean and energetic, even in repose.

I've never asked, but I judge her to be five years or so my senior. Leah is a hardworking young woman, who never seems to sit still. Although we are not yet friends, I hope we'll be, as she is pleasant company.

Today, as I approached their cottage, their dog, Shep, heralded my visit with a hullabaloo of barking. Not surprisingly, Leah stopped her chores to see what had roused his interest. When she spotted me, she raised her arm high overhead and waved cheerfully.

Her woolen shawl slipped down from her shoulders. Dressed in a plain muslin dress that she had wisely covered with a pinafore, Leah was the picture of rural wholesomeness. The only touch of vanity was a colorful scarf tucked between her collar and her apron.

Leah rested her hands on her hips. By the bevy of feathers floating around her, I guessed she'd been chasing a chicken. "Don't stop on my account," I called to her.

"Ach, this hen knows she's bound for our supper pots, Missus Rochester. Is everything all right?" Her hands flew to her breast, in an attempt to contain her worry. "Ned is fine, ain't he?"

"Yes, yes," I said hurriedly. "We are all well. I

have letters to go to London and beyond. Rather than wait for James to come by, I thought I'd take advantage of the agreeable weather and bring them myself."

"Your timing is excellent. I believe he plans a quick trip to town, tomorrow." Her frank green eyes crinkled at the corners, when she smiled at me. Shaking a fist at the hen, she added, "Today ye were lucky. Tomorrow, I plan to cook you! See if I don't!"

I couldn't help but laugh, as the hen waddled off.

"You're too right about the weather," said Leah. "Glorious!"

I raised my eyes to the cerulean sky and marveled at the beautiful blue, dotted with clouds that looked all the world like newborn lambs. "And this might be the last of the clemency we're granted. I wish I could bring my son with me on jaunts such as this. Alas, the pathways around Ferndean are rough, and his push-cart would not manage the bumps."

After looking me over, Leah's fingers struggled to tidy a stray lock that had escaped from the bun at the back of her neck. "Would you be liking a cup of tea?" she asked me, timidly. I could tell she was weighing the invitation, worrying that I'd find her too disheveled, or worse, beneath me.

"That would be most welcome," I said sincerely. "I do hope I am not intruding."

"No, ye came at a good time. Old John is sleeping in the back bedroom. Mary is out walking. James is working in the barn at Ferndean, but ye probably knew that already." Leah led me toward the cottage and swung the heavy front door open. I stepped inside to a dimly lit room, where a pot of stew simmered from a fireplace crane.

"How is he?" I whispered.

Nodding toward a bench at their table, Leah encouraged me to sit down. I did.

"He has his good days and his bad. Same with Mary. I believe that she spends her days walking, because she cannot stomach seeing her husband waste away."

Edward and I had heard that the old man's decline had a deleterious effect on his wife's health and spirits. Now, I could report to my husband that their mutual decline was confirmed. This made me sad. Would Edward and I be the same one day?

Moving swiftly, Leah hung a pot of water from an S-shaped hearth hook over the fire. While the liquid heated, she went to a cabinet and retrieved a china teapot with a chip at the spout. Two china cups, obviously saved for best, came next with their partners, matching saucers. From a tin box, she spooned out three servings of tea: one for the pot, one for her, one for me.

When all was ready, she asked, "Shall I pour for you?" Receiving my agreement, she did exactly that.

Since leaving Lowood Academy, my life has been bereft of feminine companionship. I do not count Mrs. Fairfax, because of the difference in our ages. Greater still is the gulf that separates our temperaments. I am curious about the world at-large, I love ideas and nature. Mrs. Fairfax is content with who she is and what she knows. Lucy is as dear to me as any sister, but she lives in London. I have two female cousins, Mary and Diana, but they live many miles away, and I have not seen them for two years. Sitting at the table with Leah was a novel treat. I found my visit to be pleasant, and it recalled to my mind the many friends I'd made over the years at Lowood. At the same time, this visit was also different, because at Lowood, the other orphans and I were equals. Here in the Harrigans' cottage, I was the squire's wife and Leah was married to our man of all work. To her, the inequity must have seemed insurmountable; to me, it did not seem overly large.

But of course, she did not know my history.

In companionable silence, we enjoyed our tea. When the pot was nearly empty, I admired the sweater she was crocheting and admitted my poverty of skills in that arena. Leah offered to instruct me, and I was happy to accept her offer of tutelage. I explained, "They taught us to knit at Lowood, but I was never very good at it. Is one hook easier than two needles, I wonder?"

"I think so. Certainly, there is one less tool to contend with. If I may be so bold, what is Lowood?" she asked.

I did not want to answer, as those sad memories might spoil our happy visit. Realizing my silence might be misunderstood, I relented. "Lowood is a charity school for orphans. I was sent there at age ten by my aunt. Both my parents had died, but my uncle had promised his sister, my mother, to always care for me. When he died, his widow, my aunt, decided I was a burden, and Lowood was a convenient way to shunt me aside. I stayed at Lowood for eight years, altogether, the last two I served as an instructor."

Leah struggled to maintain a bland expression, until she succumbed to her surprise. Her mouth fell open in speechless wonderment. A mist of tears clouded her eyes. "Who would give up a little girl? And only ten years of age? What sort of person discards a child like a bit of rubbish? I would do anything to have a child of my own. Anything! Even raising someone else's child would be a blessing from heaven!"

"I can answer your question. The person whose heart is hardened against an orphan is a miserable type of creature. Worse yet, she never repented of her lack of charity." My voice trembled. "I shall never forgive my aunt. Ever. Not because she sent me to Lowood, as that was intended for harm but did me good. No, I shall never forgive her for making me feel weak, worthless, and undeserving of love when I was not."

"Oh, missus," Leah whispered, leaning toward me to awkwardly pat my hand.

"Leah! Mary?" A thin voice called out in the next room. I recognized the rough tones of John Harrigan. Leah leaped to her feet to see what the old man needed.

My hostess was gone for a long time. Through the thin walls came her voice, low and soothing. John's was strident, as he made various demands. I had thought to leave, but that would seem cowardly and impolite. My departure might provoke various worries, including causing Leah to question her very natural curiosity about Lowood. No, I could not depart on such terms.

When it became clear that Leah would be a while, I withdrew the pencil stub and small sketchpad I always keep in my pocket. With rapid strokes, I captured the scene before me, a pleasant image of wholesome domesticity. The fire had turned to embers. A nearby wood carrier offered more logs, but I did not dare feed the flame, lest I ruin the stew that was cooking. Instead, I took my time, viewing the scene as any artist might. On the mantel was a pretty seashell, a souvenir, perhaps, of a trip to the coast? A few empty jugs lined the wooden lintel as well. The fireplace itself was of brick, blackened with use, but the red against the charcoal coloring was most interesting. Closing my eyes, I attempted to commit the shades to memory.

"My, you have such talent." Leah's nearby voice startled me. She stood at my shoulder and stared down at my pad. "Oh, Missus, I cannot help but share my admiration, as your work is truly a gift to behold."

"You are very kind," I said. "Most probably I should have gathered my belongings and left, as I have certainly overstayed my welcome, but I did not want to seem rude when you had gone to the trouble of making us tea. It seemed that the least I could do was wait and share my appreciation. Thank you kindly, Leah, for the refreshment and for the offer of assistance with my crocheting." I hesitated, as I got to my feet. "If I may ask, how is John?"

She sighed. I nodded and gathered my things. Of accord and without words, we stepped outside the small abode. There in the sunshine and fresh air we could speak more freely. "James's grandfather fares poorly. I believe John has lost the will to go on, and I say this, having seen my own grandfather do the same. There comes a time in life when we are tired, and our body and spirit form an agreement that we should return to our maker. That, I believe, describes what John is feeling. It saddens me greatly, but it is the natural order, isn't it? As for Mary, she keeps herself busy, lest watching her husband's decline weigh too heavily on her spirit. Today, she told me she planned to walk all the way to Millcote. Can you imagine? That's a distance of five miles there and just as many back. She claims it does her good to stretch her legs. I think she does not want to sit here and watch her husband give up on life. And yet, that is exactly what she has done in so many ways."

I squinted at the soft autumn sun. "I can understand why Mary likes to walk. I do, too, especially when the weather is this fine. Being out of doors lifts my spirits, and my surroundings bring me much solace. I suppose Mary feels much the same. If only I could take my son, Ned, along on my rambles! He would benefit from fresh air. The sights and sounds of nature are salubrious. However, his push-cart cannot manage the uneven terrain, and I do not trust myself to carry him far."

Leah cocked her head and studied me with that open manner of hers. "Why not do what the gypsy women do?"

"Pray tell me, what is that? I am unfamiliar with their ways."

Pulling the shawl from around her neck, she demonstrated. First, she wrapped the fabric, which was longer than I suspected, around her back. Then she tossed one end over her right shoulder and brought the opposing end under her left arm. As she tied the two ends together, I realized she had made a cunning pocket, perfectly sized for a child. "As long as your material is tightly woven, your little boy should be safe and snug," she said, illustrating her handiwork. "I hope you will bring him here to visit. I should very much enjoy seeing your little boy. This family has served his father, his grandfather, and the squire who came before. It will be our honor to serve your son as well."

On my way home, I rediscovered the patch of bilberries and picked the shrubs clean. I cannot say why the birds had not found the fruit, nor could I guess how they managed to ripen so late in the year, but I am not one to question such good fortune. I put the berries in my handkerchief and carried them home.

That night as we dressed for dinner, I told Edward about my visit with Leah. He had many questions about John's health. These I could answer, although only in broad terms. I also told him how Mary was doing. Rather than chide me for talking to the wife of a staff member, my husband was indulgent. In fact, I believe it pleased him to know that I was making strides toward knowing the locals better.

As if to offer further compensation for my efforts earlier that day, Mrs. Fairfax brimmed over with happiness at dinner, when Cook produced the bread-and-butter pudding made with the bilberries that I had picked.

CHAPTER 4

A fortnight later, my husband called me into his study. Of all the rooms in Ferndean, the study is my favorite, as the walls of books beckon me to assume a new persona, travel to a distant land, or live in a different time. Edward's grandfather was a voracious reader, who bought books as frequently as other men buy ale in a tavern. The heavy desk that faces a southern window has become my husband's place of business, while I use a lap desk that once belonged to his mother. On this particular afternoon, Edward assumed his accustomed place behind his desk, while I occupied a stuffed chair we had positioned nearby. I held my tongue as I waited for him to speak, although I was brimming with curiosity.

"The furnishings should arrive next week. We were fortunate that the cabinet maker had a variety of pieces set aside for a request such as ours. Also, there had been a cancellation by another customer. That's rarely the case, but in this instance, our timing was fortuitous."

"That is good news," I said. "I have not yet heard back from Lucy. I expect a letter any day now. I do hope she accepts our invitation."

"Yes," he said.

I could tell there was more on his mind. "Even if she cannot make it for the holidays, I am sure she will come and visit us at a future date."

Again, I waited, as I knew this was not the crux of the matter.

He hesitated and then added, "I've decided to sell Mesrour."

I had not expected this. Mesrour is a magnificent animal. Admittedly, the stallion would be a challenge for most riders, but he has always been perfect for Edward. The two are a perfect pair, evenly matched in their force of will! And yet, Edward was ready to say good-bye to the animal. I interpreted this as an admission of defeat by my husband.

I could not let it go so easily. "Pray tell, why? Your riding continues to improve. What is it that provides impetus for altering your plans, when you are clearly regaining your abilities?"

My husband shifted his boots under his desk. He could not meet my gaze. "All of that is true," he said at last. "After I lost my hand, I was dead certain I would never have the skill to ride Mesrour again. But the horse is in need of constant exercise, and my abilities are not up to the task. I had clung to hopes that John might recover from his injuries. If so, he could continue his responsibilities, and James could ride the horse when it needs exercise. However, that has not been the case. As it is, James is occupied from sunup to sundown with our livestock. As you saw when you visited, Mary offers no assistance, nor is she likely to do so. If she would even feed the chickens, the geese, and the pigs, James would have time for Mesrour, but she seems incapable of those tasks. Leah has become John's caretaker around the clock."

"Could Mesrour not be put at the end of a lunge line? I recall John mentioning such a method."

"Indeed, exercising him at the end of a rope would be a useful alternative. Such a program would offer Mesrour many benefits, when I am not disposed to ride him. But again, I must be honest about the limitations of each work day. James cannot drive the cattle to the pasture, round up the sheep, and feed the other animals, while exercising my horse."

"I understand," I said, casting my eyes down. The sorrow in Edward's voice caused my heart to ache.

"Could you not ride Mesrour more often?" I asked. "Perhaps over a less challenging terrain than usual? Say, along a country road?"

"Even if I did, there is a problem after I dismount. A rider is responsible for examining his horse, making sure the animal has not picked up a stone or otherwise is injured, as well as removing the tack and cleaning it. I respect Mesrour too much to shirk my responsibilities. It would not do for that beautiful animal to go lame, because I cannot see well enough to examine him as I should." Edward's exhale was long and loud. By the set of his shoulders, I could see this deficiency pricked at his heart. Mesrour is more than a mount; he is my husband's much-loved companion, a wild and athletic creature, much like Edward was, before life beat him down. This was a painful admission—

that Edward could not uphold his responsibilities.

My husband got to his feet and walked to the window. With his arms behind his back, he stared out at the trees. Soon their limbs would be totally bare, as the leaves were clinging with desperation. My husband spoke both to me and to himself, "As diligent as James is, he cannot be at my beck and call in the stable. Especially now that his grandfather is doing poorly. Without another set of eyes to check over the horse, and a fresh set of hands to brush his coat, Mesrour lacks the care he deserves. Not to mention, the animal was born to run like the wind."

But was giving up Mesrour really the answer to our quandary? I wondered, "Would it not be better to hire a new stable hand?"

"I have considered another manservant, dear Janet, so I ask you to speak plainly. Is this problem the result of my diminished capacity, or is our situation more dire than I realize?" He kept his face turned to the window rather than address me forthrightly. "Are my weaknesses creating other problems in our household? Beyond those related to my horse?"

A frown creased my forehead. Edward was asking that I speak plainly. This was in keeping with his straightforward manner in approaching all household problems. I owed it to him to be candid.

"Whilst I am hesitant to call our situation dire, I will admit another pair of hands would be welcome. We could use someone to assist in household matters. Now and again, Cook needs help. The other day, she needed more wood brought in. She and I managed by making multiple trips to the woodpile. On occasion, I have fetched provisions from the cool pantry, the smoke house, or the ice house for her. Only yesterday, Cook needed James's help in keeping the firepit hot in the smoke house. I was there, when she asked him for help. He was torn between assisting her and checking on a ewe. I also know she has called upon him to help her move blocks of ice, chase down chickens, and fetch eggs. There are a myriad of errands that take her away from the kitchen. Leah cannot help us, because she must stay close to John's bedside. Mary is…not able to offer help either."

Edward was silent for a moment, as he considered what I'd said. "It is too bad that James and Leah do not have children of their own. Then, at least, the burden of caring for the elderly could be shared. Even a young child could run and get help when needed. Or sit by a bedside and offer succor."

"Yes," I said, as I heard my own son chattering to his nursemaid upstairs. My heart swelled with love for Ned. "A child can mean so much to a family. A little one under foot might improve Mary's melancholy as well. In fact, Leah specifically spoke to me about longing for a child. The lack saddens her greatly."

"The fact that Leah is barren disappoints all members of the Harrigan family." Edward shook his head and frowned.

"The longer I live, the more I perceive how little of this world is revealed to us. There is an aspect of childbearing that is a mystery. Longing does not equate to having, does it? I think of poor Lucy and her empty arms. What a blessing Evans is to her."

"If longing were the answer," said my husband, "I have no doubt that the Harrigan home would be filled with young ones. James has mentioned to me his disappointment in regard to wanting a child. Before his injuries, John would belabor the point to any and all who would listen. He even went so far one day as to suggest that James should ask for an annulment, since Leah had not gotten with child."

"Oh, no!" I could not believe what I was hearing. "Surely James would never do that!"

"Of course not. He loves Leah with all his heart. I share the old man's complaints with you for one purpose only: to point out how thorny the situation is. Not only is Leah at a disadvantage trying to care for a crotchety old man, she is bound to the bedside of a person who has strong opinions about his lack of a great-grandchild and went so far as to blame that same young woman who is now his caregiver."

"Truly, Leah deserves more of his affection! She never gave me the slightest indication that she was unwilling or unhappy caring for John. Nor did she seem angry with Mary for her unwillingness to do for her own husband." Injustice in any form always stirs my passions. Perhaps it is because I know how it feels to be unjustly accused and punished.

"Leah has a good heart. That is one of the reasons that James loves her." Edward sighed and walked back to his chair. "Returning to the matter at hand, I can see little else to do but sell my horse. Mesrour is high-strung. Moses, that donkey of ours, can traverse any terrain with no ill effect, but Mesrour is delicately formed. Even Rashana, the chestnut mare that pulls our gig, is of sturdy stock. After a drive, the mare requires only cursory care, but Mesrour has more intensive needs. And he deserves better than I can give him."

Despite his logical pronouncements, Edward's voice held a rasp of emotion that was painful to hear. I had the impression that giving up the stallion was Edward's self-imposed penance for not being able to properly take care of his fine steed.

"Let us return to possible solutions, husband. Is there enough work here for another grown man?" I wondered.

Edward explained, "An adult man with a family would want suitable lodging and other amenities that would be costly. There is not another cottage nearby on this estate. All are filled with those who work our land. Building a new dwelling would be costly and take time. Perhaps we could find a young man, who might content himself with sleeping in the backroom of the stable. It should be warm enough there at all times except in the worst of the winter months. During harsh weather, he could sleep on the kitchen floor."

Such arrangements were not unusual. At Alderton House, a young man slept on the kitchen floor in front of the fire. Even so, as one who had known the fierce bite of cold, I was not convinced the plan was workable. Rather than argue with my husband, I said, "Before we take a step as rash as selling Mesrour, let us explore other avenues. First, we could write to those who might know of a man seeking employment. Mayhap, we can find one who would meet our requirements. Perhaps those responses will shape our course of action."

"As you wish," said Edward.

CHAPTER 5

Thus, it was decided. Taking pen in hand, I gladly adopted my role as Edward's amanuensis, writing his words on a scrap of paper. After reading the script back to him, we discussed various approaches. Our list of requirements was not long, and the amount we were willing to pay was fair. Once we'd agreed upon the language that best described our needs and our situation, I suggested, "Let me pen a letter to Mr. Carter. As the local doctor, he travels the county and knows the local families well."

"Another copy to the rector might be useful. After all, he receives his living from us, and thus we are not asking him for a favor. Furthermore, he might well know of a person in need of a position such as we are offering," said Edward.

"I could even drop off the letter to the rector," I said. "Perhaps if I speak to him in person, he'll move to make a suggestion with alacrity."

In the event, I also wrote to our agent, and to a neighboring squire, who seemed to have his fingers in a dozen pies. Our instructions explained that anyone interested in being considered for the job should send word directly to our post office box.

"Tomorrow, if the weather is clear, I can take the donkey cart into Millcote and deliver our letters," I said.

"Do you mean the dog cart?" Edward asked.

The dog cart, I had learned, was so named because hunting parties used it to pull dogs around for their convenience. Although one could conceivably harness a large dog to the cart (or to any cart, I guess), that was not the derivative of the name. Typically, a pony or small donkey pulled the dog cart.

The practice of driving the cart was new to me, dwelling as I had in town and then at Lowood. Therefore, it took me a while to master the cart with a pony attached, and Patches, as the pony had been lamentably named by its first owner, was a highly undesirable example of a quadruped. The beast would as soon nip me as walk in harness. I could never let down my guard with that devil's spawn, given the pony's devious nature. In fact, I sported two large bruises after our last encounter. One from the animal kicking me in the shin, and the other from a bite on my shoulder. Yes, I could drive the dog cart, but only if no other options presented themselves. When I complained about Patches to James, he laughed. "They always say get a pony for the young 'uns! And I am always saying, any sort of animal but a pony, if you please. Don't surprise me one bit that nasty little creature found a way to inflict pain. I told Master, from the day he bought that animal, that I didn't like him. Not at all. So, I ain't surprised to hear you don't much care for him, either!"

Shortly thereafter, we found Patches another home. Thus, I was left with no transportation except our carriage, and while the Rashana was a good horse, my skills were too meager for safely driving such a large vehicle with its bouncing springs. In despair, I had asked James to assist me in acquiring the requisite skills to drive the donkey cart. Moses, the old white donkey, proved placid and predictable. While James's time was sparse, mine was pliable, and so we found a few pockets here and there for instruction. I had not deemed it necessary to share this tutelage with Edward, lest it remind him of his own deficits.

"Yes," I planted a kiss on Edward's furrowed brow as a sweetener. "I feel comfortable driving the donkey cart. I can even harness Moses myself. You see, I have been practicing in secret for several months now."

"Indeed?"

"You know I never felt confident about driving the gig," I said to Edward. "The seat is high, the springs are challenging, and our lane is pockmarked. Nor am I an experienced rider, so I would not feel at ease on the chestnut mare. But I wanted the freedom to come and go to Millcote, if I so desired. I also longed for a way to transport small items, if need be. James suggested that I learn to drive the donkey cart, using Moses as my trusty steed."

Edward rubbed his chin thoughtfully. "Yes, that would be sensible. The cart is low to the ground, easy to handle, and Moses is a plodder. This quest of yours for independence promises to be quite a story, Jane. Pray take a seat and tell me all."

~

"Moses would be perfect for your needs," James had said, with a slight smile curling his mouth.

"Moses?" I had repeated. Was he directing my attention to a Bible verse?

"Moses the donkey," he clarified. "He is a fine animal for a beginner." Quickly, the young man regretted his remark and apologized.

"James, you have no cause to apologize. I am well aware that my skills are inadequate," I said. "I am most appreciative that you are showing such concern for my well-being. Now, please demonstrate how to harness my new friend. I shall take notes on the process."

And, so he did.

After two lessons, I could (with effort) manage the gear necessary for attaching the donkey to the cart. As for urging the animal to do my bidding, James had been quite correct: Moses was both compliant and even-tempered. So much so, that rather than worry Edward or risk Mrs. Fairfax's continued approbation, I decided not to share my new activities.

Because James had been so busy, my jaunts were not as frequent as I would have preferred. When an opportunity presented itself, I tacked up the donkey, and James examined my work, searching for flaws. Upon his approval of my efforts, I would venture forth. In the beginning, James walked alongside Moses and me. In time, James stood at a watchful distance. Eventually, Moses and I had taken several short trips. At one point in our wanderings up and down the lane, I realized I was smiling broadly, an expression most uncommon for me. This newfound freedom was as exhilarating as a flute of champagne, and I relished my accomplishment. James had hinted to me that the donkey would be a willing companion, as Moses enjoyed a change of scenery—and so it seemed. The placid beast loved a ramble nearly as much as I did. Once, when we came to a small puddle in the lane and Moses refused to move, I clambered down. Taking the reins in my hands, I guided him forward and then rewarded him handsomely with a piece of apple. Since that trip, I'd taken pains to stop by the barn and offer the donkey a bit of apple or carrot, nearly every day. In response, the animal had come to recognize me as a benefactor.

"Moses has taken a shine to you, missus," said James. "See how he perks up them ears of his? I never seen him do that before."

"Doubtless the fact I bring him morsels to eat

has more to do with his warm welcome than any nod toward my character." I sounded as though the donkey's approval did not matter, but I still felt immensely pleased.

"Apples, carrots," scoffed James, "or kind words and scratches around the ears. It don't signify any difference to old Moses. To him, that sort of small gifts are what makes his long days worthwhile."

I realized that Moses was no different from any person I'd met. We all flourish, when treated with kindness. In all of us there's a yearning to feel loved.

"So, you are the one who has been driving the dog cart?" Edward asked me. His thick eyebrows had lifted in surprise. "I noticed a variation in the vehicle's placement from time to time. I assumed that James was behind the changes."

"Yes, I own up to the fact that my efforts to park the vehicle are not always entirely successful. Although I am getting better, or so I believe."

His brows settled back into their natural position. "That is neither here nor there. A few feet left or right do not matter," he affirmed. "I am proud of you, my Janet, for applying yourself to this new skill."

"I have only driven the cart short distances down the lane, but those jaunts have nurtured my feelings of mastery." Summing up my experience, I said, "Moses and I are getting along nicely."

"I believe Mrs. Fairfax will think you are being forward, if you travel to town alone," Edward said.

"I do not doubt she will, but there is no need for her to upbraid me. I am a married woman with a child, and my purpose is for the betterment of our family. My purpose is not entirely frivolous."

Edward reached for my hand. "None would blame you if it was."

"I do not plan to take the cart, today, although perhaps I shall use it, tomorrow." I paused and gave my husband a quick kiss on the cheek. "If Mrs. Fairfax finds fault with me, I shall direct any controversy back to you, my lord, straight away."

Edward raised an eyebrow. "You do that, Janet."

CHAPTER 6

The autumn days flew by and winter nibbled at the edges of our consciousness. One morning, we found a light coating of frost on the plants in the garden. Every night seemed colder than the last. On the last day of November, Mrs. Fairfax made haste to answer the front door. I heard her determined footsteps echo in the hall, before the heavy door creaked open.

"Take that around back," she ordered in a voice that brooked no argument. A clatter outside sent us both to the window. A large, long wagon being driven by two burly men came around the side of the house.

"Ah," said Edward. "At last, our new furniture has arrived."

I was eager to see what we had purchased, especially since much of the choices had been sketched by my own hand. Leaving the warmth of Edward's office, I hurried down the hall, through the kitchen, to the back entrance. There, standing as erect as a military guard, the old woman checked off each piece of furniture, as the men unloaded it from the wagon. The items were swaddled with blankets and an outer wrap of waxed canvas. Revealing them was a laborious process. Nevertheless, Mrs. Fairfax demanded to see each new item and submit it to her fulsome inspection. Two sat at her feet, a new rocker for the nursery and part of the truckle bed.

"Jane? Do you wish to grant these your approval?" she asked, when she realized I was standing at her shoulder.

"Yes, please," I said. After a brief inspection, I explained to the movers where the furnishings should go. Meanwhile, Mrs. Fairfax went back into the Manor. She returned with a paper that detailed what we'd purchased. Wisely, she had also brought along a pencil, so she could check out items as they were approved.

The nip in the air pinched my cheeks and

chaffed my hands. "Go in and grab your wrap," Mrs. Fairfax told me. Rubbing my fingers against my skirt to warm them up, I did as she suggested. I was in the hallway, lifting my woolen cloak from the hall tree, when Amelia stood at the top of the stairs. She had Ned on her hip and she called to me from the landing. "Missus? Please come here. I want to show you something."

"Will it not wait?" I asked. Amelia is entirely competent, and this sudden request for my presence seemed unusual. I hated to step away whilst the men unloaded our much-needed furniture.

"No, Missus, I think not." Amelia's somber expression worried me. Was Ned poorly? She disappeared back into the nursery. I raced up the stairs. Amelia had left the door open. The minute I crossed the threshold I spied Ned toddling toward me with his arms outstretched. I laughed out loud. "Oh, you darling boy!"

"I did not want you to miss his first steps," said Amelia. "This is such a special moment for a mother, and I could not bear for you to hear it secondhand from me."

"Aren't you clever?" I said, as I knelt on the floor. When I opened my arms to my son, Ned gurgled happily, saying something that approximated "Mama."

Just that quickly, the furnishings were forgotten! Instead, I sat with my little boy and Amelia. Time was forgotten, as I watched Ned waddle from one of us to the other, gleeful at his newfound motility. A few of his tries were unsuccessful, and he promptly landed on his backside. Just as quickly, he was up again.

At last, a rattle followed by a slamming noise warned me that the haulers must be done with their work. Only then did I turn away from my son and run down the stairs. I hurried outside to learn from Mrs. Fairfax that most of our new purchases had been carried to their specific rooms. Because the draper's shop was only a few blocks away from Mr. Foster-Davies workshop, the two vendors had rented one wagon to transport our purchases. Thus, my soft furnishings arrived at the same time as our new furniture. The two deliverymen dutifully carried each parcel up the stairs, as none of our new items belonged on the ground floor. Finally, only one item remained, and that was a bulky shape, hidden under a loose tarpaulin. I couldn't imagine what that could be, as the dimensions did not match any I had sent to the purveyor.

"Mrs. Fairfax?" I called out. She stood at the far side of the delivery cart. Her hands were folded at her waist, and her expression was one of supreme satisfaction.

I hurried to her side. "What is that last piece? I don't recall ordering anything with those dimensions."

"Be that as it may, that item belongs here." She pursed her lips, as if to withhold more information.

Seeing that she would offer no help, I walked briskly to the covered shape. As I bent to lift the tarpaulin, one of the deliverymen stopped me. "No, ma'am. Please don't. We was given strict instructions to cover this item with a tarpaulin once we delivered it," said the man who seemed to be in charge.

The hauler continued, "Mr. Foster-Davies says it's up to Mr. Rochester to remove it. None other."

As if by magic, my husband appeared in the doorway. Edward must have overheard the worker's commentary, because he said, "Yes. Exactly so. Thank Mr. Foster-Davies for following my instructions to the letter. Take it upstairs. Turn right at the landing and set that item inside the empty bedroom. Please close the door behind you. Mrs. Fairfax will lead the way for you."

The housekeeper squared her shoulders and

walked past the men. Her ramrod straight back disappeared into the Manor as the men struggled under the weight of their burden. I was left holding open the door.

"What is it?" I asked my husband, after everyone had promenaded past.

Edward was surprisingly gruff. "Please allow me my secrets. Do not enter into that empty guest room. If you do, you will spoil my surprise."

The deliverymen came back to the kitchen after their task. Cook offered them each a cup of tea, as they had a long journey back to London. This they accepted with gratitude, huddling in the kitchen, their huge hands holding incongruously small mugs. Both men bid us goodbye and thanked us for our business. Cap in hand, the one who seemed to be the leader, turned hurriedly to say, "Oy, and we handed the post-bag to your housekeeper."

Mrs. Fairfax waited for us in Edward's office. She stood in the middle of the carpet and held a letter in her hands. The post-bag was folded under her arm. "For you," she said, shoving the envelope at Edward. "From Lucy Brayton."

He handed it to me. Opening it, I scanned the familiar scrawl, until I got to the line affirming that Adèle, Evans, Mrs. Wallander, and Lucy would all be coming for Christmas. Lucy had decided to let her lady's maid, Polly, take the holiday off to visit with her ailing mother. I could scarce contain my joy, regarding the news of our upcoming guests, and announced the visit forthwith. "Such a happy letter," I said. "Adèle, Evans, Lucy, and Mrs. Wallander will all be joining us for Christmas."

"So, Mrs. Brayton will be visiting? But who is this Mrs. Wallander?" Mrs. Fairfax's voice trembled with irritation. Wisely, I decided not to respond. Instead, I let Edward explain, "She is the nanny for Mrs. Brayton's son, Evans. In fact, Mrs. Wallander has been with him, since his birth. Lucy used all her powers of persuasion to cajole the woman into staying on to ease the boy's transition."

Edward was as pleased as I was with the news. I suggested to my husband that we had yet another surprise to enjoy. "Looking over the furniture can wait," I said, "but this cannot," and I took Edwards's arm. Together we went up to the nursery, leaving a scowling Mrs. Fairfax to herself. Amelia steadied Ned on his feet, and then our son showed his father how he was learning to walk.

"What a smart young man!" Edward exclaimed, and he rewarded our baby with a gracious number of kisses.

Taking our leave of Ned and Amelia, Edward and I toured the newly filled bedrooms of Ferndean, admiring what we had bought from Mr. Foster-Davies. All was as I might have hoped. In fact, the pieces proved to be of fine workmanship. Indeed, Mr. Foster-Davies had shown himself worthy of Lucy's patronage.

Mrs. Fairfax seemed to have overcome her irritation, except for a small grumble or two. When I decided to unwrap the soft goods, she offered me her help, and together we examined the new bedclothes for the guest room that would be Lucy's. Using my watercolors as a guide, the draper had sent damask curtains and a matching bedspread in a shade of light daffodil yellow. Although she did not remark on it, I could see that Mrs. Fairfax noted how my choice brightened up the space.

"I have secured a promise from James to hang the curtains tomorrow or the next day," she said. "He was leaving the barn, when the deliverymen arrived."

"Thank you," I said, as I opened a package with two pillowslips, both sewn from pale yellow damask and edged with soft green trim.

"That's lovely," admitted Mrs. Fairfax.

"Isn't it just?" I carefully removed the paper from the other purchases, and when I was done, I pronounced my choices to be perfect. Lucy would love the newly appointed guest room. The truckle bed was a wonderful replacement for the pallet Amelia had used. I'd asked for a sky blue bedspread for both Amelia's bed and the truckle bed. Mrs. Fairfax assisted me in setting up the new bedclothes. When I invited Amelia to see the purchases, she rewarded me with squeals of delight. "That color is so pretty! Like the bluebells in the spring. I shall knit a blanket to put at the foot of the bed, and another for the truckle," she proclaimed. "'Twas ever so kind of you, miss."

"An unnecessary expense," huffed Mrs. Fairfax, but I could see she spoke out of envy. At some future date, I would do the same for her. Her favorite color was a periwinkle sort of violet, so I would paint a swatch and then have the bedclothes and curtains made to match.

All in all, my efforts had yielded a pleasing result. True, we needed a few more blankets and such, but what we had would keep Lucy comfortable during her stay.

With that pleasant forecast in mind, I sat down and penned a response to Lucy's letter, telling her that I had every confidence she would feel at home here. I took the liberty of asking her to relay any convenience we might have overlooked, so that we could procure it for her. Once I finished my note, I dressed for dinner. Now, my only concern was making sure the letter went out.

Cook had worked all day, and so we feasted on a splendid pepper pot soup, a haunch of venison, potatoes, stewed carrots, and a fine walnut and currant pudding. After the meal, Edward, Mrs. Fairfax, and I adjourned to the parlor. That evening, the change of seasons affected all of us most keenly. A brisk wind rattled our windows. Drafts blew through the entire lodge, and a chill permeated the air. This was but a prelude to less hospitable weather to be sure. While Mrs. Fairfax read aloud from the London papers, I decided I should go to Millcote and deliver my letter to Lucy straight away. Elsewise, the snow could make my trip treacherous.

Edward seemed rather pensive. When Mrs. Fairfax finished reading several articles that my husband had found interesting, Edward said, "As the month of December is upon us, I find myself considering the upcoming Christmas holidays. Have you any special wishes, my little Janet? Any customs or habits you want to establish here in our own household?"

The questions took me by surprise. No moments in my history could be drawn upon as templates for merry-making. There was only one holiday I could remember with happiness, and even that had been tinged with sadness.

When I learned that Edward was not free to marry, I was sorely tempted to toss convention to the wind and live with my love, forgoing the benefit of sacrament. However, say what you will about my upbringing in a charity school, I will admit that a strong sense of morality is ingrained in the deepest regions of my being. And to be honest, I could not bear the thought of having to hide our union from the ugly sobriquets of the world, at large. I would not allow others to turn a love so pure into a foul joke, as I knew full well they would. I could not stomach being near to Edward every day and knowing we must live as friends. Instead of following my carnal desires, I decided to run away from Edward and leave Thornfield Hall immediately.

How vivid is that sad memory! First, I told

Edward of my decision. He could not dissuade me from saying goodbye, as I knelt beside him. Touching that strong jaw and turning his head toward me, I kissed his cheek and stroked his hair. "God bless you. God keep you from wrong and from harm. Reward you well for all the past kindnesses you have shown me." What a struggle it was, trying to keep my voice level! Every particle of my being cried out, "Stop, Jane!" I was walking away from my one true love. How I wanted to stay with Edward!

But I could not.

Overwrought with emotion, I stumbled out into the world. All I knew was that I had to go away, and to stay away, I must travel to a place where Edward had no connections. My lack of preparation was appalling. My entire savings, twenty shillings, were not enough to buy me a coach ride, but the driver took pity on me. Once I had exhausted those meager funds, I determined to walk…but where should I go? I had no place. None in this big wide world.

The pain of my breaking heart drove me to put one foot in front of another. Nature was my hostess, as I slept in a mossy bower. For sustenance, I ate a handful of ripe bilberries! By the time I found a nearby town, my disheveled appearance caused good people to shun me, even while I begged for work. When they drove me away, I had no choice but to keep on walking, the gripping hunger in my belly seemed a fair penance for the wrong I had committed, by loving a man who was not free to return my affection. At some point far beyond sanity, a choice presented itself. On the horizon appeared a hamlet, where a gleaming church spire pointed directly toward God. I reckoned He was signaling to me that I should keep going.

I meandered like a lost dog, hungry, dirty, and tired. Once I gained that village, I went from door to door, asking for work, but all who answered my knock turned me away. Despair piled upon despair, as I trudged the cobbled streets, enduring what any beggar must, that sickening blend of inhospitality and repulsion. My last hope was a parsonage, and a glimmer of possibility lightened my steps. Surely a kind clergyman would know of a position I could fill or, at the least, find me a bed for the night. Christian charity had saved me once before, if one could consider my life at Lowood a boon. Perhaps I could call upon God's help yet again. Lifting one foot and then another, I forced myself to draw nigh unto that white church spire. The rectory was but a small distance away. With trepidation, I used the door-knocker. This time I was turned away by the rector's housemaid, even as I tried to barter my gloves for a crust of bread. "Is there not a clergyman inside who cares for the poor? The desolate? The needy? Am I not still one of God's children, even in these miserable straits?"

But my cries were lost in the howl of a cruel wind portending a winter storm. With that solid door shut in my face, I considered curling up on the stoop and letting Mother Nature do with me what she will. But a stronger force from deep inside me drove me on. So, I staggered away from the church and the rectory. More weak than ever, I went forward, following no particular direction, but praying I might find shelter somewhere, somehow.

I cannot tell you why I was granted intervention from the good angels. All I can say with surety is that they delivered me to safety. Surely, I could not have lasted much longer in the cold, as a soft drifting of snowflakes quickly turned into a stinging blast of icy rain. Wet, weary, hungry, and in desperate need of shelter, I literally stumbled onto the front steps of Moor Cottage, a tidy dwelling shared by the Rivers siblings, Diana, Mary, and their brother, St. John. Finding me too ill to stand, the Rivers took me in and nursed me back to health. Some months passed, and to the outward observer, my health had mended. My soul would never be repaired, but my stay there at Moor Cottage allowed me the time I needed to patch up that torn portion of my psyche. Thanks to the care and friendship of the Rivers siblings, I was able to heal, while safely hidden from the world of Edward Rochester.

After we became better acquainted, and they had the opportunity to witness the fruits of my education, they helped me find work as a teacher. Much later, we learned that I was an heiress. The fortune was left me by a distant relative who was also kin to the Rivers. More important than money, I had a loving family! St. John, Mary, and Diana were not only my saviors but my blood kin. The beggar that my cousins had taken to their bosoms was actually a woman of means, and I repaid them by sharing my newfound wealth with them.

Shortly thereafter, on a day when the Rivers siblings had been called away, I found yet another opportunity to repay their kindness. Christmas was but days away. With the help of their housemaid, I cleaned the small house from chamber to closet, only to turn around and polish it with beeswax and oil. The small domicile fairly glowed with my efforts. My labors were finished shortly before Mary and Diana returned. Their boisterous pointer, Carlo, and I greeted the sisters on their doorstep. He signaled his affection with happy barking and vigorous wagging of his tail, while I embraced my cousins and clasped them to my heart. St. John joined us shortly thereafter. The four of us celebrated Christmas week in merry, domestic dissipation.

Curious as it sounds, at the lowest point in my life, I'd found shelter, fortune, and family. All that I lacked was the one person I loved more than life itself, Edward Fairfax Rochester.

And now that we were married and marveling at the joy we experienced with our son, I truly did have everyone anyone could ever want.

"Jane?" Edward was waiting for my response to his question, even as these thoughts renewed their presence in my mind. His gentle prompt returned me to the present, as I gave myself a tiny shake to focus. Looking at me curiously, he repeated his question, "I asked if you had any particular holiday wishes that we can assume for our own. The commission of even the smallest details would be pleasurable to me. Though Ned is yet young, I aim for him to grow up remembering happy times with our small family. Naturally, that means his mother must be well looked after."

That pronouncement brought an unexpected hitch to my voice, and I fought the tears prickling behind my eyes. Clearing my throat, I talked about my time with the Rivers. "I did once spend a quiet Christmas week with my cousins. We talked, read books, and I translated a passage in German. That is the most pleasurable holiday I can remember. Otherwise, I have naught to contribute, when it comes to the execution of a happy Christmas. I am sorry to say, sir, that my experience with merriment has been severely limited."

"Did you not play snapdragon?" asked Mrs. Fairfax. The cant of her head spoke volumes. The older woman was disbelieving of my past.

"Snapdragons, like the flowers in the garden?" That made no sense to me. Where would one get those in the dead of winter?

"No." She clucked her tongue. "Snapdragon is a game, whereby raisins soaked in liquor are tossed into a bowl and set aflame. The object is to snatch one up and eat it."

That shocked me. "And children do this?"

"Not babes, but young ones do." Mrs. Fairfax set aside her knitting to stare at me. Seeing the socks she was making reminded me that I needed to buy yarn in town, if I hoped to learn to crochet. Although I could turn to Mrs. Fairfax and try again to master knitting, I decided that I would rather use crocheting as an excuse to spend time with Leah.

Edward was back to wondering about my holidays. "Did you never spend hours staring at a Yule Log, as it was slowly devoured by flames?"

"How is the fire from a Yule Log different from peat or coal? Or any other log?" I asked. My curiosity was rewarded with a gasp from Mrs. Fairfax.

"Do not tease us, Jane," she scolded.

"Mrs. Fairfax, it is not in my nature to poke fun. You know that." I spoke evenly, whilst nudging the housekeeper back toward the truth. I had not experienced a happy holiday. Ever. Indeed, most of my life had been bleak.

And she should realize as much, because she often chided me for my inability to settle my features into a smile or a tableau of contentment. Instead, she ofttimes complained that I looked melancholy. When she queried me, I would only say that I came by that emotion honestly. My gratitude for my current life notwithstanding, I shall always remember those times when I was alone and without comfort. They formed me. They taught me how much suffering there was in the world.

"Allow me to try again," said Mrs. Fairfax. "Surely, as one who grew up on this green isle, you'd enjoyed your share of caroling. You did, did you not?"

To that I nodded. "We sang hymns while I was at Lowood, but I would not say I enjoyed caroling. Those songs repeated religious themes appropriate to the season. None of them was particularly cheerful. Nor did we sing any place other than inside the church. It was not allowed."

Mrs. Fairfax shook her head. "That's regrettable. There are many hymns of exultation."

"Tell us about your holidays at your Aunt Reed's house." Edward stirred in his chair, so he could see me more clearly.

"I believe the holidays at the Reed house were much the same as most people might enjoy," I said honestly. "Presents were exchanged. Guests were invited. There were dinner and evening parties."

"And did you enjoy them?" Edward raised an

eyebrow.

I turned to him with a blank face. "Excuse me, sir?"

"Did you enjoy the parties? The visits with guests? The presents?" He studied my face.

"I was not a participant," I said, doing my best to overlook the growing expression of anger on his face. "Aunt Reed did not think me fit company for her children, much less for visitors. I was confined to my room during those festivities. Therefore, I cannot say whether those activities were enjoyable or not. When Bessie, the maid, was not minding me, I would press my ear against the bedroom door, so that I could listen to the music and singing. That's when I would overhear the music. I had a doll that was a cast-off from Georgina, a figure with a few wisps of hair and a hard body. Her facial features had been rubbed away, so that I could not discern any expression at all. None. Even so, I often took my doll to my crib and held her all night long, when there was merrymaking. I very nearly took the doll with me to Lowood, but at the last minute, Georgina reminded me the doll belonged to her."

A heavy silence followed. It was terribly uncomfortable for all of us. I wondered if I had ruined all prospects of a happy Christmas.

At length, Edward said, "It makes me angry to think of how vulnerable you were! You were only a child, and every child needs—deserves—love. If it were in my power to change those bitter memories, I would do so."

That brought a smile to my face. "You talk of magic, sir. Winding a clock backwards? Then why contain such wizardry to changing my past? I am happy today. I have survived. No, if I was granted a magic wand, I would use it to care for all the unfortunates in the world today. Especially for the children. At the very least, I should cast a spell so they had food and shelter."

"It seems like so little to ask," my husband admitted," to give a child nourishing food and a warm fire. Are you sure that would not spoil them?"

This was said in jest, and I knew it as such.

"Spoil them? Coming from you, sir, that is rich indeed. I have watched you shower Adèle with dolls, sweeties, new ribbons, a rabbit fur muff, and colored pencils. Now that, my kind husband, would come closer to spoiling the poor than what I propose. No, I would only hope to make the children's lives bearable. Feeding them and keeping them warm would still prove deprivation, if they lack affection and love."

Edward frowned in thought. "Were all of the girls at Lowood orphans, Jane?"

"Oh, no, sir. One or two were from large Christian families, with parents who could not afford to feed or house them. Five were sisters, the daughters of a clergyman. His wife was often ill, and he was a great believer in education, but he could not teach all the girls by himself and do his parish work. Also, the reverend had a son, and he determined that all of his resources should go to his male issue. He fooled himself into believing that the girls would somehow find suitable husbands or occupations, such as teaching. To me, it seemed clear they had no chance of that, being without proper dowries or proper introductions to suitors."

"What happened to those sisters?"

"Two of them died of typhus straight away. Another, weakened by the loss of her sisters and her own heartbreak, died shortly after." And a thought came to me. A voice from long ago whispered in my ear, those wise words from my dear friend, Helen Burns, "Life appears to me to be too short to be spent in nursing animosity or registering wrongs." Perhaps Helen had been right.

It was odd to reflect on how short her life had been. I'd only known Helen a brief while, before she died, and yet her loving nature had shaped my guiding principles. Helen had been the soul of forgiveness. I did my best to model my behavior after hers. Thus, I had concluded that the cruelty I'd endured at Lowood was not worth fretting over. In day-to-day life, I did my best not to think about my past. When I did go back to Lowood, it reopened the bandages that I'd carefully applied to my wounded soul.

Edward spoke with great weariness, "Your pleasures, by your own account, have been few, Jane. I cannot change them, but I shall endeavor to make up for those early deficiencies."

A teardrop rolled down my face and splashed on my hand. Oddly, I had not realized I was crying. Fishing a handkerchief from my pocket, I wiped the moisture from my face. Edward sensed my sorrow. He reached out for me. I took his hand in mine and comforted him. "Sir, I have endured many a sad time in my life, but how can I regret the road that led me to you?"

Slowly he smiled. "Ah, Jane. What a pair we are! Survivors in the storm-tossed seas of life. How I love you. Thank you for saving me, my angel."

"And thank you for loving me," I answered him.

CHAPTER 7

Mrs. Fairfax had been listening, quietly. Her knitting needles had stilled, and now they rested in her lap. "Jane, despite the deprivations, surely those who taught at the charity school found a way to invoke a modicum of holiday cheer. Did you observe St. Stephen's Day, or maybe you called it Boxing Day? How about when Lowood employed you as a teacher? Surely then you were given that day off. Perhaps they even slipped you a coin or two in a box with food?"

My puzzlement must have shown on my face. "One year, yes. The day after Christmas was set aside for a few of our staff to visit their families.

To avail yourself of the day off, you had to have your mother write the headmaster. Of course, my mother had long since passed away. So, I was one of those who stayed at the school. The cook disappeared, and we were treated to a cold collation for our meals. I believe we spent the day reading."

"Is that all?" Mrs. Fairfax sounded desperate.

"One year," I said slowly, "when I was eleven, one of the girls went home for the holidays. She came back with a small bag of sweets and fudge, I believe. She did not share her spoils, but she did eat them with great gusto. The head teacher discovered the treasure trove and promptly took it away, explaining that such frivolities would distract us from the true meaning of Christmas."

"And that true meaning was?" Edward prompted.

"I was taught that the birth of Christ is but the preface to a sad story that ends with death and sacrifice. Time and time again, we were cautioned that this season of light was a precursor to the crucifixion that must inevitably follow, as it was ordained by God our father."

Edward's countenance displayed a perfect look of disgust. "When explained that way, why should we celebrate any portion of life, given that we are all headed for the grave?"

This philosophy was one I embraced with fulsome understanding. "As one who loves nature, I have come to accept that brevity is part of its charm. If we do not gather rosebuds today, we cheat ourselves and lose an opportunity to experience the profound gratitude that is incumbent on all of us. Looking ahead to our inevitable demise is useful, if only to remind us to savor each day."

"This philosophy of dire inevitability does not improve your life, Jane. In fact, I would argue that any repudiation of joy flies in the face of our more natural instincts. Tell me, was this impoverished viewpoint foisted on you or did you nurture it yourself? I ask, because the miserable circumstances of your life cannot have fostered a belief that life bends toward bounty." Edward's tone was gentle, probing as if he were touching a festering sore.

Rather than answer without thinking, I took my time and gave the matter full consideration. As I think best when I am in motion, I rose and picked up the nearby tongs. With care, I stirred the fire, causing a small blaze to flare amidst the embers. Mephisto noted my restlessness. Rising to his feet, he arched his back and stretched in a languid manner. His stomach dragged against his bedding, no doubt the result of Cook slipping him choice tidbits in the kitchen.

"Thinking back," I said, "this dim view of the future was inculcated within me by those around me. They claimed to know better than I." My words were plain and true, without adornment or exaggeration. I returned the tongs to their vigilant position beside the other fireplace tools. Then I settled back in my armchair, feeling the need to elaborate. "My Aunt Reed never included me in any familial celebrations. Nor was I invited to sit at the table for the elaborate meals contingent on the holiday. Never did she offer me a single Christmas present, even though she showered my cousins with all sorts of toys, sweets, and other prizes."

I continued by saying, "I never asked her why I was excluded. She introduced her reasoning, shortly after I came to stay with her. According to my aunt, I was the product of a deceitful alliance. Aunt Reed said my father tricked my mother into marriage, hoping to lay claim to her family fortune. When my mother was discovered to be with child, she was promptly disinherited, and Aunt Reed said I was only barely legitimate. Certainly, I was not welcome in the Reed family. Aunt Reed could tell by looking at me that I was a nasty, selfish girl, and I did not deserve presents or any special treatment at all! She explained that I should count myself fortunate not to be in the poorhouse."

"Blast it all, Jane," said Edward through clenched teeth. "No child is responsible for how she is brought into this world. Your Aunt Reed promised her husband to care for you as one of her own, and yet, by all accounts, she did you no favors. Her weak attempt at Christian charity is a farce! As for being selfish, as you have no doubt observed, it's the nature of children to concentrate on their own needs, and rightly so. The youngest among us have no power. They have no real responsibilities except to grow into adulthood, a task that can only be accomplished with rigid self-absorption. Can we rightfully call Ned selfish? Of course, he is. He demands to be fed, to be held, and to have every one of his needs fulfilled. If he did not, would we know how to care for him? Pray consider, what duties can he perform for us? What can he exchange for this caregiving? He has nothing to give back but the occasional smile. And yet, your aunt would no doubt find his character wanting. From what you have told me, your aunt offered you nothing, save the necessities required to sustain your tenuous hold on life. Considering that she was an adult, and a woman of considerable resources, I can offer her memory no sympathy, and I strenuously urge you to reconsider her spurious conclusions."

When I substituted my darling son, Ned, for my younger self, the import of Edward's words found their mark. Edward was right! Had I been selfish? No more than any other child and assuredly less than some. By way of comparison, I held up Adèle as an example. She was a bastard child with no real claim to Edward's continued patronage, and yet he had always treated her with care and affection. Even though she had been abandoned by her mother, Celine, and despite the fact she was not even related to Edward, he had extended sincere affection to the child. Never once did I hear him disparage her or chide her or castigate her as a drain on his resources. This was despite the fact that Celine had walked away from her daughter without as much as a fare-thee-well. Furthermore, the woman publicly humiliated Edward, by running off with another lover! Even so, my husband did not attach the sins of the mother to her child. Moreover, if Edward had not concerned himself with Adèle's future, we would have never met, because I had come to Thornfield in order to serve as Adèle's governess.

Edward's analogy, my comparison of my situation with that of Adèle, was a revelation. With a new clarity, I saw how Aunt Reed had tried to blame me for her cruelty. In truth, I had always suspected that her unkindness toward me was unwarranted, but I had never before considered how truly blameless I was! Bessie, the Reed's maid, had told me repeatedly that I was a wicked girl. Now I was forced to review her remarks as well.

Had I been a bad seed?

Using pure logic, divesting myself of emotion, I reviewed my childhood. I had only the haziest of memories of my father. My mother had been ill for a long time, before she died. I could barely recall sitting next to her on her bed, playing quietly with a picture book, telling myself a story. There had been an older woman, a landlady? A maid? She had mopped my mother's brow, and it was she who pronounced my mother dead and closed her eyes one last time.

After a long time, Uncle Reed sent for me, but

the trip to his London home was long and... dusty. I remembered choking on dust. Uncle Reed was dying, when I arrived at his home. Aunt Reed sobbed and sobbed, and I knew immediately that my arrival was taken as a bad omen. My Reed cousins teased and tortured me. Bessie was kind but brusque. To Bessie, I was yet another responsibility added to her list.

But had I really been selfish? No. Never. Unless wanting to be loved was a product of selfishness.

Mrs. Reed insisted I was a liar, but that was quickly disproven, even while I was at Lowood.

An ingrate? Perhaps. But then, I was given very little other than life's necessities.

A thief? Mrs. Reed said I was. My only companions were the books in Uncle Reed's library. I borrowed them, it is true, but I did not steal them.

Violent? I did defend myself from my cousins, but all three of them were older and bigger than I. I never started a fight, but after being pummeled and slapped many times, I grew weary of their attentions.

Of course, this mental review took only seconds, measured by the mere ticking of the coach clock on the mantel. The answer came to me, as bold and brilliant as a strike by lightning. No, I had not been a bad child. I had only been a sorrowful child, who lost her parents. Every child deserves to be wanted and loved. If one were to call me selfish, then it would be because I wanted a crumb of affection. That is all.

Edward and Mrs. Fairfax had waited patiently for my reply. I continued to stir the fire, whilst thinking of a suitable answer. At last, I said, "You are right. My past has been injurious to my sense of self-worth. Certainly, I have not been a participant in those portions of life that others take for granted. Through no fault of my own, I have never been treated to a happy Christmas, save for that time that I spent with my Rivers cousins. And then, I was the architect of our merriment. Looking back, I can see now that I have been cheated of the joys of this season. Pray, tell me what I have missed, as from this day forward, I intend to rectify the deficit." I put down the poker and stepped away from the hearth, so I could look Edward and Mrs. Fairfax in the eyes. I said, "With your help, of course."

"Jane, I cannot change your past, but I am determined to set the course for your future," said Edward.

"Let me offer my assistance as well," said Mrs.

Fairfax. "I hadn't realized...well, let's all look to the future, shall we?"

The evening marked a turning point. Pursuant to this conversation, a multitude of plans were put forth, and a few were immediately put into action.

CHAPTER 8

The next morning dawned rainy and cold, so my trip to town needed to be postponed. Sitting in the open cart would make for a miserable five-mile journey, and my errands could wait one day. Perhaps the inclement weather was for the best, as it gave me more time to plan for the holidays, especially since I'd been given my marching orders. With the proper preparation, I had no doubt that Ferndean Manor would be the site of a wonderful holiday season.

After a breakfast of toasted bread and tea, I went to the kitchen to visit with Cook. She was standing in front of the close closet, looking quite fierce. Her fists rested on her hips, and she shook her head at an empty bowl streaked with the remnants of the walnut and currant pudding. "Did Master eat this during the night?"

"I cannot see how. Edward and I slept soundly all evening," I said. "Perhaps Mrs. Fairfax indulged her sweet tooth?"

"Nay, she swears she had none of it."

"Perhaps Pilot stood on his hind legs and helped himself?"

"Not likely. That big dog has never been a thief before. Besides, as ye can see, this crock was in the close closet. I always keep it latched. Pilot could not have forced his way inside." With the air of a woman badly treated, Cook set the bowl in the dry sink. "Food was meant to be eaten, of course. It's only that I like to plan out what to serve ye, and it's hard going when the victuals disappear."

I could only commiserate her loss and then change the subject. "Last night, Edward, Mrs. Fairfax, and I decided that we should make this a festive holiday season. Toward that end, we shall need appropriate menu items. What might you suggest? What do we need? If this rain lets up, tomorrow I shall take the cart into town. Is there anything in particular that you lack for our larder?"

"A happy holiday, eh? Too right, I say." Cooke

interlaced her fingers and rested them on the waistband of her apron. "I can write down the supplies I need, but I'd like to go over the upcoming menus with ye, if ye please," said Cook. Her voice dropped to a lower pitch, as she spoke quietly to make eavesdropping nigh unto impossible. "Mrs. Fairfax has requested several recipes in particular. I done told her I'll submit them to ye, Missus. I hope I ain't speaking out of turn, but ye're my mistress, and I'll be taking my orders from none but ye. I ain't sure that Mrs. Fairfax liked what I said, but that's that, to my way of thinking."

"I see," I said. On occasion, Mrs. Fairfax sought to retain the upper hand and styled herself as the decision maker for our household, despite Edward's warnings that she was overstepping her boundaries. I was the lady of the manor, for better or worse. True, I relied upon her, but she often tried to ignore me. Old habits die hard, especially when they are fueled by hidden agendas. On occasion, Mrs. Fairfax still had trouble seeing me as her cousin's spouse, and therefore, as her mistress. Once, when she had seriously gone too far by making a decision without consulting me, Edward reminded me we could send Mrs. Fairfax packing. But to my mind, that was going too far in the other direction. The woman had served Edward and his family most of her life. Most impressively, she kept the household humming along, no matter what calamities befell us. My only quarrel with her was that too often she circumvented me, in order to do exactly what she wanted. I believe this was more a matter of habit than of malicious intent.

Cook continued, "As for the menus, I've got them right here."

With a flourish, she produced a folded paper from the pocket of her apron. I looked over her scribblings quickly. Misspelling abounded, but I could still understand the gist. Cook continued, "What exactly would ye wish for me to prepare for the holidays? A nice punch? A roasted peacock? Blood sausage? Maybe loaves of rye bread to give to all our visitors? Mince pies and boiled puddings are always nice for giving to the tenants."

"To the tenants?" I repeated. Having never been the wife of a squire before, such niceties were beyond my ken. But Cook's commentary sparked a buried memory of the one Christmas I'd spent at Thornfield Hall, before it burned down. Vaguely, I could recall a procession of visitors to the Hall's kitchen. None came into the

Hall proper. All seemed to have a sense of purpose, but I could not tell why.

When I asked Mrs. Fairfax what these guests signified, she explained, "Master Edward's father, the Old Squire, George Howell Rochester, was always a kindly benefactor to those who rented and worked on his land. On Boxing Day, it was his habit to give each of his tenants a box with a token amount of cash, a nice bit of cheese, a loaf of bread, and a boiled pudding. I expect that hubbub you heard is naught but our renters stopping by the kitchen to claim their own."

The revival of that memory allowed me to confirm Cook's suggestion. "Yes, exactly so. Thank you for thinking about the tenants. A sausage, a loaf of bread, a pudding, a hunk of cheese, and a coin. I believe that would be sufficient, don't you?"

Cook smiled in satisfaction. "Aye. That takes care of the tenants and their kin. What is it that ye fancy for your own table, missus? Being a fine lady yourself, ye must have enjoyed many a holiday feast or two."

How little she knew of my past! Once again, I was surprised at the assumptions made by other people. Cook thought I'd led a grand life, but this was not the time and place to correct her thinking.

Instead, I turned my mind to that holiday with my Rivers cousins. And yes, that had been joyful, although not necessarily extravagant. Hannah, their maid-of-all-work, and I had spent days in happy culinary pursuits, chopping sweetmeats, grating spices, stirring batters, and concocting a multitude of cakes, puddings, biscuits, and breads for the Christmas celebration. I had committed to paper several of that good woman's recipes, including a mulled wine that scented the air delightfully with clove and nutmeg. But surely, Lucy and Edward might expect a bit more than that? It had been rather humble.

"My experiences are not as fulsome as you might imagine. But I do have a recipe for mulled wine," I managed at length, by choosing to be honest and stopping there. "What dishes have you made in years past?"

Cook tilted her head and drew in a long inhale as she parsed her memory. "Of course, I can do what's been done before, but if there's one dish or another ye are especially fond of…"

"Goose," I said. I could not tell you where that came from, but a distant corner of my memory dredged up the fragrance of a goose roasting on a spit. I could vaguely recall that I'd had a cold portion of the bird for my meal, when I had lived at the home of my Aunt Reed.

"Then goose, it is." Cook clapped her hands together, joyfully. "I know how to make a roast goose that's so lovely, it'll bring tears to your eyes."

Imagining a fine Christmas dinner and a Boxing Day, that would fill the bellies of our tenants, sent my spirits soaring. Edward had been right—we could fashion this winter celebration in any manner we pleased! This would be a wonderful adventure. "Cook, what else would you suggest?"

"I'm a daft hand at making marzipan icing for Christmas cakes. Also, I'm partial to Charlotte Russe. Are ye familiar with that?"

She sketched out the ingredients, sponge biscuits, whipping cream, and liquor. The Charlotte Russe sounded like a perfect addition and perfectly suitable for company. Lucy rarely ate much, but the sweet inducements would make a marvelous menu addition. "Yes, make the Charlotte Russe," I said, and then it occurred to me to ask, "Perhaps you were hoping to take Christmas Day off and visit your family?"

"Ye are too kind, missus," Cook said, shaking

her head. "Truly ye are. My family and I will celebrate on Twelfth Day, the Feast of the Epiphany, if that's satisfactory. That's our tradition, and I'd like to keep it as such, if it won't inconvenience ye none."

"Of course, it won't," I said. "We shall open the bulk of our gifts on New Year's Day, unless Edward decides to break with tradition."

"Then, it's decided." Cook gave me a brisk nod. "I'll get your hot meal started early on Twelfth Day. I can leave a cold collation for ye to eat for the day after. I know Missus Brayton is coming, and I would never leave your guests wanting."

"Cook? I am thankful for your good planning."

"I aim to put all my skills to good use for the benefit of your family and Mrs. Brayton. Mayhap, this will be your best holiday ever, missus, and as the years go on, God willing, each one will be better yet." Cook clapped her hands together. "I shall write a list of supplies that ye can take into Millcote."

"Let me find that recipe for mulled wine and bring it to you." I headed upstairs to the master bedroom to fetch my journal from the bedside table. As I mounted the steps, I realized Cook had not asked me how many guests were expected.

That seemed curious. She had mentioned Lucy, but only her. Furthermore, I hadn't mentioned Lucy to Cook, yet she had known about our friend's visit.

In fact, that seemed exceedingly odd. No doubt, either Edward or Mrs. Fairfax had warned Cook. Yes, that made sense. As I retrieved the journal, my mind whirled with ideas.

There was one other person I could consult about holiday festivities, another person who might share a favorite recipe or two with me.

That person was Lucy.

After copying out the recipe for the mulled wine and giving it to Cook, I sat down and wrote a letter.

Mrs. Captain Augustus Brayton

24 Grosvenor Square

London

Dear Lucy,

News that you are joining us has set off a flurry of activity and a bevy of hearts overflowing with joy. Edward and I have decided to make this the merriest holiday ever seen here at Ferndean. This celebration will serve as a rebuke to all the sad times in my past. Or at least, that is what we have planned. Whether we can manage this, I shall soon discover, and I must admit I feel a certain burden of responsibility. I am sure you, and you alone, will understand my natural trepidation. I have no knowledge of such festivities. I want this to be everything Edward (and you) might hope for and more. In short, I am committed to creating a family event that we can look back on, and add to, from now on. Certainly, I hope for a celebration that Adèle, Ned, and Evans can look back on, fondly.

That is but one reason I am writing you, dear friend. (Another, of course, is because I owe you a letter.)

What ideas can you share with me for merriment? Does your cook have any recipes that you think are especially delicious?

I know that Adèle will firmly approve of a high-spirited affair. Since she is there with you, could you take her shopping for holiday gifts? And if it isn't too much trouble, could I trouble you to make a few purchases for me? I have noticed that Edward needs a new pair of riding boots, so I've traced the sole of his old pair on a sheet accompanying this letter. Adèle has enjoyed her time with you. Could you choose a gift for her that would come from us? Perhaps she has seen a bonnet that might be suitable? Or a reticule? Or a pair of earrings? Since I am not there, I cannot guess what might please her in the same efficient manner that you can, so would you be my surrogate?

I cannot emphasize this enough: We are delighted that you and Evans (and Mrs. Wallander) will join us here at Ferndean Manor. Although I recognize that we shan't be able to offer you all the amenities of a Christmas in London, we will try to make up for any deficiencies with our deepest affection.

As for any news from our little corner of the world, John Harrigan is still unwilling or unable to leave his bed. His wife, Mary, goes on long rambles to bolster her spirits. Their granddaughter-in-law, Leah, is doing her best to care for her husband's grandparents, and that means that all of the responsibilities for animal husbandry and other errands fall to their grandson, James. Therefore, Edward has decided to sell Mesrour, claiming that his horse cannot get proper care. As an alternative, I have suggested trying to hire a helper, but thus far, our efforts to find a new person have not yielded any candidates that would suit.

I do enjoy my visits with Leah. She has promised she can teach me to crochet. I hope so. Of course, they expected us to learn knitting at Lowood Academy, but my clumsy efforts disappointed my teacher immensely. Eventually, she threw up her hands—and sent a ball of yarn flying—in disgust.

Instead of knitting, I was permanently designated as the person who would wind the balls of yarn for other students, a task I found enjoyable because my mind was free to wander. I have high hopes that crochet will be easier than knitting, as there is only one implement to manipulate. We shall see.

Why do I want to learn this needle art? I long to fashion small items for Ned, such as a jacket and a hat. Assuredly, I could purchase these in Millcote, but the pleasant daydream of producing them with my own hands has cast a spell on me. Likewise, I would happily make a new scarf for Edward to wrap around his throat, when he goes out. Moths attacked his woolen muffler and made quite a hash of it. The poor man still tries to wear that old thing, but the holes are growing at an alarming rate.

That leaves me asking you for help finding suitable gifts for you and my cousins, Diana and Mary. Do you have any requests I can fulfill? As for Diana and Mary, I know their needs are simple, but I haven't seen them in nearly two years, so I am at a loss as to what to do. Do you have any good ideas? Have you seen anything at the craft fêtes? I know Adèle was much amazed by what she saw on your expeditions.

Much love,

Jane

P.S. I am learning to drive the dog cart. Being able to go where I please, when I like, is exhilarating.

When I finished my letter to Lucy, I wrote a note to Hatchards, the London bookstore. Addressing myself to the proprietor, I requested books for everyone on my holiday gift list, including Cook, Mrs. Wallander, and Amelia. For good measure, I asked the bookseller to choose a few more tomes that might be popular. In most cases, I knew the titles I wanted, because I'd taken notes as I read the newspapers, and in others, I added a quick description of each person's interests, and trusted the bookseller with choosing the titles.

"If the books could be wrapped securely and delivered to Mrs. Lucy Brayton at 24 Grosvenor Square in London, that would be most satisfactory." Feeling happy with my plans for procuring books, I folded the letter and applied sealing wax.

CHAPTER 9

The next morning dawned bright and cheerful. Although colder than the previous days, the clear skies assured me I could easily make the trip to Millcote, if I bundled up appropriately. After eating my toast with tea, I visited Cook in the kitchen. She was in a decidedly bad humor, as she stood in front of the close closet and glared at an empty porcelain plate on the shelf. "Gone! An entire pigeon pie! It was to be your luncheon," she sputtered. "I never!"

"Have you asked Edward? Perhaps he came down early to eat the pie?" I peered into the closet, following the direction of her gaze. Whoever took the pie did not leave any clues as to his identity. Nor were there any crumbs. Just an empty dish.

"I asked the Master when I made him a pot of tea earlier. That ain't all," said Cook. "I found the rind of a piece of cheese."

Fishing around in a basket, she produced a black waxy crescent moon. "That's all! Only the rind, as if the cheese itself chewed neat as ye please. If folks are hungry, I can always add dishes to the table. All ye must do is say as much!"

"I would gladly do so," I responded, "but I have not seen nor heard any complaints. Have any others been in and out of the kitchen? Perhaps Amelia has been hungry?"

Cook scoffed. "That girl don't eat enough to keep a bird alive."

"James?" I wondered out loud. "Mayhap, he has taken food for his family and forgotten to tell you? Certainly, we're always willing to share with the Harrigans. Perhaps he wanted a special treat for his grandfather?"

"Not likely. He's the one who discovered the missing cheese, when he was tucking a bowl of fresh eggs into the close closet." Rolling her eyes to the heavens, Cook sighed. "This is a mystery to me."

Changing the subject, I asked if she had completed her grocery list. She had. Before I set out, she wanted to review the menu items with me. We did so quickly. "I've also asked my friend, Lucy Brayton, for suggestions for holiday meals," I said. I did not want to spring a surprise on Cook at the last minute. "Since she'll be our guest, I'd like to be accommodating. I shall post this letter to her today. Surely she will respond quickly."

"Ye can count on me. I think that if we stick to this list I've made, we'll have all we need. I did my best to make the list as detailed as possible, short of being wasteful." Cook handed me her hand-written shopping list. Her spelling was indecisive and often varied, when it should have been uniform, and the teacher in me was hesitating, wanting to correct her. I resisted the urge. Overall, Cook made herself clear enough, and frankly, most of our tenants probably would not have done so well. I studied the collection of items and made a few notes, whilst discussing them with Cook. Once I was sure that I understood what she needed, I readied myself for the journey ahead. My trip could not be postponed, and I was equal parts excited and anxious.

Realizing that I would be driving into the wind, Cook warmed a brick for me in the oven, as I put on my spencer and my bonnet. I thanked that kind lady for preparing the warm stone and carried it to the stable. James was nowhere to be seen. By prior arrangement of a note tucked into his message box, the young man had moved the cart out from the stable and down to the end of the drive, which meant the donkey and I had an easy stroll to the vehicle. Ever thoughtful, James had also put a neatly folded wool blanket on the driver's seat. Surely, I would not be too cold on the way to town. I reminded myself that I would have to leave well before the sun went down, to avoid being cold on the trip back to Ferndean.

Hearing my footsteps as I approached his stall, Moses pricked his ears. His collar was heavy, but I managed it. I also struggled a little as I tried to fasten the padded breast strap around his chest. A piece of carrot was the reward for his cooperation. Only once was I forced to refer to my notes and a small diagram that I'd drawn to guide my efforts. As a matter of fact, harnessing the donkey went better than I expected.

Cook must have told Edward what I was doing, because he came out from the Manor and asked if I needed help.

"No, sir. I believe I'm all set," I said, hearing the pride I was feeling.

He took a quick walk around the cart and checked for loose straps. "Excellent job, Jane."

Stooping toward me for a quick kiss, he bid me goodbye. As he headed back toward the house, I noticed that Mrs. Fairfax stood at the front window and stared at me. I had no doubt she would put a flea in Edward's ear about the impropriety of my traveling alone. I was ready to slap the reins to urge Moses forward, when Cook hurried out, calling for me.

"Missus!" she shouted. "All my eggs is gone! A varmint must have slipped past Mephisto and gotten into them. I can't make my puddings without. Could ye pick up two dozen more eggs from Leah on your way to town? If ye don't mind, could ye drop off this jar of piccalilli for John? It is his favorite."

"Of course," I said, glad that I could provide a necessary service that would benefit us all.

Cook produced a wrapped package inside a basket and handed it to me. "John takes particular enjoyment from my relish, and I made that up just for him. He don't eat as much as he used to, so I'm hoping this'll help his appetite."

"That's kind of you," I said.

She colored. "Eh, I thought about waiting for the holiday season, but why? He'll enjoy it now, I reckon. The other days of the year, well, them's the times when we ought to help each other out, don't ye think?"

"I do indeed," I said, and after that happy exchange, I was on my way. My timing had proved providential, as Cook needed those eggs. Until John took his tumble, she would have asked him to bring more on the morrow. But James was too busy to run an errand. As Moses hurried down the lane, I speculated on the sort of man servant we needed at Ferndean. John's condition had forced so many changes, not the least of which was leaving us without conveniences we relied on. It was just a matter of time before Edward returned to the idea of selling Mesrour. Late last night, he admitted to me that he still worried over his inability to properly exercise his horse. Would that someone might reply to our letters! Perhaps we wouldn't hear anything until after the holidays. The celebrations so abundant this time of year might be hindering someone from answering our request.

Even so, surely, we could find someone who needed the work, but who did not need lodging for an entire family. I determined I would make an effort to hurry along the process. Although I hadn't planned to visit the rector, I would do so.

Perhaps a face-to-face request would add importance to our request for assistance.

Moses was a congenial travel partner. The tilt of his ears, the quick lift of his hooves, suggested he was happy to be out and about. The slight chill in the air did not bother him. In fact, I think it encouraged him to step lively.

A frisson of nervousness trilled through me, but the longer we processed down the road, the more I chalked it up to excitement rather than trepidation. As long as I could harness Moses and drive this donkey cart, I was free to come and go as I pleased, in a way I'd never experienced.

Admittedly, Moses was not an elegant mount. No one would see us and think how fine we looked. But that was beside the point, as the opinions of other people mean very little to me. Instead, I concentrated on being a good driver, looking ahead for possible problems, such as a rough spot in the lane. James had warned me that even the most easygoing animal could become frightened by the unexpected. He had emphasized that it was my job to remain vigilant. "Old Moses won't let you down. Not if he can help it. But for all his good qualities, missus, he's still a dumb beast. You must always remember that.

You're the one in charge. At the helm, so to speak."

Even so, Moses seemed perfectly happy, and when a leaf fluttered down and slid along the bridge of his nose, he remained calm. A smile crept over my face. The warm brick did its job admirably, keeping my feet comfortable. The wool blanket proved an excellent choice for shielding me from the cool temperature. But it was the sun smiling down on us that lightened my spirits. All in all, I was happy. My mind tried to soak up every moment and take in every impression, so I could share it with Edward. I noticed the smell of the donkey, the fragrance of freshly mown hay, the way our pace caused a breeze that fluttered a lock of my hair, the hopeful call and warning response of birds as we hurried past their perches, and the way the bare branches scratched the belly of a clear blue sky.

More delights awaited me. The post office in Millcote bustled with activity. I posted our letters. First, I submitted my missive to Lucy and tried to tamp down my expectations of a quick reply. I posted several other pieces of mail, including my missive to Hatchards and a new letter written by Mrs. Fairfax to Edward's agent, Mr. Brisben, in London, outlining our request for a helper. Since we hadn't heard from the doctor or the rector, Edward had chosen to expand our search, by reaching out to another personage, who might lead us to a new man servant. I hadn't mentioned to my husband that I planned to speak to the rector, furthering our efforts to move our quest ahead. After all, the man might not be at home, when I called. But I had to think that arriving on his doorstep would impart a sense of urgency to our earlier request.

Stepping out of the post office, I allowed myself a quiet sense of satisfaction. Surely, at least one of our queries would generate a positive response.

In fact, I decided that my next stop would be the rectory. That way, if I missed the rector, I could try again after my shopping.

St. Francis of Assisi, the Anglican church in Millcote, was a quaint little building at the end of a short high street. Edward's grandfather had overseen the building of it, himself, as the Rochester family's gift to the town and surrounds. My husband sent money every year for the upkeep of the place, including payment for a fresh coat of white paint. Thus, covered in a never-changing cloak of white, the church spire could be seen for miles and miles. The white rectory was set back and a little behind the church. The rector's home was surrounded by a white picket fence and a garden that, despite the autumn chill, was well-tended and lush. Late blooming roses graced white trellises, pansies lined the walkway, and cabbages of all shapes, sizes, and colors vied with marjoram and herbs in the flower boxes. Reverend Jones-Smythe owed his living to my husband, and yet, curiously enough, after his appointment last year, the parson had not even dropped by Ferndean to visit. Nor had his wife.

Mrs. Fairfax had remarked upon the lack of courtesy, an unusual reaction on her part, as she tended to regard the clergy with the gravest sort of respect, because customarily, a rector was usually most appreciative of his benefactor. "One would think a visit to see the Master might be a high priority," she'd said, clucking her tongue. "I never! Even if the rector is too busy to call, his wife should have asked to see Edward and thank him in person for his generosity."

Edward had merely shrugged that off.

Of course, since he and I do not attend church, it was possible that the priest figured we would just as likely like be left alone.

No matter. I was bound for the rectory,

hoping to hand deliver a second copy of the letter I'd written, requesting that the reverend help us in our search for a person to assist James. I was more than willing to overlook the absence of a courtesy visit, if the clergyman or his wife could promise help. Of course, all that seemed dependent on finding one or both of them at home.

Moses proved unconcerned about the noises of the bustling high street. He trotted along like the finest of equestrian mounts, never bothering to falter when a door slammed or a voice rang out calling for a friend. I was ever so proud of my four-legged friend. Tying his reins to the picket fence and rewarding him with a chunk of apple, I told my trusty friend, "I shall return. Please wait for me."

On the door stoop, I rapped on the large walnut door. The murmur of skirts and the hollow ring of footfalls told me the dwellers were within. Voices spoke to each other inside the house. When no one answered the door, I knocked again. I had begun to feel foolish, when a sour-faced woman opened the door a crack and said, "Don't need none. Whatever you're peddling, go away."

This curt brushing aside of a visitor did not endear the maid to me. Servants take their cues from their masters, so my impression of the rector grew rather dark, indeed. By the quick manner in which she attempted to dispatch me, it was obvious that this maid was in the habit of turning visitors away. Given that the church should always provide sanctuary (although this was the rectory and not the church, proper), I was not amused at this breach of etiquette. My knuckles did more violence to the door. Voices and footsteps on the other side assured me that my knocking had been heard. At length, the door was slightly opened again.

The woman who stood before me was wearing a maid's uniform, but the garment fit her poorly. Her starched collar needed pressing. Her skirt was too long and dragged the ground. Her apron had seen better times, judging by the stains. Again, I took a mental inventory and decided the rectory was collecting ticks in the deficit column.

"I am here to see Mr. Jones-Smythe," I said, drawing myself up to my full height. Admittedly, my stature is not impressive, but the authority in my voice should have signified I was not to be trifled with.

"I done told ye, we ain't buying nothing from

ye. Go on! Get!" This was punctuated by tiny shooing motions of the maid's hands.

Rather than respond to her ridiculous assumption, I stuck one foot inside the doorway and continued, "Please tell Mr. Jones-Smythe that Mrs. Edward Rochester, the wife of his benefactor, is standing on his front stoop and would like a word with him. Right now."

At my expanded introduction, the woman's face turned pale. She threw the door open, but did not invite me in. Taking two steps backwards, she stumbled and nearly fell. After recovering her balance, she hurried down the hall. Given how unimpressive this welcome was, I removed my foot and waited on the doorstep. A quick glance behind me was enough to ascertain that Moses was placidly watching this folderol. The maid's speedy exit did offer me one advantage: I was rewarded with a view inside the rectory.

From what I could see, the furnishings were uniformly garish. Most pieces would be out of place anywhere other than a palace, and since I've visited King George IV, our Regent, at Buckingham Palace, I can point this out with authority. Beyond being garish, the proportions of the pieces were completely out of scale and, therefore, not at all pleasing to the eye. Side tables crammed the hallways. A large clock with gilt trim extended beyond the wall behind it. In short, the home reflected the same sort of disarray that I'd encountered with the maid.

With a shuffling gait, the maid returned. Standing in the middle of the hall, she said in an awed voice, "I'll show you in. The rector and the missus are in the orangery."

The word echoed in my head. Orangery? Since when did a rectory aspire to an orangery? Surely, none of the rectors who lived here previously had the means to add large stone pillars and a glass roof. I doubted that Edward would have approved such a vast expenditure. Was the maid mistaken in her terminology? There was only one way to find out. I followed behind the woman, doing my best to dance around the myriad of furniture pieces competing for their share of the hall.

As I wended my way back to what the maid had enthusiastically called the orangery, I marveled at the total lack of taste and its obvious triumph over good sense. When we arrived at an open door, the maid pivoted and said, "Please enter the orangery."

I need not have wasted my time wondering how a rectory could afford such a costly addition, because the overheated room was anything but an orangery. I'd been led to a room at the back of the house, furnished with wicker and stuffed with a good deal of miserable looking plants. Parting the drooping leaves of some sort of palm, a man in a dog collar and an extravagantly dressed woman stood to greet me.

"Mrs. Rochester, how nice of you to come and welcome us," said the rector. He had the features of a weasel, small and pointed and mean looking. His coloration was a washed out blond. "Please sit down and join us. We find it ever so pleasant to sit here amongst the greenery, when the weather is cold outside."

I chose a wicker chair, as far from the two of them as possible. He continued talking. "I was only this day telling my dear wife that I hoped to see you and the squire one Sunday at services. Unless, of course, you prefer for me to come and conduct a mass in your family chapel, instead. I am, of course, at your service."

Mrs. Jones-Smythe wore more ribbons than a Maypole. They streamed from every inch or her. Her brown hair was twisted into hard curls to frame a blocky face. A generous dusting of powder had settled into many indentations left by a bad case of smallpox. I'd seen people who adorned themselves like this before. Mr. Brocklehurst, the supervisor at Lowood Academy, saw nothing wrong with dressing his daughters in velvet, silks, ribbons, and finery, while chastising innocent orphan girls for the slightest hint at self-preservation. He forced us to wear woolen hose and brown dresses of thin stuff, with little pockets made of cloth that were tied to our smocks, so that a bag of work would be our constant companion. In the coldest days of winter, our cloaks were far from adequate to keep us warm. Each Sunday, we were forced to march to church, although we were afforded no gloves or boots. Our hands and feet sprouted painful chilblains that itched and stung. Mr. Brocklehurst's wife and daughters indulged in fur muffs and fur trimmed cloaks of fine wool.

The rector's wife appraised me, sweeping in an arc from my feet to my bonnet and back down again. Of course, her eyes lingered on my simple wool cloak. Where my outer garment was not tugged tightly closed, she probably saw glimpses of my pelisse-robe, a coat-like dress often worn to go walking. I'd chosen it for the dark color of blue that would hide any mud splatter. All in all, my apparel was simple and free of any adornment. The opposite of the woman seated across from me.

She simpered, "Although the trip would be tiresome, I would be willing to accompany dear Cornelius, when he conducts service in your chapel, as I have been told by none other than the bishop that I embody the womanly virtues a good wife aspires to achieve. Therefore, you might look upon me as a role model. I am sure you need such guidance, given your background as a . . . governess."

This last word was offered in an uncomplimentary way. Whilst I feel no shame for my former occupation, the way Mrs. Jones-Smythe fairly sneered, when she said governess, was an affront.

"Mr. Rochester and I would not dream of importuning you," I put in quickly. "There's no need for you to come to Ferndean Manor."

"Ferndean Manor?" The rector's eyebrows shot up in surprise. "I was given to understand that Thornfield Hall is the Rochester family home."

"Thornfield Hall has been burned to the ground for some time now," I said briskly. Surely, he knew this. I wondered what his game was, and I decided to play along. "We are in the midst of rebuilding. Therefore, our chapel is in disrepair. It will take time to restore it to its former beauty. Meanwhile, my husband and I are living at Ferndean, the Rochester family's hunting lodge."

"Oh, my! How awful for you." Mrs. Jones-Smythe tittered. "A hunting lodge! That must be very unfortunate."

"I do not find it problematic," I said in return. There was a curt edge to my tone. Her definition of civilized and mine were likely to be very different.

"If you are rebuilding, I am sure you will need the counsel of a woman such as myself," Mrs. Jones-Smythe said. "I have grown up in fine surroundings, and I am particularly attuned to the requirements of the church. If the chapel needs to be rebuilt, you'll want expert help. Planning and equipping a sacred space can be rather a daunting prospect."

"I am sure my husband's architect has experience he can draw on," I said. However much Mrs. Jones-Smythe fancied herself a paragon of good taste, by twice that amount she had missed the mark entirely. "James Gillespie Graham came highly recommended. He has designed both country houses and churches. His specialty includes interiors as well as exteriors."

My rejection of Mrs. Jones-Smythe's help displeased her. With a calculated toss of her head, her tight curls bobbed franticly. "Be that as it may, you might still find yourself contemplating a variety of choices. Your background may not qualify you to make good decisions."

"I shall keep that firmly in mind," I said. I watched with fascination as the many ribbons on her frock fluttered in harmony. Although the rector's wife was closer to Edward's age of forty-six than mine of twenty-two, she dressed in the pastel colors usually associated with young women and not suitable for matrons.

"I am here for another purpose entirely," I said, noting that I had not been offered tea or any other refreshment. Given how stuffy the room was, I longed to return to the cool weather out of doors, so I decided to dispense with any other attempts at niceties. "My husband and I wish to hire a helper to take on sundry tasks at Ferndean Manor. Specifically, we want someone who can assist with the livestock, run errands into Millcote, and help Cook by fetching wood and water and so on. A man who is good with horses and other beasts would be most desirable. We have already sent you one letter regarding the need we are facing."

The rector gave me a weak smile. "Surely, you recognize how busy I am. I did see your letter, but I cannot be expected to ask each and every member of my parish, if they know someone who might be right for the job."

His wife must have read the letter, too, because she added, "One does not ask one's congregation personal questions. My husband could hardly know if a churchgoer needs employment."

I nearly gasped. Instead, I said, "Of course the rector should know! He of all people should care for his flock!"

"Mrs. Rochester, you forget yourself," Jones-Smythe chided, wagging a finger at me.

Bile rose in my mouth and heat rose in my face. How dare he? The rector's behavior was exceedingly rude.

He continued, "I hardly think you should be chastising me for not consorting with those who refuse to work for a living."

"You are right, sir. I do not expect you to consort. I expect you to comfort and care for your flock. Surely, among them is a man who needs a job—and wants one!"

"I sincerely doubt that my husband can help you," the wife quickly said. "After all, he is an ordained priest, and not a vicar who associates with the rabble."

"So true," said the rector. "I see myself as a servant of God and a man to inspire the *hoi polloi,* not one to walk among them, Mrs. Rochester. I assume the term has meaning for you? If not, I can translate." His smile reminded me of a polecat baring its teeth.

"No need for you to translate. I am conversant in both Greek and Latin," I said coldly, answering his question. For good measure, I added, "As well as being fluent in French and German."

The rector and his wife looked surprised. As well they should be.

Hoi polloi, of course, translated into the public area, is a ghastly reference to the parishioners that this man was charged with loving and leading to salvation. These were the people that Jesus sought to nurture and comfort.

I rose to my feet. My whole body reacted with revulsion. I had dealt with such people my whole life. People who spouted Christian virtues but chose pride over penance, commerce over compassion, and fashion over faith. It angered me to realize my husband was responsible for supplying this man with his living. But I reminded myself that news of this unwelcome attitude would anger Edward, too. And Edward had the power to do something about this caitiff excuse for a man of God.

With a shudder, I turned my mind to the task at hand. "Perhaps you might reconsider. Allow me to give you this letter. The contents detail what skills we are requiring. Surely, there is someone in your flock who would like to find employment. We are looking for a single man, a person without a family. Even if you do not mingle with the *hoi polloi,* you might hear of someone needing such a position as we are offering."

The Reverend Jones-Smythe did not move to take the letter. Mrs. Jones-Smythe intercepted the correspondence, as I held it in my outstretched hand. I withdrew the letter and added, "This is for the rector, only."

The face she pulled was ugly, and her tiny eyes grew mean, as I handed the envelope to the rector.

"I shall do what I can," he said, without opening the letter, "but I urge you to turn your attention elsewhere."

I thought to myself, *Believe me, I shall!*

As quickly as possible, I took my leave. As I climbed into the donkey cart, I distinctly heard

Mrs. Jones-Smythe's voice. She was staring at me from behind her curtains. "A donkey pulling a cart! One would think a fine lady would ride in a gig! With livery men!"

Indeed, and one would think the wife of a clergyman would possess a charitable soul. It seemed that neither of us was what the other expected.

CHAPTER 10

That unpleasant task accomplished, I took Cook's shopping list into the general store and handed it to the owner. That good man promised to collect the items himself and drive them out to Ferndean.

Next, I also indulged myself by doing a bit of shopping on the high street. Inside one shop, I found a new shaving kit for my husband. For dear little Ned and for Evans, I purchased sets of wooden blocks painted with the alphabet. The boys were too young to appreciate these at present, but they would enjoy them later. For John and Mary, I found a twist of peppermints. For James and Leah, I found butterscotch candies. For Amelia, a new length of printed muslin that she could sew up into a dress. For Cook, I found a cunning implement for mashing potatoes. For Lucy, I found an adorable trug, a wooden basket, that she could take along on rambles. In the jeweler's window, I noticed a small pearl pin that Mrs. Fairfax might enjoy. It was rather like a pin I owned that she had admired, so I bought it. For Mrs. Wallander, I found a small painted tin filled with candies. Satisfied that I had done all I could toward making our Christmas jolly, I climbed back up in the driver's seat and urged Moses onward.

The way to the Harrigans' cottage went more swiftly than my trip into town. Perhaps that was because I felt more confident of my skills with Moses. Whatever the reason, Leah waved happily to me, as I pulled up. With her open manner and true Christian spirit, she served as a pleasant counterpoint to Mrs. Jones-Smythe. The jug of piccalilli for John was received with much praise for Cook. This time, Leah did not even ask me, before brewing a pot of tea for us to share. While the tea steeped, she went to a basket and withdrew a small package wrapped in brown paper and tied with string. "This is for you," she said, with a pretty blush.

Inside the paper was a carved wooden crochet

hook. Someone had put a great deal of work into shaping and smoothing the outside of the tool. "James carved it, in the evenings," she said shyly.

"How extraordinarily kind of both of you," I said. "I shall cherish this. Please thank him for me, and thank you for instigating this."

"That is not all." She went over to another basket, a waist-high one, sitting next to her spinning wheel. From this container, she withdrew a small ball of yarn, dyed with woad into a color much like a stormy sky. When she handed it to me, I took it to the window and lifted the soft orb to the light, so I could admire the shade. The blue-grey tint was both pleasing to the eye and calming at the same time.

"Did you dye this yourself?" I asked, as Leah came and stood beside me.

"Indeed, I did. I hope you like it. You seemed to appreciate peacefulness, and thus I came upon that color as a way of giving you what your heart desires."

Friendship is always an unexpected gift. To take up residence in another person's heart is a privilege. I thanked Leah profusely. Her eyes danced with happiness as she said, "Come now and have a seat. Let me teach you to crochet. You begin with a chain; that is the hardest part."

"Is a chain like casting on with knitting?"

"Yes, missus."

"No, no, no! You must call me Jane!"

"All right. Yes, Jane, a chain is like casting on. Were you taught that as a child?"

"A teacher tried to teach me the skill while I was at Lowood, but her patience with me was limited. After a while, she punished me by making me stand in the corner. She was sure I was knotting my yarn on purpose. Of course, I was not. Eventually, I redeemed myself enough to help by winding balls of yarn for the other girls."

Leah frowned. "What a shameful way to treat a child. If I had a young one, I would endeavor to be the soul of patience. All of us are different. One might learn to cast on easily with knitting needles and another might take to making chains. What matters is to practice. I'll do the chain for you, but first, I need to know what was it you were hoping to make? I trust you will choose a simple piece to start." Her voice was bright with enthusiasm, and I felt that excitement transfer to me.

"I should like to make something for my husband. I wondered if I could make him a muffler. Would that be possible?"

"I am sure you can do that, and it is a very

good place to start. A piece like a muffler will accustom your hands to the hook and your mind to the rhythm of the stitches. You cannot go too far wrong, because I shall be here to help you at every turn," said Leah. "Now let me show you the mufflers I have made for James and John so's you can see, in your mind, what we're on about."

A little later, Leah gave me three dozen eggs, one more than Cook had requested.

"Cook will be pleased," I said.

"Good. You are always welcome to come here…Jane. Even if it's not to run an errand," said Leah.

"I know. Thank you," I said, and we shook hands.

CHAPTER 11

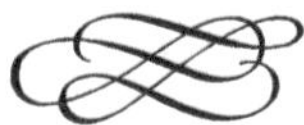

On the way back to Ferndean, the seasonal changes seemed more pronounced to me. Perhaps the quickly cooling temperature was the reason. The bare gray branches stood out against the varied shades of the conifers and evergreens. Bright red berries dotted the holly bushes. Ripe rosehips were being plucked off their stems by fat jays. The juxtaposition of red against blue-green delighted my artistic sensibility and reminded me that, the one Christmas season I'd spent in Thornfield Hall, there had been a surfeit of greenery, ribbons, and candles. Likewise, the holiday that I'd passed with my cousins featured similar frivolous accents.

Surely Ferndean Manor deserved to be dressed in similar holiday finery!

Here again, I might call upon Lucy for advice.

I arrived as dusk began to darken the sky. Shivering, I unhooked Moses from his harness. Edward came out to help me. Working together, we freed the donkey from his tethers. "Was he good for you?" asked Edward, as he led Moses to his stall.

"He was wonderful," I said. "Truly, he was the soul of patience. I could not have asked for a better traveling companion. Do I need to brush him? Or otherwise care for him?"

"He doesn't appear to be lathered up, so I think he'll be fine until tomorrow, when James will inspect his hooves. Let's toss a blanket over him, to be sure he doesn't take a chill." Edward opened the gate to Moses's pen and led the donkey inside. Hearing Edward's voice, Mesrour whinnied. After locking the stall gate, Edward walked down to the stallion and scratched the horse's nose. My husband's sadness was palpable. There was nothing I could do but redouble my efforts to find us a helper.

"Truly, he was an admirable companion," I said, changing the subject as Edward returned with a blanket. Edward handed me one edge of the fabric. Together we centered the plaid cloth over the donkey's back. I buckled it on, so it wouldn't slip off. At Edward's direction, I measured out the proper portions of wheat bran and sheaf oats for my four-legged friend. "Too much would make him ill," my husband explained.

"Let me go back to the cart and fetch my purchases," I said. I retrieved a market basket, a flour sack, and a box with the eggs.

Edward raised an eyebrow. "What did you buy?"

"I have my secrets, too," I retorted, slipping my free arm through his.

The very next day, I wrote Lucy and asked, "What should I do for decorating Ferndean? There are many evergreens nearby. Stands of holly, too. Would they be sufficient?"

I was fortunate, in that James came by that morning and took my letter to the post bag.

Over the upcoming days, I struggled to master the skill of crocheting. At first, I held onto the hook for dear life, choking it, so that my hands ached. As a result, my loops were too tight, making it difficult to slip the hook in them and almost impossible for me to add more stitches. I found myself unraveling a lot of work. As time went by, I loosened my grip, trusting the hook, and the piece began to take a more regular form. I doubted that I would ever find the process relaxing, but I vowed not to give up easily.

One cold morning, James brought me two letters, one with a foreign postmark and a second from Lucy in London. "James? Could you wait for a few minutes? Maybe have tea in the kitchen? I need to respond to these immediately."

"You know that language? That one there?" He pointed to the envelope with the German stamp.

"Yes, I do," I said. "It's German. I can read it well and speak it a bit. This message is important, because it concerns a surprise for the Master. I'll need your help, if I am to truly give him an unforgettable Christmas. May I tell you all about it?"

"I'd be much obliged," James said. With cap in hand, he listened eagerly. Once I finished, he tapped the side of his nose, thoughtfully. "Sure, and I can pick your gift up from the coach station in Millcote. I'll toss a clean blanket over it and bring it here, directly. Do you think it would fit in your larder or your butler's pantry?"

"I believe so. Shall we go and see?" Thus, we became co-conspirators. Since the larder is

Cook's domain, it was necessary to include her in our discussions.

"Absolutely, ye can put the gift here," she agreed. "James, will ye help me shift things around? Once we're done, we should have plenty of room. Master will never think of looking here, I reckon."

"Cook? Please make sure James has a cup of tea, won't you?"

"Aye, of course I will! I'll even offer him a scone, if they haven't all disappeared mysteriously," she said, finishing her comment with a disgusted "huh."

"Food is still going missing?" I asked.

"Aye. Complaining about it makes no difference. No one admits to sneaking down and eating it at night. There's naught I can do but serve other victuals and make a gracious plenty extra."

"That must be unsettling," I said. I couldn't imagine what was happening, but I suspected we had vermin that slipped past Mephisto. The cat had grown increasingly fat and lazy. These days, he barely climbed out of his bed.

I thanked the kind woman for entertaining James and walked swiftly to the parlor, where I kept my lap desk.

The timing of Lucy's message suggested our

correspondence had crossed in the mail. Her letter was actually more of a report on Adèle and Evans than anything else. "Adèle is learning to write proper thank you notes after we finish our social calls," Lucy explained. "As you know, when she was at Alderton House, the headmistress demanded that the girls copy word-for-word the letter she herself had written. That way she could control what the girls were sending out. Of course, that will never do. Coming up with one's own thoughts takes more effort! And the result is much more personal and, therefore, likely to delight the recipient."

She went on to tell me that Evans was crawling so fast that Mrs. Wallander could scarcely keep up with him. Her brother, Bruce, was ever the carefree bachelor, or so she wrote, and Lucy despaired of him ever finding a wife. In regard to herself and her state of mind, I detected a hint of loneliness in her patter. Her husband, Augie, had been banished to India after calling out Prinny, the nickname given to our king when he was Prince Regent. Prinny had been a card-sharp, a cheat. He was unaccustomed to people who stood up for themselves. Everyone knew that the heir apparent did not play fairly, but most who played cards with him were too much under his thumb to call attention to his sins. Augie didn't mind losing his own money, but he was angered when Prinny bankrupted a young soldier. That infuriated Prinny.

For the most part, Lucy has accepted her husband's banishment with good grace, as she does not blame Augie for calling a spade a shovel. He had watched too many other men lose money to Prinny, money they could ill afford to part with, and Augie was determined to stop the nonsense, when the young soldier gave up his monthly stipend.

Alas, Augie has paid dearly for his decision. Prinny could not publicly punish Augie, as that would be too transparent, so he sought to make both Augie and Lucy suffer in a more circuitous manner.

I know that Lucy longs for her husband. I have seen with my own eyes how she writes him, every day, and the eagerness with which she attends the silver tray that her butler uses to serve up the mail. Never before had it occurred to me that, at certain times of year, that longing is more painful than at others. Now I realized the holidays must be particularly lonely for her. I set aside her letter and thought about how lucky I was to have my husband here by my side.

I quickly penned a reply to the vendor in Germany, sealed the letter, and handed it to James. I thanked him for his help in all its forms and sent the young Harrigan on his way.

In reviewing my plans for the commission of a happy holiday, I allowed myself to take pleasure in what I had accomplished: the menu was planned, the guests were invited, their rooms were made ready, Adèle had been recalled to our home, and I had set about procuring gifts. I had even made arrangements to provide the boxes that tenants would be given on Boxing Day. Until I heard back from Lucy, decorating the Manor seemed to be the only task remaining to make our home festive in a manner befitting the season.

That night proved the coldest yet. As Mrs. Fairfax, Edward, and I sat huddled around the fire, a strong draft lifted a portion of *The Times* right out of the housekeeper's hands and nearly carried the newspaper into the fireplace. Had I not been nimble and alert, the paper would have surely burned.

"Blast it all," Edward said, slamming his fist against the arm of his chair, "this is intolerable. I will not put up with drafts such as these. Tomorrow, I shall take the gig to Thornfield Hall and tell the workers that their presence is required here, instead. No doubt they can remedy these cursed leaks before our company joins us."

"This lodge has always been miserable in the cold months," Mrs. Fairfax responded mildly. "If you recall, last winter was unseasonably warm, so we were spared, but typically, the Rochester family avoided being here in December and January. I remember your father laughing about his own guests complaining. He suggested to them that staying here was a test of their fortitude. More than a few did not appreciate his sense of humor. They never came back. Squire Rochester would brag that these stone walls were sturdy, and they had seen decades upon decades of rough weather, and they would proudly stand for yet at least a dozen or more centuries. Of course, the old squire was right, as stone is practically impervious to decay. However, the mortar between the stones has begun to crumble. In many places, it has fallen to the earth. The wind whips right through those empty spaces left behind." Mrs. Fairfax concluded her commentary by plucking her knitting from the basket at her side.

Edward was displeased to hear such a straightforward example of his father's cruelty. As I understood it, the squire actively sought ways to excuse his harsh behavior, by bragging that a man was a man by virtue of his ability to withstand challenges. As a father, he insisted upon raising up strong sons, financially set in life. As a country squire, he prided himself on associating with men who regularly tested their mettle by participating in sport and a myriad of opportunities, where they suffered duress. So, it seemed that living in a draughty house was yet another opportunity for a man to test himself.

I shivered and turned my attention to poking away at my crochet project. Mrs. Fairfax had offered to teach me to knit, but actually, I was very happy to have Leah as my teacher. Since she'd given me the carved hook and the yarn, I'd walked twice to her cottage in search of assistance. Each time, Leah proved to be a patient teacher. When one of her explanations did not help me understand a concept, she kindly found another way to word her thoughts. This, I have learned, is the hallmark of a good teacher. A good instructor keeps trying to find new ways to share concepts, until the student finally comprehends the information. Leah was not only generous with her explanations, she was also encouraging of my efforts, even when she was correcting my mistakes.

"Be more trusting of the hook," she told me. "Rotate it as you work. Let it become an extension of your fingers. Your loops can be looser. They won't slip off the hook. I promise you. Remember, you have until the first of January for gift giving. That's more than enough time, Jane, so do not worry. I shall help and guide you."

I repeated Leah's advice in my head, while I crocheted. Slowly, I noticed an improvement. Once in a while, I would realize that the repetitive act of hooking and pulling through the yarn was soothing.

Neither Edward nor Mrs. Fairfax thought to ask me what I was working on or what I was making. Most likely this was because my efforts had not produced a piece big enough to notice. However, I was getting faster and more sure, as I continued. A habit was being drilled into my hands. Soon, the repetition would not even require a modicum of thought.

"Before now, no one ever considered turning Ferndean into a home, and mayhap, that's as it should be," Mrs. Fairfax was saying. "For the amount you might spend plugging the holes, you could easily rent a nice house nearby."

"The stones that shelter us today dotted the moors for eons, before they were collected in the

1600s to build this lodge. I'll not give up on them so easily," Edward said. A long lock of his dark hair fell over his thick eyebrows. "I blame myself for letting these aggravations go on too long. The act of reaching out to our guests and planning for the holidays has called attention to Ferndean's deficits, and now I have seen my way clear to making amends. Those corrections are much needed. When they are, we should have a very merry season indeed."

Edward was as good as his word. James hitched up the gig for him shortly after first light, and my husband drove Rashana to Thornfield Hall. That very afternoon, a crew of workmen arrived. They brought along a dray loaded with lumber, various stone-working supplies, and other items intended for sealing the multitude of gaps and crevices in Ferndean Manor.

Cook paused her work and joined me to watch from the kitchen, as the men hopped off the dray and listened to their foreman's instructions. "I made a cold collation for them to have for their tea," Cook said, jerking a thumb in the workers' direction, "and I got out mugs to make them hot drinks. It's miserable cold out there, and they'll be working without shelter until the sun goes down."

I thanked her for thinking ahead.

"No bother," she responded, returning to a crock she'd covered with a linen towel. "Well, nearly none. I would have liked to have fed them a ploughman's lunch, but someone ate an entire loaf of bread overnight. Helped themselves to a generous scoop of fresh butter as well."

According to Cook's complaints, we were being robbed of foodstuffs on a daily basis. I asked, "Could it be mice or rats?"

"I doubt it." Cook moved the crock to a marble slab and took out a lump of dough. After dusting her hands with flour, she began kneading the thick mass. "I promise you, missus, I can't figure what's happening to the food. I've given up on tracking down the culprit. Maybe it is a horde of rats that come out, when I ain't looking. Mephisto hasn't been slinking around like usual. Right now, your cat is curled up in sleeping. Not much use as a mouser these days."

"Do we need another cat?" I asked.

"Ye don't seriously mean to drown that poor puss!" Cook's pink cheeks paled to a shade that matched the flour on her hands.

"No, no, no. I did not mean my question as a prerequisite to killing the beast, only a reasonable question that might be answered by adding a second feline to our retinue. Edward has mentioned there are feral cats out in the stable. Could one of them be tamed?"

Cook shrugged. "Perhaps. If you took one when he was young, I guess. Or we could wait and see. Things have a way of working themselves out, they do. If those stone masons do a right good job of patching up the holes in this lodge, then maybe critters won't be able to find their way inside so easy like. That'd give Mephisto a chance to catch whatever's running around and get ahead of the game."

She might be right, I thought. Somethings have a way of sorting themselves out.

"Jane?" My husband called to me from the study. "The workers will go back to Millcote this evening and stay at the inn, before returning on the morrow. Do you have mail that needs to go to the post office?"

"Yes, thank you," I said, moving to his study to speak to him directly. "I shall pen a note to my cousins and to Lucy." When James came over to help Edward hitch up the gig, he'd dropped off a fat envelope from Lucy. She'd graciously shared her favorite recipes, and in turn, I'd shared them with Cook. We were thrilled to have such a variety of suggestions to choose from.

"Make haste, my darling," Edward said.

While Edward was in his study and talking to a tenant, and Mrs. Fairfax was indulging in a nap, I opened my lap desk and wrote several letters. The first one was directed to Lucy:

Mrs. Captain Augustus Brayton

24 Grosvenor Square

London

My Dearest Lucy,

The chilling days are upon us. Oh, how the drafts have bedeviled us here in Ferndean. Do not worry, dear friend, as we will not ask you to submit to such misery. Only this morning, Edward has brought in a crew (formerly working at Thornfield Hall) and instructed them to plug all the cracks and crevices that cause us distress. Thus, your visit has done wonders to bring joy to me—even before your arrival!

As you can tell, for oh so many reasons, I am delighted that you have accepted our invitation. I passed your recipes and menu suggestions along to

Cook, when they arrived in the post this morning. Cook was very pleased with your recipes.

Please come prepared to share any games you know. I have heard that people play one called "snapdragon." Do you know of it?

Mrs. Fairfax has warned me that I cannot festoon the Manor with evergreens until Christmas Eve, lest I invite bad luck. However, I can gather boughs and branches and hold them to one side in waiting. What should I collect? Should I go to town and buy ribbons? How much would you suggest? Please share all of your thoughts, no matter how random.

I am afraid I have taken advantage of your helpful nature without asking you, and I'm asking your forgiveness. You see, I supplied a list of books to Hatchards and instructed that they be delivered to you. If you could bring those when you come, I should be most appreciative. (Please do not peek inside the package, as one is my choice for you.) As always, we shall plan for a feast on Christmas Day and open our presents on New Year's Day.

Edward has discovered how impoverished my previous celebrations were. Thus. he has fully committed himself to improving my lot in life. Of course, your presence will be more than sufficient for supplying all my needs and requirements, this holiday season. That said, my husband has gone ahead and made grand plans of his own. Knowing his generosity, I expect that a surplus of gifts will play a large part in our general merriment.

As for the news here, I am at last learning to crochet. With the assistance of Leah Harrigan (you'll remember John Harrigan, Edward's faithful retainer, and that she's his granddaughter-in-law), I am seeing a modicum of success with my efforts. In fact, I am making a new scarf for Edward to wrap around his throat, when he goes out. Moths attacked his old muffler and made quite a hash of it. The poor man tries to make do with his old one, but the holes are growing at an alarming rate.

I am eager to see Evans and judge for myself how much he has grown. Of course, we have missed Adèle terribly, so having her at home will be a treat.

Until then, I remain your "sister,"

Jane

After dripping on sealing wax, I turned my hand to writing another letter.

Dearest Cousins, Mary and Diana,

You cannot imagine how much I have relied on

my happy memories of that Christmas I spent with you at Moor Cottage. Such fondness does not wane, even though the years have passed. Nor do I think it will ever be erased from my mind.

I think of all three of you so often. Is St. John still abroad? I am sure he is happily spreading his love of God. I am confident that his words will not fall on deaf ears.

Edward and I are well. Our son, Ned, is happy, healthy, and growing quickly. He babbles, and his attempts to say "Mama" and "Dada" amuse us greatly. We are blessed to have him.

Adèle has been in London with our friend, Lucy Brayton, but both she and Lucy will be here at Ferndean for the holidays. I am looking forward to seeing them. That leads me to ask, "When will the two of you come and visit?"

It has been far too long, dear cousins.

I shall end this abruptly as I have the chance to get it into the post in Millcote. Giving this correspondence short shrift does not imply any the less love for you both

Your devoted cousin,

Jane

CHAPTER 12

Another week passed. The temperatures dipped lower every night, and the days were briefer. Brisk winds ripped the remaining leaves from their branches, leaving behind the naked trees and shrubs. The cold seemed more severe than it probably was, because the bitter winds whistled past and sliced through the landscape.

Meanwhile, the workmen came daily. In my ignorance, I had expected they would mix the mortar and spread it on, much like one might put butter on bread. Alas! I was wholly ignorant of the repairs to be done.

First, the stone masons assessed the damage. In more than a few places, the original stone had deteriorated to such an extent that an entire rock needed to be changed out. In other spots there was spalling, or chipping off, and this required a decision as to how bad the damage was. The weak surface would need to be removed, typically down at least an inch to be safe. New stones had to be chosen to replace the old. The surfaces of these new pieces had to be chiseled so that the texture matched what remained. I joined Edward in his study where one of the master masons explained that it was well to take the least intrusive approach possible. The mason said, "If what I find ain't broken or too bad, we'll leave it alone."

"Even if there is a crack or fracture?" Edward asked.

"That's right. Them we patch, unless they bear a load. Like over a window or a door. Otherwise, you'd have a motley looking wall, squire. No, 'tis much better for us to only do what needs done. Find the crevices and fill them with new stones, find the parts likely to crumble and take them back to where they're strong, and patch the fissures as we go."

I lingered long enough to listen to the man assure Edward that soon we'd be much warmer, but frankly, I had lost my faith in their abilities. They'd labored over the walls for a week, and I could not tell any difference regarding the draughts. Indeed, I now bundled up with two shawls, instead of one. After working steadily on the muffler for Edward, I realized the sides were badly skewed. I could not continue without guidance from Leah, so I put my work aside.

When a mild day surprised us, I made a decision—this would be the last of my chances to get help. I might as well take Ned along, when I visited my new friend.

With Amelia's help, I concocted a sling for Ned, in the manner demonstrated by Leah. The nursemaid stepped back to admire our handiwork. "Oh, missus, that arrangement of your shawl is clever by half! Ned loves looking around, and you have found a way that will allow him to take full advantage of your walk."

"Just in time," I said. "This promises to be the last of our fine weather."

I begged another jar of piccalilli from Cook, by promising to trade the relish for a dozen fresh eggs. The jar and my muslin bag with all my sketching supplies went inside a good-sized market basket, along with a small jug to hold any autumnal fruit that had been overlooked by wild animals. That poor muslin bag of mine had been mended so much that it looked entirely disreputable, but I still relied upon it to hold my art supplies.

"I doubt that ye'll find any bilberries left, but if ye do, please pick them. Mrs. Fairfax has her heart set on a bread-and-butter pudding with them," Cook explained as she handed me the jug. "Maybe even a handful of rosehips? I can dry them to put in tisanes. Whatever ye find, it'll be a gift, to be sure."

"I shall do my best." My mind was fixed upon of that clutch of bilberries I had marked on an earlier walk. Perhaps a few more had ripened and eluded the birds; I did not know, but I hoped it was so.

Ned was delighted with every aspect of our walk to the Harrigans' cottage. After cooing over him with delight, Leah produced a quilt that we spread on the floor. Thus supplied with a warm and cushioned surface, Ned busied himself admiring a ball of yarn. Meanwhile, Leah and I enjoyed a cup of tea. After we finished, she showed me the error of my ways with the crochet hook. Correcting my mistake took her no time at all! I'd neglected to start the first stitch of each row right after the turning chain. True, I'd done this exactly right for most of my project, but somewhere along the way, I'd gotten confused. She helped me unravel the errant portion and watched as I regained my lost ground. Leah also went out of her way to praise my efforts. "Your husband will be most pleased with his new muffler. You've done fine work, missus."

"Please call me Jane," I begged her, again.

"Jane," she said hesitantly.

We sat and worked on our projects, while Ned admired his new surroundings. Briefly, my little man fell asleep. His pose struck me as particularly charming, so I pulled my art supplies from my bag. Using a pencil in my sketchbook, I quickly roughed in an outline that I might use later.

"What a gift that will make for the Master!" Leah exclaimed.

She was right, and her suggestion was perfection itself. Edward would very much approve of a finished rendering of our son. "I am never sure what to buy for my husband. He has traveled the world, and I have not, so I feel at a disadvantage. As for Mrs. Fairfax, I found a small pin she might like, as she's commented frequently on one a friend gave me long ago. Otherwise, I know little of what she likes, except that she seems to crave bilberries," I said.

"Then I have the perfect gift for you to give her," said Leah. From the farthest corner of her larder, she withdrew a small jug. "This is bilberry jam. I make a half of a dozen pots every year. Take this to Mrs. Fairfax."

"Let me pay you for this," I said. "I'll send money home with James."

"Of course, you will not," Leah protested. "The berries were collected on your land, after all."

"But this is a result of your labor! Please, Leah, let me send James home with a few coins. I am certain you can find something useful to spend them on. If you don't take them, I shall feel like I have taken advantage of you."

"Keep the coins, please, and let me beg a favor. Would you sketch John for me? I want his image as a remembrance, especially for James and Mary. I fear the time is near that he'll no longer be with us. In fact, he's sleeping right now. He spends much of the day in slumber. I daresay you could go into the bedroom and he'd never stir."

"Of course, I'll do that for you. Gladly! I shall do my best to capture him on paper."

While Leah played with Ned, I slipped into the room where John was snoring loudly. I eased into the nearby rush-seated chair and studied my subject. Rather than use pencil, I chose charcoal to capture an image in bold strokes. I would later refer to these to animate a portrait. More light was needed to do an adequate job with shading, but once I'd gotten the basics on paper, I could expand on the limned image at my leisure.

When I was satisfied that I'd done what I could, I returned to the main room of the cottage. Leah was holding Ned on her lap and singing to him. The yearning on her face touched my heart. All of her concentration was fixed on my baby.

"He is such a darling, Jane. You are so lucky! If you ever need help with him, please call on me," she said. Blushing furiously, she added, "I know you have a nursemaid, but if she ever takes a day off, or, well…if you have cause, just call. This baby is so good! In fact, if John were not here and needing me, I would even come up to the big house and help out if you wished. Say, if your nursemaid went visiting family or such like."

Her offer was actually a plea. I could not help but respond to the hunger that played nakedly on her face. Why had God not seen fit to bless this woman with a child?

"You are very kind, Leah. I shall keep your offer in mind, as it is obvious that you have won my son's favor. His smiles tell me how much he likes you. I find them beguiling, don't you?"

"Not just beguiling," she said. "Heart-melting. Oh, missus. He is adorable. You are so lucky!"

Ned and I took our leave of Leah and headed toward home. Along the way, I stopped to pick up walnuts and drop them into the market basket. Ned thought my bobbing up and down the finest entertainment ever. My son and I entered the kitchen, as Cook opened the door on the heavy iron baking oven. Ned startled as the hinges squealed, when Cook centered a loaf of bread on the rack. Once she finished finding the perfect spot for the pan, she let the cast-iron door close with a thunderous clank. I jumped at the noise, and this time Ned made a tiny squeak of surprise. I reached down and stroked his hair to comfort him. Cook slowly turned toward us.

"Good afternoon, Cook."

"Oh, missus, there you are! I didn't see you come in. How was your ramble? Your walk put a lovely pinch of color in your boy's cheeks."

"Yes, it was quite enjoyable. The last bits of foliage are still clinging to some of the shrubs. The trees, of course, are bare. The leaves of bramble bushes have turned the most exquisite color, like that of a fine claret, and the privet berries are the darkest blue I've ever seen! I brought you the last of the walnuts. I am assured you can find a good use for them. Lamentably, the bilberries are all gone."

Her eyes widened. "Those walnuts are a rare treat. Good on ye, missus. I can think of a dozen ways to put them to good use."

"I could not search for more. As you can see, I lacked the needed agility to stoop down too often to find them." Hoisting Ned higher on one hip, I smiled at my son.

"Aye, and aren't you clever to carry your child that way?"

"'Tis naught of my doing. Leah showed me how. She says that gypsy women do this, and it works well for them. I can attest that it is true."

Cook observed how awkwardly the market basket dangled over my arm. "A new muslin sack is in order for ye, I daresay."

"That is true. If I continue these rambles, I shall also need a trug. I bought one for Lucy, and I should have purchased one for myself as they are more sturdy than baskets woven of wicker and rush. I believe it is safe to say that I shall always bring back some sort of treasure from my trips. You are quite correct, Cook. My poor muslin bag has seen better days. I have sewn up the loose stitches twice. Since then, other stitches have come loose." I shook my head in dismay. "The fabric is too fragile for new stitches to hold fast."

"Aye, ye could have lost the whole kit and cargo on your walk. What a shame that would have been! What's in that bag that you treasure it so much?"

"My sketchbook, a pencil, and a nub of charcoal."

"Then if that bag comes apart, all your lovely pictures would be gone in the blink of an eye." Cook shook her head. "That would be a shame!"

"Maybe not too much of a loss," I said. "I have no illusions that I'm a great artist. I am only tolerable. However, I do enjoy this pastime. Leah asked me to work on a portrait of John. A good idea, I think. She says he sleeps all the time. I am not sure how long he'll…well."

"Aye, John's given up, I think." Cook sighed. "Respectfully, missus, I beg to differ regarding the quality of your artwork. Matter of fact, my sis told me there's going to be a spring fête down at the church hall. The money will go to buy food for the poor families of the parish. Would ye consider donating a picture or two for them to sell?"

"You don't honestly mean to suggest that anyone would pay for my work? Cook, that's nonsense!"

The stricken expression Cook's face told me that I had embarrassed her. I regretted my declaration immediately. "Please understand! All I see are the flaws in my work. I have so much more to learn. I find it hard to believe that my work is worth sharing. I can't even imagine offering it for sale!"

"Well, I can," she retorted.

I could see that I'd injured her pride. I hastened to say, "Perhaps I am prejudiced. Mayhap, I am not the best judge of my own efforts. Let us come to an agreement. Cook, if you think that folks would exchange good coin for my artwork, and if you think that some charity might benefit, that's good enough for me. I would be honored to offer up one or two of my landscapes."

She studied me. Her face had returned to its natural color.

I added, "Certainly no one would be interested in purchasing my baking or needlework."

"Ha! That's true!" Cook burst out with a hearty laugh. The tension between us disappeared. "We're mightily agreed on that, missus. Ye spent a lot of time with Leah today. Is she doing poorly?"

"No, she's fine. I visited Leah, because she kindly agreed to teach me how to crochet. I had a problem with the piece I'm creating, and I didn't know how to correct it. I worried that I had botched everything, but she put me back on the right path. It was a perfect day for a walk, and the weather was gentle enough that I could take Ned outside. And of course, I enjoy Leah's company immensely."

Cook smiled at me. "She's a dear girl, ain't she? As good as they come, she is."

CHAPTER 13

Each day, I eagerly awaited our mail. The workmen brought it to the house, when they came, so our deliveries were daily. I opened each correspondence with hope, as I was sure that we would receive responses to our request for a man to help James. No, the rector wouldn't help, but I'd written to the bishop, and he'd promised to ask around. Mr. Carter, the doctor, finally dropped by and said he'd been making inquiries. Edward's agent wrote back to say that anyone he recommended in London would more than likely need lodging, but he would still do what he could.

Despite all of these persons being vigilant on our behalf, our efforts had come to naught. How could it be that we lived in the largest county in England and no one wanted a steady job? A roof over the head and food in the belly?

Edward patted my hand. "Remember, dear Janet, we are miles from a bustling metropolis, and thus the few city dwellers who would be suitable for work in a stable cannot imagine being isolated out here. For others who might be right for this job, there is no way to contact them, if they are scattered around, working at other estates. Winter is not the time for most to go wandering in search of employment."

"Please do not give up. Please do not sell Mesrour. Not yet." I grasped him by the shoulders and pleaded with him. "Give it until spring, won't you?"

In my mind, selling Mesrour had become tantamount to Edward giving up on life. Such a desperate solution would mean my husband would never be the man he once was. Whilst there was truth to that, there was also folly, as Edward's spirit was unbroken, even if his body had suffered from the fire that consumed Thornfield Hall.

"Ah, my loving wife," he said. Since we were alone at the breakfast table, he reached over and caressed my face. I kissed his hand. I loved these quiet moments at the start of each day. Mrs.

Fairfax typically carried her tea and toast into her bedroom, leaving me and my husband a bit of privacy. Occasionally, she would join us, but more often than not, this was a time for the two of us, husband and wife, to discuss the day ahead.

"The weather will soon turn raw." We had moved to his study, where my husband leaned back in one of the armchairs near the fire. His boots stretched toward the fireplace. Outside, workmen chiseled away at new stones. Where the old stones showed stair-stepping cracks, the master mason suggested replacement. The surface of some of the new stones would need to be chiseled flat to match the existing ones. This proved to be exacting work, as the man with the chisel had to have an artistic sense of sculpture to properly do this job.

Much of the replacement had been accomplished. Since today dawned mild, the masons were bustling around repointing, removing crumbling mortar and replacing it. This, too, required an artistic skill, as the texture, color, and composition of the original mortar had to be carefully matched.

A light rap on the study door turned our attention to the lead worker, a man in his forties with a leathery skin. Besides a heavy wool jacket, he held a cap in his hands, as a nod to the chilly weather. "Begging your pardon, sir and missus. I was dispatched to ask ye a question."

After Edward nodded his agreement, the man continued, "I know they's some that think we should tear down the ivy that's partially covering your walls. In my experience, that ain't a good idea. I'm bound to do as you wish, however, so I await your instruction."

"Do not the tendrils of the ivy destroy the mortar?" I put it as a question. I did not really know whether that was true or not.

"Some think that, but it ain't true, missus. Think of it like this: that ivy's like having a waxed jacket wrapped around your house. Them leaves shield this place from the wind, the rain, the heat, the cold, and all sorts beyond."

That made perfect sense to me. There was more.

"Of course, ye don't want it creeping into your window frames as it'll damage the hinges and the joints. I can cut it back by the windows and the roof so's little critters can't use it to climb in, if you catch my drift," he said, all the while turning his cap in his hands.

"Excellent thinking," said Edward. "I appreciate you bringing this to us, and we trust you to do as you think best, as you have the better of us in the way of your superior knowledge in this area."

The man practically preened like a peacock. "Then, if ye don't mind me saying, I'd also suggest moving some of the ivy from one side to the other. See, you ain't got any on the south side of the Manor, though it's plentiful on the north and east. It'd be grand for it to get started on the south and maybe on the west, too."

We concurred with his suggestion and thanked him again for his efforts. Day by day, the draughts were growing less severe. The workmen were doing an excellent job at stopping up the holes between the stones. Of course, there was naught they could do to ward off winter, and at night, the temperatures dipped lower and lower. Once the brutal temperatures set upon us, we would be burning logs in earnest to stay warm. Even so, I was happy that no meandering breezes invaded our home as they had before. Really, the men had done a remarkable job, and I amended my prior thinking.

I spent much of the day working on my sketch of John, as I wanted the piece to reflect him accurately. The weak winter sun came through the windows of the front parlor, so I set up my lap desk there. Occasionally, I grew frustrated, as a line or shading did not progress as I had hoped. In those cases, I put my portrait in the desk and pulled out the rough sketch of Ned. Thus, I went back and forth between the two projects. In between, I picked up the scarf I was crocheting for Edward. That was coming along better than I had anticipated, and I was pleased.

That evening after our tea, Edward stared into the fire. "This promises to be a long, hard winter."

Mrs. Fairfax added, "Already mice are shifting their households indoors, preparing for the harsh reality that will come. I saw one in the hallway outside of the kitchen."

"Mephisto will be busy," I said. "He has proven his talents as a mouser."

"Not as much lately," Edward said. "He seems to have lost his taste for the hunt."

"Perhaps he is a touch under the weather," I admitted. My affection toward the cat was unexpected. I have never owned a pet. I would not have sought Mephisto's company, nor would I have brought him home with me, except that, when his old mistress died, he was destined for the streets of London. As a domesticated animal, he was not accustomed to life on the streets of London. He stood a good chance of being crushed under horses' hooves or the wheels of a carriage. Mephisto deserved better, and so I had petitioned my husband for us to bring the cat to Ferndean.

To my surprise, Edward had been willing to add the cat to our household. "In a lodge like ours, surrounded by fields and copses, mice and shrews are a never-ending challenge. The barn cats are wild in nature, whereas Mephisto is accustomed to being treated as a pet." Mephisto took to Ferndean and his new hunting grounds with admirable gusto. Until recently, the vast population of rodents had declined precipitously. The fact that Mrs. Fairfax had seen one was not in keeping with my cat's typical prowess, and I said as much.

"Of late, that cat has been a slug-a-bed." Mrs. Fairfax scowled at the curled up kitty.

I could not leap to Mephisto's defense because she was quite right. He had seemed lethargic. Whereas once he would have leaped up on our bed in the morning, he seemed to be content to stay in his crate. I missed the cat's efforts to win my heart, no more purring against my leg nor rubbing his face against mine.

"To be fair, perhaps he *is* doing his job," said Edward. "We have no way of knowing the number of interlopers Mephisto has eradicated. Mayhap, one slipped past the cat."

"Maybe, but the fact I saw a mouse worries me," Mrs. Fairfax continued. Where there is one mouse, a dozen surely follow. I have also noticed that the cat has gained weight."

Whilst Mrs. Fairfax had not objected when we added Mephisto to our family, she was never enthralled with him. From the start, Mephisto had chosen to be my pet, and subsequently, he had ignored the housekeeper. I had witnessed her attempts to win over his affection by offering him small delicacies, but Mephisto did an admirable job of ignoring the older woman.

"We might want to instruct Cook to cut back on any scraps she feeds the cat." My husband has had considerably more experience than I have with animals, although he admitted to me that he'd never had an inside cat before Mephisto came to live with us.

Our conversation encouraged me to stare at the crate near the fire. Mephisto was snugly curled up among the old bits of blanket. In fact, he had not even raised his head at the sound of his name. That alone was worrisome. I chewed on my bottom lip. "To be sure, he doesn't seem as active as he once was. Indeed, he rarely seems to leave behind the comforts of his crate."

Edward stood, stretched, and leaned one arm against the mantelpiece. "That's hardly surprising. The cold is coming. All of nature slows down to preserve its vitality. The changing of the seasons and the early onset of dark makes one's bed seem enticing. If you wish, we could try to tame one of the barn cats and bring it indoors. Maybe if you select a kitten, you'll be successful in domesticating the animal. Perhaps Mephisto is lonely, or he's grown lazy and needs a young helper."

I tugged at a strand of yarn that irked me. I was nearly done with the scarf, but a moment of inattention had led to a skipped stitch.

Mrs. Fairfax glanced over at me and shook her head. "Jane, are you still puzzling over that mess of yarn? Whatever is it that you are trying to make?"

I'd kept the scarf a secret so far, and I intended to continue as I had started. Rather than be honest with the housekeeper, I said, "'Tis naught but a dishrag."

"My, my. The color is extraordinary," Mrs. Fairfax continued. "Seems like a waste of yarn for that to go into the kitchen to mop up spills."

"True. Leah had this left over." That was close to the truth. "So, I am trying to learn to crochet, and I am practicing on a dishrag." That confession, I hoped, would satisfy the housekeeper.

But I was wrong. She managed to knit as easily as most of us breathe, which goes a long way, I presume, to explaining why she has such a paucity of skills for teaching. When an activity comes to one with ease, enumerating the steps can prove difficult. Teaching requires a certain bent of mind, an ability to form a mental heuristic, and to break an activity down into steps. Mrs. Fairfax lacked the patience to be a good instructor.

Casting an inquiring eye my way, Mrs. Fairfax sighed with disapproval. "One would think that needlework skills would have been integral to your education."

I agreed. "One would think." Even though there were many deficits to my education at Lowood, I cannot blame the school for my inability to learn the more basic needlework skills. Eight years should have been enough for me to grasp abilities that seemed to come naturally to others.

"From all I've heard and read about Lowood," started Edward, "their expertise was in nurturing human suffering and hypocrisy. I can in no manner forgive that charity school for the many cruelties it dealt Jane and the other denizens of the institution."

"Good schools can seem overly strict," began Mrs. Fairfax, "in their zeal toward improvement."

"There is truth in that," I agreed, warming to the subject. I put the crocheting down, as my hands desperately yearned to punctuate my thoughts. "However, I cannot approve or understand the school's reliance on physical suffering as a teaching method. Ongoing cruelty was meted out with the explanation that these hardships were important and necessary steps toward our salvation. Such a doxology presupposes that I and my sister orphans were sinful from birth, an assertion I cannot accept. When I look around at the evidence of God's love, I cannot square his beneficence with any catechism that features as a central tenet the suggestion that children, the youngest and most tender of his creations, are inherently evil. And yet that is exactly what Mr. Brocklehurst, the institution's supervisor, told us over and over again. Even as his daughters and wife sat on throne-like chairs in front of us and displayed finery such as ribbons and silks and furs and woolen cloaks, we students were forced to walk several miles in rain and snow, only to sit and shiver in an unheated church while listening to protracted sermons. When illness befell us, as it inevitably would, the weakest among us were struck down first. Many did not survive."

An uncomfortable silence ensued. No doubt Edward and Mrs. Fairfax were mentally comparing my experience with that of Adèle's recent stint at Alderton House. Yes, a girl died at Adèle's school. True, Adèle hated her time there. But by all accounts, the food was plentiful, and the girls were never forced to withstand deprivations of simple comfort. Nor was there an overweening religious philosophy built on the premise that the young girls, the students, were innately evil.

That was what separated Alderton House from Lowood Academy. At Alderton, students misbehaved. At Lowood, girls were believed to invite the devil to dwell within—and as such, an exorcism must be performed. No, not a formal ceremony to cast out demons, but an informal, ongoing program of purging, predicated on the victim's innately evil nature.

Rather than persist in discussing a sad time in my life, I changed the subject. "Ned will be thrilled to see Adèle. And Lucy and little Evans."

"Jane, have you firmed up all of your menus?

What is left to be done? May I assist you with your preparations?" Mrs. Fairfax was on solid turf here, as her ability to run the household is unparalleled. I thanked her.

"I believe all is well in hand. After making several lists, Cook has assured me that she has everything she needs. The menus are set. I have done all of my holiday shopping. I have appealed to Lucy to share any particular desires she might have, so that we can accommodate her." I paused. "All is in order, except for decorating Ferndean. I asked Lucy to tell me what to gather, but I haven't heard from her."

"James is coming tomorrow, so you might plan to take the cart out with him. I suggest you head out first thing tomorrow morning. As the day goes on, the temperatures will dip."

I agreed that would be wise.

Mrs. Fairfax added, "Cook says that a wet northern wind is kicking up. That may mean we'll get snow soon. You'll want to do your collecting before the weather covers up all the best greenery."

I agreed that going tomorrow would make sense. Turning to the housekeeper, I said, "There will be much to do, when the time comes to actually decorate. Your assistance in choosing the most advantageous placement of any greenery would be much appreciated."

Mrs. Fairfax sat up a wee bit straighter. "I should be delighted to do so."

My husband came over to plant a kiss on the top of my head. "Jane, Cook told me you've done a lot of planning. She's very impressed by your efforts. I believe we will have a delightful holiday season, and I thank you for your efforts."

I blushed. "I'm doing what I can with my paucity of knowledge. If this season is deficient, we can always take note and make amends for next year. I did not know you consulted with Cook. What other schemes have you embarked on?"

"If I tell you all of my Christmas plans," Edward said, in his most stern voice, "I would deprive you of a generous portion of the joy of the season. You will have to be patient and see what happens, as anticipation is a delight unto itself. Suffice it to say, I have a plentitude of surprises in the works. Visitors are but one of the many gifts I will be giving you."

"You say guests? I know of Lucy, Evans, and Mrs. Wallander. Are you suggesting that more visitors will join us? How will I prepare the Manor, if I don't know how many people to expect?" My question sprang from my curiosity, more than from my needs. In truth, there's not much I would need to do to make Ferndean ready for guests, except perhaps to air out the older bedclothes in the linen press cabinet.

Edward regarded me gruffly. "Your attempt to cadge information from me will not do, my darling. I am wise to your trickery. You'll glean no nuggets of gold from me. I am promised to make these twelve days of Christmas the merriest you have ever known, and I am not above ignoring your questions, if that aids me in reaching my goal."

CHAPTER 14

Immediately after breakfast the next morning, I threw on my warmest spencer and wrapped a shawl around my shoulders. With a quick goodbye kiss for Edward and a cuddle for Ned, I hurried into the kitchen. There stood Cook, with fists on her hips, staring into the larder. "I cannot understand this. Every morning 'tis the same. One thing or another disappears. I've come to believe that either we have a very hungry ghost or someone amongst us wanders around in my kitchen at night and helps himself!"

This complaint was never-ending, and I had no remedy for it. James stood in front of the glowing coals in the hearth and warmed his hands. From behind Cook's back, he winked at me. She'd wisely served him a mug of hot tea with milk to warm him before our expedition. I could only surmise that she'd decided he was not to blame for the disappearance of the victuals.

"I certainly wish I could supply you with an answer, Cook, but the mystery of the disappearing food is beyond my ken. So, you've heated a couple of bricks for us?" I nodded toward the oven. The heat from the iron box was palpable.

"Aye, first let me wrap them in these wool sleeves that Mrs. Fairfax knitted for them. They'll stay warm longer this way. I'll have hot cocoa ready for ye both when ye return." She folded her hands across her waistband and surveyed me. Checking, I presume, to see that I'd chosen my warmest apparel. "Ye're taking your muslin bag? Hoping to do some art?"

I nodded.

"Well, see if ye can find a sprig or two of mistletoe while ye're out and about. I wager the Master would appreciate any excuse to kiss his bonny bride."

"Don't ye worry," James chimed in. "I have instructions regarding what to look for, and mistletoe is on that list. Mrs. Fairfax already lectured me on that which she wants us to gather."

That was well and good, as our expedition was a new one for me. Since I could offer no answers, I adjusted my bonnet and pulled the hood of my cloak up and over my shoulders for added warmth. This day had dawned clear as a fine crystal decanter, but a darkening swell of clouds to the north of us suggested the mild weather might not last.

"Feels to me like a snow is coming," Cook warned us. "My toes ache and my back is complaining like a mean devil for certain. Best for ye both to be out and about while ye can."

Moses watched me solemnly, as I approached him with a bit of carrot from my muslin bag. I kept back another tidbit for after our drive. The young man had thoughtfully parked the cart close to the mounting block for my convenience. After I caressed the donkey's ears as a friendly sign of appreciation, James offered me his hand to help me climb on the stone step. Once I was settled, I put the bag on the floor at my feet.

James walked around to the other side and hopped in. "Me grandfather has a poem about such," he explained with a backwards glance at the mounting block. With a slap of the reins, he recited:

A loupin' on stane is a very good thing,

For a man that is stiff, for a man that is auld,
For a man that is lame o' the leg or the spauld,
Or short o' the houghs, to loup on his naggie.

I laughed. "I'm not a man who is lame, but I am too short to easily get into and out of the cart."

"But ye managed fine when you took old Moses out, didn't ye?"

"Yes, I did. He was as patient and mild as you had promised. I look forward to taking him to Millcote again."

"Aye, well, but that'll have to wait, as we're in for a spot of terrible weather."

This reminded me of the conversation I'd had with Cook back in the fall, so I asked James, "How can you tell whether the winter will be mild or cruel?"

He considered this, cocking his head and thinking my question over. "I am canny, when it comes to watching out for changes. My own grandmother taught me to do so, and the indicators are plentiful. I saw a fat squirrel in the garden, tucking seeds into the ground. The hens are growing extra of their downy feathers. Old Moses has a thick undercoat on him, as do Rashana and even Mesrour. We best better enjoy this time in the sunshine whilst we can, missus. We'll be shut in for months, I dare say."

The weak sunlight cast interesting shadows as stems bearing the last seed vessels of the rose-bay willow herb waved cheerfully above the other sparse vegetation. New catkins appeared on the alder and hazel trees. A song thrush trilled a melody before flitting to the spent seed heads of a cow parsnip. My mind is stimulated by the out-of-doors, and I itched to sketch what I saw.

First of all, James drove us past a stand of silver birch. Beyond those spare trunks with their paper-thin bark in its distinctive silvery hue, James pointed out a group of juniper bushes. These sprawled their way up a rocky slope, sheltering other bushes, including yet another bilberry bush. Alas, the berries were all gone, but I drew myself a quick map so I could explore this spot in the spring.

"Ye'll want to hang these bits outside the Manor, as juniper will keep away evil spirits," James said as he jumped down to cut an armful of branches. The smell was spicy and aromatic. When I remarked upon it, James smiled and said, "I'll grab a handful or two of the berries. Leah uses them, when she cooks squirrel. Says they flavor the broth just right."

Next, we stopped by an evergreen tree. "I'm not sure how to tell spruce from fir," I said.

James pulled on a branch to show me. "Spruce have cones that hang down. That's how ye can always tell. And pine has shorter needles than spruce. The needle-shaped leaves will look good against the dark wood in the Manor hall."

This time, he went to the back of the cart and grabbed a small hatchet. From tree to tree he went, chopping off the nicest branches. I carefully climbed down and grabbed one by the butt end. Dragging the spruce cutting to the cart helped me warm up considerably. Thereafter, I assisted by hauling one branch after another, until James was free to work beside me.

Not far away was a gleaming holly bush. The shining surface of the leaves reflected the waning sunlight. "We'd better hurry," James observed. "The snow might not hold off long." I admired the red berries nestled among the blue-green leaves. The deep red orbs set off the pointed leaves perfectly, and I said as much.

"Aye, some folk think there's naught to see when winter comes 'round, but I say there's much to delight the eyes as long as ye take your time to look." James climbed out and chopped off an armful of branches.

Our last stop took us back to the area I'd explored weeks before, that spot where the walnut and chestnut trees stood tall. Behind them was a trio of oak trees. "I'm betting there'll be mistletoe up there, amongst those limbs of the oak," James explained, jerking his chin at the spreading limbs. As I waited in the cart, he chose one of the trees to climb, selecting a low branch that offered an easy foothold to others. Remembering what happened to his grandfather, my heart beat hard and fast, as he moved from one perch to the next. To distract myself, I reached for my dilapidated muslin bag. Pulling out my sketch book and colored pencils. I sketched the dull hues of the landscape around us, hoping to paint them later. For reference, I climbed down and picked various bits of foliage, thinking I would commit their shades to paper at my leisure.

As I labored over my drawings, James tossed sprigs of mistletoe onto the ground. The leaves were shaped like small thumbs, and the berries were white and waxy.

Descending through the branches, James carefully navigated his return to terra firma. "That such be more than enough for decorating the hall, I should think." I agreed and stooped to pick up a piece of the mistletoe.

"Nay, missus. Ye finish your artwork. I'll gather the gleanings here. Leah told me how rare a talent ye have. Any dogsbody can pick up these cuttings."

"Dogsbody?" I repeated.

"Aye, 'tis a term they use in the navy for someone who does menial work."

Seeing that the weather would not allow many more opportunities, I acquiesced to his offer. I was still sketching, when he finished and came to stand at my elbow. "Leah says ye can draw like she never seen before. My, and it's a wonder, it is." His wide-eyed gaze told me that he was entranced.

"We all have our talents. The crochet hook you whittled for me is a treasure, James, and your wife's ability to spin and dye yarn is amazing."

He hung his head to hide a blush. "Aye, well, I expect that's true, missus. God never creates any of us without a touch of his majesty, does he?"

I thought that one of the most poetic truths I'd ever heard.

As usual, when we returned to Ferndean, Cook was bent over a boiling pot. Clouds of steam rose and fogged the air around her head, blurring her profile and making it indistinct. Since she had not heard James and me approaching, and the water she stirred was violently sending up bubbles, the young man and I waited quietly, until she directed her attention toward us.

James and I watched carefully, while Cook held a muslin bag over the water. The sack was tied at the neck with a long piece of twine, and the tail of the string was tethered to the handle of a wooden spoon. With great concentration, she lowered the bag and let it slowly sink into the water, until it was completely covered. The twine leash on the bag kept it from drifting to the bottom of the pot. A froth of bubbles rose to the surface, bringing with them the heavenly odor of cinnamon. I could not help but breathe in a little more deeply, enjoying the robust spicy fragrance.

"Oh," said Cook as she turned around. "Missus! James! How are you both?"

Without waiting for an answer, she found the pot she uses for making hot cocoa.

"We are fine," I said, speaking for both of us. "Our foraging was productive. Now tell me about boiled pudding. Is there a secret to making it come out right?" I wandered closer to the pot and watched the bubbles rise and break.

"Aye, of course there is." She chuckled. "If the water don't keep boiling, the pudding will get soggy. Ye have to keep your eye on it every minute. That can be tricky, as I need to make the sauce whilst that pudding cooks. Don't it smell delightful? I aim to make one pudding for each of the household staff members, but I reckoned that I'd start with this one and let ye taste it as the recipe is from Mrs. Brayton. See if it's seasoned to your liking. I can adjust the amount of fruit and sugar as you please."

The milk was in the pan and heating slowly. James watched Cook's labor with obvious appreciation. The woman was adroit, and I was entirely happy she had come to work for us. I hoped she would never leave.

I sighed with pleasure and appropriated a tall stool. "If the fragrance is any indication, your boiled pudding promises to be glorious. Could you also make one for Lucy Brayton? When she comes to visit, I'd like to shower her with gifts. She's always so generous to us and to Adèle."

Cook nodded. "I'd already planned to do as much. I also planned to make extra for any of the local farm families. Now some squires, they only were generous on Boxing Day, but Old Squire Rochester, for all his faults and his sins, God rest his soul, he was good to his people on Christmas Day as well. Mr. Edward's father made a big show of handing out victuals to the tenants and even strangers on Christmas Day. I've put my niece to work, oiling paper. If we can get enough twine, we can wrap up neat packages and fill them with a hunk of cheese, bread, slices of ham, and small puddings. Those'll keep in the cellar. If you don't mind me dipping into our supply of sugar, I might even add a biscuit or two."

All the while she talked, she kept one eye on the warming milk. Without skipping a word, she added cocoa and sugar, stirring the mouth-watering mix, until it was perfect. James and I accepted the hot beverages with gratitude. Once we had, she went to the close closet. From there she removed a scone for each of us, and after plating these, she handed them to us.

I marveled at her thoughtfulness. "Of course, you are free to use any and all of the sugar you require. Cook, you do us proud. Your knowledge of the old days is a godsend, as I should like to always err on the side of doing more for folks rather than less. Thank you kindly for your good planning. Pray tell me, how can I help you? Have you discovered any more supplies that will you need?"

"Since ye already approved the menus I gave ye, we should be fine. As we are getting an early start, if I did miss any ingredients, I suspect we can send James to Millcote."

James nodded. "As long as John is not fretful and I get my other chores done in time to lend assistance."

"If the weather doesn't change, I could take Moses there," I said.

"Nah, missus. This time of year, it's too changeable for ye to take the chance," Cook said. She added, "I could walk there myself on my half-day off. Too bad we don't have a tweenie to help out here in the kitchen, or a stable boy to run to town for us. Then we'd really be set and not have to worry."

I sighed. "It's not for lack of trying. Edward and I sent letters to the rector, the doctor, and the estate agent. I fervently asked them for their recommendations. In fact, I made a call upon the rector and his wife."

Cook sent me a sly glance. "Oy? And I'd imagine ye were surprised, eh? Me and my sister went to church twice, since the Reverend Jones-Smythe came here. We've vowed to never go again."

I couldn't blame the Cook and her sister.

During and after my visit, the rector and his wife had struck me as wholly unsuitable. Moreover, the Jones-Smythes had made no attempt to get in touch since my visit. In fact, they hadn't even sent us a note, expressing their regret that they could not help us. Nor had they scheduled a courtesy call. No, the Jones-Smythes had shown a brazen disregard for the hierarchy of our positions.

James and Cook waited for me to speak. I said, "I hate to advertise for a helper in the county newspapers, as I much prefer those who come to us through references. However, I answered an ad for a governess, so perhaps that is the way for me to proceed. Indeed, that might be our best option. I shall revisit the topic, after the holidays."

"I regret I can't do more," said James, somberly. "Leah feels badly about it, too. Yesterday, my grandmother wandered off. We're accustomed to that, but yesterday, oy, she didn't come back, until after nightfall. Leah was sick with worry. A neighbor brought my grandmother to the door. Her mind's beginning to wander, and her feet are following wherever her thoughts seem to go."

My mouth fell open. "Oh, no! Are you saying her mind is going?"

James nodded. "Sad to say, I believe that's the

truth. I have suspected as much for a while, but yesterday, Leah said we can't pretend any longer. She said that John and Mary have to be watched every minute."

"And yet," I said, as I shook my head, "Edward tells me there are no vacant cottages on the property. I don't know how we'll find lodging for a man with a family."

Cook folded her hands over her belly and watched as James and I finished our cocoa. "There's more than enough work for another pair of hands, if you don't mind me saying so."

I agreed. "The stresses on you, James, and on Leah are real hardships. Beyond finding help for Cook and a way to exercise Mesrour, you two need a helper. Someone who can sit with John and who can entertain Mary. Otherwise, they are at risk. Tasking Leah with their care is but a partial solution. As good as she is, and your wife is saintly, she cannot watch two people at once!"

James studied his empty mug. Cook poured him a second portion. The young man nodded. "We both reckoned that my grandmother was losing her way, but she's gotten so much worse, since my grandfather has taken to his bed. Last night, she told me she was looking for him. 'Who?' I asked, and she said, 'Your grandfather.' I walked her into the bedroom, and she didn't recognize Grandfather. Asked me who he was, cool as you please. I fear she'll wander out in the cold and die of exposure or take a tumble off one of the crags and break her leg."

"That must be a terrible worry," In years past, Mary had served the Rochester family. She had always been devoted to her husband. I could picture myself in her position. How heartbreaking it would be to watch your spouse's decline. However, I had not realized that Mary's wandering was dangerous. I had thought she was only soothing herself by going on a ramble. Now I knew differently. She was like a little child, searching for a lost friend. Undoubtedly, she would continue to roam farther and farther afield.

It also struck me that whilst we thought ourselves only down one man, in actuality we'd lost four helpers: John, Mary, James, and Leah. Perhaps the best course of action would be to build a new cottage on the estate and hire an entire family to help us out.

The melancholy conversation had its effect on James. "I better get back home, missus. I'll unhook the cart and throw a tarp over the greenery.

That should keep it nice and fresh until ye are ready to decorate with it."

I thanked him for the pleasant morning. Cook pressed a parcel into James's hands. "'Tisn't much. Only a few sausages, a bit of cheese, and a half a loaf of bread."

James was very appreciative, thanking us and taking his leave.

With a sideways look at me, Cook asked for my approval.

"You're a good woman, Cook," I said. "Thank you for thinking of the Harrigans."

"Ye have a kind heart, Miss, sure you do," said Cook. She dragged the back of her sleeve across her eyes to brush away the tears. "I expected you'd been in favor of a wee indulgence. I've known Mary and John since I was a little one. They're salt of the earth, just like the Bible says, and they're devoted to each other and to Master. Even if John were feeling up to snuff, we'd still need another bit of help. See, her problems with her mind aside, Mary is not as spritely as she once was. For a year or more, John's been covering up for her."

"I didn't know that."

"Ye weren't supposed to know that. We conspired to keep it to ourselves. Oh, we never discussed it, but we all knew what we were doing, deep down. Besides, what I need help with is a bit of hauling and lifting and dragging and such, and that's not something Mary could do on a good day."

"I know," I said.

The problem was vexing, to say the least.

CHAPTER 15

When I walked into the parlor that evening, Mrs. Fairfax and my husband sprang apart like two naughty schoolchildren caught gossiping. As I took my accustomed chair, they avoided my eyes and blushed. Both seemed at a sudden loss for words. I reached over and picked up the most recent copy of the newspaper from London. Edward cleared his throat. "Jane, Mrs. Fairfax and I were talking about what to do for my tenants as a holiday gift."

"Oh?" Of course, I knew that Cook was working on comestibles. Hadn't I seen as much this morning? I had. After James Harrigan left,

Cook and I reviewed our plans for supplying the tenants with comestibles on Boxing Day.

Then why was Edward lying? Rather than call out my husband for his prevarication, I nodded and kept silent.

After the awkward lull that followed, Mrs. Fairfax took over. "Jane? For years, Edward's father invited tenants to feast and make merry on Christmas Day in the Great Hall at Thornfield Hall. He would hire a fiddler and another instrument or two to play. The large oak table was moved from against the wall and centered at one end. That left the rest of the floor cleared for dancing."

"It sounds very festive," I said. This came as news to me. I was still trying to form a way to share what I'd learned from James. Edward already felt guilt, regarding John's tumble from the roof. Hearing that Mary's mind was going would further complicate my husband's sense of responsibility. There was no way we could build a new building for a new family. Not until spring. We'd been fortunate that the stone masons had found a span of nice weather so they could patch up Ferndean. To start a new project would be asking too much, even as we knew the workers would not be able to continue rebuilding Thornfield Hall, when the weather turned bitter.

Quickly, I made a decision not to relate what I'd learned about John and Mary. The holidays were nearly here. There would be time after our merrymaking, and thus, nothing I would say would spoil the efforts we'd planned for a good time.

Fortunately, neither Edward nor Mrs. Fairfax noticed I was quiet. Instead, they described how Thornfield Hall had been appointed, who had been invented, and how the estate celebrated in years past. I did my best to imagine their descriptions, but I could not. The juxtaposition of merrymaking and Edward's melancholy were too vast. When I had first arrived at Thornfield Hall, Edward had not even been at home. Due to his despair, he'd come to avoid the family home, visiting the place as infrequently as possible.

His father, Old Squire Rochester, had foisted marriage on Edward, even though the old man knew that the women in Bertha Mason's family suffered an aggressive strain of madness. But the squire wanted his second son to have access to Bertha's fortune, and her parents wanted her married and safely removed to another place, hoping they could gloss over the intermittent signs she'd shown of losing her mind.

Edward had walked into a trap, as Bertha had been a renowned beauty, who played the pianoforte skillfully. My husband is, and has always been, a great admirer of music. So, he was strongly persuaded that marrying Bertha was in his best interests. Their meetings were carefully chaperoned. She was never alone with him, and he attributed this to her religious upbringing. Instead, this was the family's way of limiting his exposure to their daughter's eroding equilibrium.

After Bertha repeatedly tried to stab Edward in his sleep and then moved to setting his bed on fire, he locked her up in one of the top floors of Thornfield Hall. Her minder, Grace Poole, was a large woman, capable of handling Bertha, and very well paid for her silence. Sadly, Grace loved a drink or two, and as time went on, her drinking continued until she was more often drunk than sober. Thus, she must have been inebriated when Bertha managed that last act of defiance, setting the Hall on fire.

Edward had a good reason for ignoring most of his responsibilities toward his ancestral home. Shortly before he pledged his love to me, he had entertained for the first time in years. Even back then, the Great Hall was unused, so of course, I'd never seen the place in its glory.

I tried to push away my gloomy thoughts. Instead, I turned my attention to where we were now. Soon this place would ring with laughter! Lucy would bring with her a strong sense of joie de vivre. Adèle might pout and sulk upon leaving London, but she would quickly change to her sunny self, when she saw how much Ned had grown. The many preparations we'd made could not go unnoticed. All that was left to do was to decide—yes, to make a decision—that we would be merry.

Edward and Mrs. Fairfax were waiting for me to comment on their ideas. "I suppose we could open the Great Hall here," I said. "I could appoint it with greenery on Christmas Eve. The old dining table has been laid on its side and pushed up to the wall, but it would be easy enough to set it right again."

Edward's face brightened with interest. "Capital idea, the greenery. I remember that from my youth. We could burn a Yule Log in that large fireplace. I know just the fallen oak tree. James and I were discussing what to do with it the other day. You'll find it a marvel, as it is nearly seven feet long. As a matter of fact, I have several bottles of wine not worth drinking. We could borrow a French custom and pour that miserable wine onto the wood. Then, the fragrance of the vineyard would mingle with the burning oak. Believe me, the result is a delight."

"I can make requests of all the old minstrels, the ones who used to play for the Old Squire. If those musicians cannot come or if they have passed on, perhaps they can recommend younger players willing to take their place," said Mrs. Fairfax.

"Since Christmas falls on a Saturday, Boxing Day will be celebrated on Monday," said Edward. "Thus, we shall have two opportunities to send food home with our guests. All natural signs point to a harsh winter, so I believe our guests will be doubly glad to have more victuals for the harsh days ahead."

I agreed. "I have instructed Cook to make foodstuffs that we can give to all at Boxing Day. Certainly, Lucy and Adèle will be happy to help us pass out the boxes." That left me wondering what our dear friend Lucy Brayton was doing with Adèle this very evening. No doubt they were at the theatre, as the London paper was full of news about performances at the Opera House. I continued exploring our plans, "As for opening

Ferndean to the tenants and sending them home with food, certainly we could do that. What is the purpose of a Great Hall, if it is never used? And I can well imagine what a difference the extra comestibles might make to a local family."

"How did you and James do collecting greenery?" asked Mrs. Fairfax.

"I think it went very well. James determined that leaving the pieces in the cart and covering them with a tarp would be best. I hope you concur."

Her face was suffused with rapture, which surprised me, as Mrs. Fairfax is typically serious and occasionally dour. "Absolutely! That was a wonderful plan. Tell me. Do you know what it was that you collected?"

"We found great bunches of holly, bows of juniper, large portions of spruce, and mistletoe. Lucy has suggested as much to decorate the Manor. She has promised to bring yards and yards of red ribbon."

Her letter had arrived while James and I were out collecting greenery. The last of the stone masons had brought it here from Millcote. I'd opened it eagerly and read it with great joy. "Lucy has promised to be here in time to help us make everything ready for Christmas Day."

I added almost as an afterthought, "James has promised that he'll come over on Christmas Eve and help us hang the boughs."

"Do you not think you should invite the new rector?" Mrs. Fairfax looked almost eager. "We have not yet met him. Or his wife. He could bless the people, our home, and all of our endeavors."

This was met with a heavy silence. Edward and I were not churchgoers, even though he provides the local reverend with a living. After my sad experiences at Lowood Academy and his personal disappointments with his disastrous first marriage, we have grave doubts about the way the Church represents the word of God. Mrs. Fairfax's suggestion that we turn to the Church could generously be called unexpected at the least. Furthermore, although Mrs. Fairfax and Edward had not met the rector and his wife, I had, and I'd mentioned as much in passing to my husband.

Edward did remember, and he prodded me to share what I knew. "Jane? You met the new rector, didn't you? Mr. Jones-Smythe? And his wife?"

Before I could answer, Mrs. Fairfax went on, "Of course, I dare say the rector has his own plans for Christmas programs."

"I'm sure he does," said Edward, amiably. "But

given my patronage of the church and the nature of our request, I harbor happy expectations that he can be persuaded to find a way to assist us in feeding his flock."

A frown creased my face.

"What did you think of them?" Edward asked me directly.

This was not idle chatter on the part of my husband. Edward has always valued my opinions and, in particular, my impressions of people. He has made it perfectly clear that he considers me to be a keen observer of human nature. I think of it as a survival skill. With some degree of hesitation, I said, "Not much. I was singularly unimpressed by both of them. Nor did I find them disposed to sharing Christian charity. It can do no harm to invite them to come and say a blessing, especially if our tenants would appreciate the gesture."

My husband made a noise rather like a snort. "Do no harm? Jane, your generosity exceeds your honesty. On the contrary, in a season meant for making merry, in a few days filled with hope and anticipation, a sour note may well spoil our milk of human kindness. You were unimpressed? Say no more. That's all the validation I need for revoking an invitation. I say we let our actions speak volumes and any sanctified tongues remain where they belong, on hallowed ground."

It was then that I realized I had been holding my breath. "I concur," I said with evident relief. "Whereas my cousin, St. John Rivers, lives his faith, I could not discern any signs that the rector and his wife hewed to the tenets of theirs.

"After the holidays," Edward continued, "I shall call upon the rector myself. If I do not find an inkling of those traits mandated by his position, I shall see that he is replaced."

That was fine by me.

"Speaking of removal, has Cook mentioned to either of you that food keeps disappearing from the kitchen?" Mrs. Fairfax asked. "She was in a state of fury earlier today, when an entire mince pie went missing."

Edward chuckled. "I heard her complaints all the way into my study. I must confess I find her amusing. She obviously has mislaid items. There can be no other explanation. It's not like any of us are roaming the hallways at night and raiding her larder. You don't think Amelia is taking food, do you?"

This he directed toward me.

I had a quick rejoinder. "No. The girl is too skinny by half. Besides, Amelia knows that she need only ask and we'd supply her with whatever she wants. I've said as much many times."

"Could James be letting himself in? Picking up food that might entice his grandfather to eat?" asked Mrs. Fairfax.

"That's all I can figure," I admitted. "And if so, I am loathe to ask him about it." Editing my words carefully, I said, "John and Mary are doing poorly. If James is taking food to tempt them into eating, I say hurrah for him and his ingenuity."

"Surely James would say something, if they need more food." Edward looked perplexed. "He and I have spoken several times, since Cook began her complaints. The man knows I'd do anything in my power to help his ailing grandparents. I thought we had such an understanding that he would come to me with his requests."

I shrugged. "Perhaps you can approach him after the holidays."

"Yes," said Edward. "I think I shall."

With a sigh, I pulled a soft wool blanket over my skirt and turned my attention to my crocheting. Edward dozed in front of the fire, and Mrs. Fairfax picked up the newspaper. She would have read to us, but I bade her to cease, as the newspaper was several weeks old, and Edward seemed happy enough to be drowsy. Pilot groaned, as he folded his long legs and rested his head on his paws. Within minutes, his ears twitched and he whimpered, caught up in a dream that sent him running in his sleep. Upon realizing that the dog was in distress, I dropped to my knees and stroked his hoary head. "No need to do that, Jane," Mrs. Fairfax corrected me. "He's an animal. Let him be."

"He's one of God's creatures," I responded, as I rubbed Pilot's ears. "Although he cannot speak, his loyalty is evident. Do you realize he sleeps outside the nursery door all night? It is true. After we go to bed, he wanders down the hallway and picks the same spot night after night. Of late, I've taken to putting down an old blanket for him to ease his aching bones."

As a matter of fact, the idea came to me that, if my skills with a crochet hook grew, I could produce some sort of bag for the dog and fill it with fresh hay.

"You waste your time on that old dog," said Mrs. Fairfax.

"No," I said firmly. "A kindness is never wasted, be it for a dog or a cat or a person."

Edward surprised us by rousing and saying, "When I think of all the years that Pilot has run alongside me, keeping pace with Mesrour, waiting outside of inns, and resting at my feet, I cannot imagine any other creature more deserving of comfort in his old age than my dog."

When his Master pronounced his name, Pilot's brown eyes opened halfway, recognized his benefactor's approval, and quickly fell back asleep.

CHAPTER 16

Two days later, a wagon arrived at the back of the Manor. James drove and brought along two farm hands. Cook came and found me in the parlor, where I was working on my portrait of a slumbering Ned, since I'd finished the picture of John Harrigan. "A wagon's here and James is driving it. I think it's that present ye commissioned for the Master," she whispered in an urgent voice. "The one from Germany."

Normally, Edward would have heard the clatter and gone to meet the delivery, but fortunately for me, Edward was out making the rounds with his agent, doing a yearend check on all of his tenants. His intention was to visit them and hand out the invitations I'd drafted the day before, the notice of a party on Christmas Day in the Great Hall as well as a distribution of boxes on Boxing Day.

Cook was all aflutter, as two men lowered the bulky object from the wagon to the ground. A quilt had been hastily thrown over my gift, and I resisted the urge to look beneath the covering. Edward's gift would, therefore, be a surprise for me as well as for my husband. The men lifted my purchase and carried it into Cook's pantry, where she'd already prepared a vacancy. I congratulated James on his timing, but he demurred, "'Twas no accident, missus. I knew Master would be making rounds of the estate. This here actually arrived two days ago, but when I got word, I asked the stationmaster to keep it safe, until I could fetch it. When he heard it was for Squire Rochester, he were more than happy to do as I asked. I told him I'd need two strong men to help me, and a wagon for delivery, and he arranged it all. I'm sure the men'd be glad of a coin or two. I put the wagon hire on your account, and I told Squire Rochester that I needed such to transport the Yule Log."

"Of course, I'll take care of the men," I said. "That was wonderfully devious of you, James."

"Oy, wait until ye see," James winked at me. "That Yule Log is the biggest tree I ever did see."

He motioned to the workers, and in concert, they walked out of the house and back to the wagon. I stood in the kitchen doorway and watched. A good deal of grunting and groaning commenced and the men lifted down an enormous tree trunk wrapped in willow switches. As they carried it past me, James said, "'Tis from an oak tree at the other end of the estate. It's to be your Yule Log. I know we're to be dragging it, but it's far too big!"

"So I see!" I ushered the men and the log through the Manor to the Great Hall, where the fireplace was large enough to shelter a small cow. There the log was gently set down in front of the huge brick hearth. The tree trunk brought with it the scent of the forest, a fragrance both earthy and primeval. A pang hit my heart, as I contemplated all that the tree had seen in its long life. I comforted myself by thinking that at least it would leave this mortal plane in a blaze of glory, providing light and heat and merrymaking for so many. The men worked as a unit to move wood from the nearby log box, building up a platform for the Yule Log. Once all was in order, they counted to three and heaved the Yule Log into its place of pride.

Whilst Cook served the men a cup of tea and biscuits, James busied himself, slowly saturating the wood with Edward's castoff wine that my husband had thoughtfully put aside in the pantry for this purpose.

I was happy to give the men more money than they expected. I also paid James a bit extra with the explicit command that he "spend that on Leah."

"You planned this perfectly, James. Thank you ever so much," I said.

He pocketed the coins and said, "I know just what she's wanted. They sell a special soap at the chemist. It smells like a bouquet of lavender, and she loves it."

An hour of my day was spent finishing the last of the invitations. Mrs. Fairfax had been kind enough to look over the list created by our agent. She pronounced it very complete. I'd methodically put a tick mark next to each name, as I'd finished writing out the details. Most of them had gone with Edward, but a few were still needing to be addressed.

"It wouldn't do to leave anyone out," Mrs. Fairfax said, approvingly.

I heartily agreed and went back to handwriting the addresses. There was no need for our guests to respond, as we would manage, no matter how many or how few came to rejoice with us.

That same afternoon, Mrs. Fairfax showed herself to be exceedingly useful, because she announced that she had succeeded in contacting various musicians. She had tasked herself with developing a list of songs for them to perform. I left her to it and went back to working on the portrait of Ned. I added chalk to his portrait with a happy heart, lightened by the knowledge that there would be sufficient music to add a festive air to our Grand Hall.

Two days before Christmas, I woke up, wide-eyed with excitement. This would be my last chance to put the final touches on my gifts. According to her letters, Lucy would have an early departure from London by coach on the morrow, Christmas Eve. The plan was for James to drive our carriage to Millcote and meet our house guests there. Edward would be finishing his rounds with the estate agent.

I had much to do before Lucy and her entourage arrived. James had agreed to watch his grandfather and grandmother for a few hours, freeing Leah to come and pick up the portrait I had made of John.

But my friend wouldn't arrive until midday, and so I had determined that I would serve her a meal called a luncheon, which Lucy had assured me was fast becoming all the rage for the ladies in London. She'd even sent me a list of foods served for such a repast, and Cook was eager to try making them. The dainty "sandwiches" of thinly sliced ham and egg salad would be a treat, along with tiny cakes and tea. Although Mrs. Fairfax disapproved of the fact I'd be entertaining the wife of a servant, I did not care, as such distinctions mean little to me. Leah was fast becoming a friend, and I was pleased to be able to cultivate the bond between us.

That left me several hours, at least, to perfect my portrait of Ned, whilst taking full advantage of the bright morning light streaming in through the windows, so I ate a hurried breakfast of tea and toast and went into the parlor. I focused all my concentration onto the image in front of me, adding and correcting strokes of my pencil so that my son's well-loved face began to take shape on the paper. In fact, I was so engrossed in my labors that I did not hear Amelia enter the room. She must have stood at my elbow for several minutes, before clearing her throat to request my attention.

When I turned to her, she grinned. Smiling at my son, she said, "That's Mama, isn't it? Come on, Ned. Say Mama for us, little sir."

He tucked his head under her chin as a wave of shyness overcame him. I stood up and held out my arms. Immediately, he reached for me and said, "Mah-mah." My heart nearly broke with joy. True, he'd attempted the word countless times, but never had he been so successful until now. He repeated his triumph with another clear, "Mah-mah." I cuddled and kissed him.

"Thank you, Amelia," I said, as I spoke to her over the downy hair on his sweet little crown. "I wouldn't have missed this for the world!"

"Ah, and I was lucky, because I was able to watch you as you drew. 'Twas fascinating, Missus. Truly so. That picture is the very image of Baby Ned, if you don't mind me saying so." The young woman edged closer to my lap desk to stare down at my drawing.

"There's a bit more I wish to do, but I hope to finish it by this afternoon, and I have one I did of John, so Leah can take it home with her." I handed Ned back to Amelia. When my hands were free, I found the portrait of John and showed it to the nursemaid.

"Coo, missus, that's the very image of Old John. You got him perfectly. Is this for James?"

"Yes, but it's for Leah to give to her husband. She requested it," I explained. "As much as I'd like to hold Ned a little longer, I better get back to my work. I need to finish this one for Edward, especially since he's out with the estate agent. I can only work on it in this good light, when my husband's not at home."

Indeed, clouds on the horizon were grey and threatening. Snow was coming, of that I was sure. I hoped that Leah could visit and still get home before the fat flakes came pelting down. If need be, she could spend the night, since her husband had agreed to watch his grandparents while she and I met. But I knew she would feel awkward here as a guest, and whilst staying, she would worry about the burden on James. Leah was experienced in taking care of both of the elderly Harrigans; however, James was not. Leah worried her husband would take his attention away from his grandparents for a moment, and a calamity would happen. She'd said as much to me. "It's not that I don't trust James. He's a good man, through and through, but I know how easy it is to get distracted. He doesn't. He hasn't had to watch them nonstop like I have," she had confessed to me.

If we were lucky, Leah would be able to come, visit for a short while, and walk home before the weather turned nasty. I hoped so.

After Amelia took Ned and left, I continued to refine the baby's image. At some point, I decided that I needed to stop. Learning when to quit is hard for any artist, and yet, if one continues working and refining too long, there's a realistic chance of ruining the piece. I knew I'd done all I could with my rendering, and adding anything more would detract rather than enhance.

I was putting aside my pencils, when Mrs. Fairfax entered. "Jane? Leah Harrigan is here. She says you were expecting her later in the day, but she came early to avoid the threatening weather."

I abruptly got to my feet. "Thank you. Please show her in, and could you ask Cook to bring us some tea and the luncheon repast? I'm sure Leah will be chilled after her walk."

"As you wish." Once Mrs. Fairfax had gone, I collected my various papers and tucked them into my lap desk. I tucked the portrait of John between two pieces of scrap paper, hoping to protect the portrait. Rather than wrap the package with string, I hesitated. Leah would want to see what I'd done, and there was no reason for her to wait. I had placed the gift on top of my lap desk when firm footsteps announced a visitor. Leah, bless her, had carried in the tea tray herself, rather than tasking Cook with the chore.

"Hello," I said, as I gestured to the empty tea table. "There would be fine, I think. How kind of you to carry that for Cook. It looks to be heavy."

"Nay, no more than what I usually carry on any given day." Leah laughed and set the tray down. "'Twas my pleasure to help that good woman of yours. Cook was elbow-deep in flour and making pie crust." My guest had taken off her heavy cloak whilst in the kitchen. Now she unwrapped the woven shawl she'd tied around her head and hair. The walk and the cold had brought a bloom of pink to her cheeks and a sparkle to her eyes.

Before she took the seat opposite of mine, I removed the scrap paper from the portrait of John. "See if my work will suit," I said, setting the picture on the lap desk. Slowly she walked toward the drawing. Her mouth fell open. My heart sank. She found it wanting, I decided. It's not to her liking. I adjusted my posture and waited for the inevitable disappointment I expected to hear.

"Oh, Jane! It's glorious!" She whirled to face

me. "I cannot believe how lifelike it looks. You've well and truly captured John, even to his spirit! James will be so pleased!"

My shoulders relaxed, and I allowed myself a smile. "I am so glad that I met your expectations."

"No, you did not. You exceeded them!" Leah hugged herself with happiness. "Oh, my! This will be the best gift ever."

I touched my friend on the arm. "We'd better drink our tea before it gets cold."

Seeing her confusion, I lifted one of the sandwiches. "My friend Lucy tells me these tiny sandwiches are all the rage in London, so she sent instructions for Cook. I hope you like them."

Following my lead, Leah lifted an egg salad sandwich to her mouth and took a bite. Keeping one eye on me, I assume looking for hints as to how to behave, Leah ate the repast with gusto.

I asked how John and Mary were doing. She sighed. "With the advent of cold weather, I shall need to stay closer to home, lest Mary go wandering. That could be dangerous. Sadly, that will be difficult and means that James will be restricted. I can't even feed the hens! Mary could slip away. So, one of us must stay with her at all times."

"We are doing our best to find a helper, but it's

been a futile task. No one seems to want to work, unless we can supply them with a cottage. Currently, none is vacant. We've sent letters to the rector, to the doctor, and to the estate agent in London. After the holidays, we've decided we shall advertise."

"That's very kind of you, but if you don't mind me saying, it won't help us. Not directly. True, if James isn't here helping you, he can take turns with me at home, but we need a pair of eyes to watch over Mary and a pair of ears to listen out for John." Her lower lip trembled. "If only we'd been blessed with a child."

I decided to change the subject. "As I'm sure you know, we are opening the Great Hall for Christmas Day. I shall be heartbroken, if you are not among our guests!"

"Oh, Jane, would that I could! But John's too poorly to ride in the dog cart. I dare not abandon him of an evening. Mary's mind is going. Whilst I can make a short trip such as this during the day with James watching them, she seems more and more confused at night. Believe me, there is nothing I would like better than to see the Great Hall done up in greenery or to twirl around the floor with my husband, but I would be sick with worry. I hope you'll understand."

I did, but the news did not make me happy. I thought about her problems, as I sipped my tea. "James has agreed to come and help decorate the Great Hall. What if James took the carriage home, rather than the dog cart, after we finish? Surely you could put John and Mary in the carriage for the drive here? With warm bricks for their feet, they should be comfortable enough. We can carry in wingback chairs from the parlor exclusively for them. They'll feel like royalty sitting on a throne. After all, I dare say we won't have a lot of holidays with them, so why not celebrate their years of service? Can we not try?"

Leah's eyes filled with tears. "That is exceedingly kind of you. Don't you need to check with the Master?"

I reached over and took her hands. "No, I do not. On this I am firm, and I know Edward would agree."

Impulsively, she hugged me.

Over the course of the next hour, Leah showed me how to finish the scarf for Edward. I repeated the finishing stitch, until I felt confident I could carry on without her tutelage. As we worked, we talked about the tenants who might come to the Great Hall. Leah did not know all of them, but she knew more than I did, and she shared bits and pieces, so I could be a better hostess. Meanwhile, the snow had held off. I had little doubt she'd make it home before the flakes came down and made walking a misery. With the shawl wrapped around her head, Leah strode out of Ferndean's kitchen, pausing on her way home only once to turn and wave at me.

Shortly thereafter, Edward came home. "How was your tour of the tenants?" I asked.

He regarded me somberly. "Not good. I think I shall have to dismiss the agent. At the very least, I am committed to warning him that his efforts are disappointing. Many of the cottages are in disrepair. A few of the tenants had complaints about the lack of help they've been given on a variety of issues."

Running his hand through his hair, he sighed. "I have been negligent. I trusted this man too completely, and I fear that I have been a poor steward."

I put my arm around his shoulders. "It is not too late, is it? You are alive and aware, and I am sure you can make amends."

Gripping my hand in his, he said, "Dear Janet!

I am more pleased than ever that we are inviting so many to the Great Hall for Christmas Day and happier still that we've arranged for a generous Boxing Day."

I went back to the parlor, thinking that if I applied what I'd learned from Leah immediately, there would be a good chance I could follow her directions and not ruin my project. As the light faded from the window, I lit the oil lamp and moved to the chair nearby. Creating a fringe was not really hard, but it was time-consuming. One edge was done and only a quarter of the other was yet to be finished, when I heard a far-off sound, a jingle, like the noise bells would make. This sound was so unusual that I thought I must be dreaming. Opening the window might help to clarify, but the cold air would fill the parlor, making me loathe to do that.

Instead, I moved closer to the glass. Was it bells I heard? If so, from where did the noise emanate? Was there a horseback rider bringing a message? A courier from London? Carefully drawing a tail of yarn through the scarf, I left the project in such a manner that I could easily pick up where I'd left off. As I rose to my feet, I heard Mrs. Fairfax scurrying along the hallway. Knowing that she would answer the door, I took my time tidying up the area and picking up stray bits of yarn. The scarf could be finished later. After all, Edward still thought I was working on a dishrag, and I was all too happy to keep up the deception.

The bells grew louder and louder. Horse hooves clattered along our paved driveway, until they stopped. Our heavy front door creaked in protest, as Mrs. Fairfax opened it. A proper lady of the house would sit in the parlor and wait until her guests were announced. After all, it was probably a courier who would want Edward's attention, not mine. Rather than hurry to the foyer, I tucked my portrait of Ned into the lap desk, securing it under a handful of loose papers.

That's when I heard my name.

"Jane! Where are you! Won't you come and greet me?"

I froze. Could my ears deceive me? No, surely not. I ran out of the parlor, turned sharply into the hallway, and stopped to stare. There in the grand foyer stood Diana Rivers, my cousin.

Off on one side of the big oak door, my husband watched, as I realized he had, indeed, surprised me with one of his gifts. He'd brought me my cousin! I hadn't seen Diana in years! We hastened to embrace. Tears mingled with snowflakes on her collar, and we were both wet, but I could not turn loose of my dear cousin. As ever, she was scented with a hint of lemons, a fragrance infused in the soap she favors. When at last I'd assured myself that she was real, I stepped away and threw my arms around my husband. "Thank you," I said. "What a wonderful surprise."

Formal introductions were in order. Diana, always grave, shook Edward's hand and thanked him for his hospitality. Edward excused himself to see to it that Diana's trunks were moved to a guest bedroom.

Diana was equally pleasant to Mrs. Fairfax and Amelia, but upon meeting Ned, all semblance of restraint broke down and my cousin gushed with tears. "What a darling! Oh, Jane! May I hold him?"

Of course, Ned was a little shy around this new stranger, and he burrowed himself deeply into Amelia's embrace, so I suggested that I take Ned, while the nursemaid relieved my cousin of her wraps. Then all of us could repair to the parlor. The excitement that accompanied Diana's visit had thoroughly confused my little boy, and he hid his face against my shoulder. Even Diana's obvious delight in him could not pry Ned loose from my arms. Yet after a while, the change of scenery worked a charm, as the parlor is familiar territory for Ned due to me keeping one of his favorite stuffed toys there. Moments later, cuddled in my lap, Ned ventured a shy smile in Diana's direction.

That was enough to melt her heart all over again.

Visitors being a rarity and my enthusiasm being so great, I fear I forgot my good manners and began to pepper Diana with questions. When I realized she'd had a long journey, I put Ned on my hip and ushered my cousin upstairs, hoping to find a suitable bedroom where she might freshen up. Mrs. Fairfax stood outside one of the doors and announced, "I have prepared this bedroom for your cousin. I shall be up directly with a ewer of hot water."

How fortunate we were that other bedrooms besides the one designated for Lucy were fit for habitation. That's when I realized that Edward and Mrs. Fairfax had been involved in subterfuge. Elsewise, the bedroom would not have been ready for Diana!

The coachman had carried my cousin's trunk upstairs and placed it in a logical position. Diana was pleased with the dark burgundy quilt and counterpane, as well as the matching wingback chair sitting in front of the fireplace. "I shall sleep like a queen," she exclaimed. "Oh, dear Jane, what a lovely holiday we are bound to have!"

Whilst it was true that this particular room lacked the delightful yellow color scheme I'd selected for Lucy, the bedclothes were fresh and the place was ready for a guest. Later, I would bring up a sprig of juniper in a vase, to brighten the space and make it smell like a winter holiday. But first, I was determined that Diana should have a nice cup of tea, as our supper would not be served for several hours. Bidding her to meet me in the parlor when she was ready, I left my cousin and walked down the hall.

Amelia stood outside the nursery, so I handed Ned back to her, before I walked to the kitchen and requested that Cook prepare a pot of tea and a plate of biscuits. She was already heating the water, and a fresh batch of gingerbread was on the sideboard cooling. I carried the tea tray with the warm and spicy gingerbread into the parlor and waited there for Diana. When she arrived in the parlor feeling refreshed, I plied her with questions about her journey.

"In all ways, it was uneventful," she said, "and I have Mr. Rochester to thank for making the preparations in such a manner that they were seamless." She had taken a coach to Millcote. There, a hired coach had met her in order to complete her journey to Ferndean.

Diana was full of news about her sister and brother. "Mary is hale and hearty. She is much engrossed in her studies. She is now able to translate nearly any German passage, even those written long ago by scholars. Soon, she'll be equally proficient in Italian. Have you kept up with your language studies?"

I admitted that I hadn't, but I hoped that during her visit we could practice.

"Of course," she said with that sweet smile of her. "St. John sends us regular letters from India. Truly, he seems happy in his work as a missionary."

CHAPTER 17

Preparing for dinner that evening, I spoke to Edward, recounting my visit with Leah. "I hope you won't mind that I suggested James swap the donkey cart for the carriage on Christmas Eve. That way John and Mary can join us to celebrate on Christmas Day. They are much too fragile to ride in the cart, but the gig with its springs will not jostle them around. I fear they will not be with us for long, and I want to honor and enjoy them while we can."

"Of course, I do not mind. As usual, you showed kindness to someone less fortunate, and I heartily approve." He gathered me in his arms and kissed me. "As a matter of fact, I seem to approve of everything you say and do. Or had you noticed?"

"Indeed, I had, and I wanted to say again that I am most appreciative that you brought Diana here. It is such a perfect holiday present, my love." I paused before adding, "I cannot imagine anything better."

"Well then, your imagination needs to stretch its wings, and I aim to remedy the situation. There are more holiday surprises afoot, dear Janet." With a kiss on the tip of my nose, he set my heart aflutter.

Cook had outdone herself by preparing a particularly fine roast with potatoes, turnips, and carrots. Yorkshire pudding served as the perfect compliment. The dining room table was set with a white damask cloth that glowed in the candlelight. Edward offered a toast of thanksgiving that Diana was with us, and we all lifted our glasses of wine high. Diana admired the lovely silverware, the fine crystal, and the beautiful china, painted with a variety of native pheasants. I blushed with happiness that I was able to provide Diana such a fine meal in such elegant surroundings.

After we ate, Mrs. Fairfax joined us. We sat in the parlor, and Diana amused us with stories about her students, as she'd recently been teaching at the village school. Even Mrs. Fairfax was charmed by my cousin's ability as a raconteur. As we rose to go up to bed, Diana reached out for me and brought me close in an embrace. "Now, Jane," she said, "tomorrow we shall review your German. I want to see if you have progressed at all."

Edward asked her, "Are you another polyglot, Cousin Diana? I hope so, as I want Jane to be well-versed in a variety of tongues."

"Indeed, sir, I value learning almost above all else, and that exception would be family and friends," she replied pertly. Pilot had been resting his head on her knees for most of the evening. Now that she had disturbed him by gaining her feet, he followed along behind her with adoring eyes. Using her free hand, Diana reached down to caress the dog's ears. "Although that might well be an incomplete list, as I also have a particular fondness for animals."

That evening, as we climbed into bed, Edward said to me, "No wonder you set such store by your cousin. Diana is an animal spirit, a person with such inner strength and vitality that being in her presence is a tonic."

I wholly concurred and said, "When first we met, our natures dovetailed: mutual affection—of the strongest kind—was the result. Thank you, my darling, for bringing her here for the holidays."

"Not only the holidays," he whispered. "She is welcome to stay under my roof as long as the two of you wish."

~

The next morning, after serving himself from the sideboard, Edward asked Cook if there were more blood sausages.

Cook made a huffing sound, as she rested her fists on her hips and glared at us. "Aye, and someone knows very well that's the last of them. I made a special trip out to the smokehouse yesterday and grabbed a fair dozen or so, thinking our guests might relish them. Lo and behold, this morning there were but three. I ask you! Who is that hungry to raid my larder at night?"

Diana stared at me with large questioning eyes.

Edward shook his head. "No, Cook, you know it is not me. I say, we must be in possession of a hungry ghost. The disappearance of food is the only trail this phantom leaves behind."

Not wishing to frighten Diana, I asked my

cousin how she slept. "Very well. Much better than the person in the next room, I daresay."

Edward put down his fork and examined Diana's face carefully, in case she was jesting. Seeing no signs of a joke, he turned towards me. I, too, was surprised by her remark. None of the other bedrooms near hers was occupied. The nursery was at the other end of the hallway, closer to the master bedroom, with a dressing room in between. Why on earth would Diana think she heard a person rustling around in the night?

Edward laughed, but it was a mirthless reply. "The ancient sounds of Ferndean must have tricked you, Cousin Diana. The room next to yours is empty, save a few odds and ends of furnishings. There is the nursery and our room, but no other rooms have occupants."

Diana cocked her head to study Edward. Her bright eyes narrowed. "Really? I could have sworn I heard footsteps. They seemed to come from the next room. I could tell someone was trying to be quiet as they crept around. The door protested, as it was opened. A little later, the mysterious wanderer returned. I distinctly recall a creaking board making a protest under the person's weight."

"That could have been Pilot," said Edward.

The dog was sitting at his Master's feet. He lifted his hoary head, when he heard his name. Edward continued, "Pilot slept at the foot of our bed all night. I remember, because I tried to roll over, and he was a heavy burden to shift. I would have dispatched him and shuffled him to the floor, but given his age, he finds it difficult to get comfortable However, it is conceivable that I am mistaken and he was your midnight wanderer. Already he seems most attached to you and stares at you with undisguised affection. Jane and I often leave our bedroom door ajar, in case there might be an emergency with Ned. Pilot could have hopped down and gone wandering, seeking you out."

"That must have been it," said Diana agreeably. "Jane, do you remember St. John's old dog? Carlo? He used to wander around at night. He's been gone a long time, and I miss having a dog around."

"As for the theft of the blood sausages, the culprit can only be James," said Edward, pushing back from the table. "He must be hungry, when he comes in of a morning to set the fires. I suspect he's too proud to tell me that he needs help. Try not to fret over this, Cook. After the holidays, I shall sit down with him and have a chat. Better yet, I plan to make a trip out to the stable today. With luck, I'll run into James, and we can talk freely there."

Silently, I wondered why Leah had not mentioned anything to me. I had come to regard her as a friend. If they were in need of food, surely, I had proven I could be helpful. Had I not suggested a way to bring John and Mary to the Manor for Christmas Day? Was the gap between us still so large that she dare not cross over to ask for help? The very idea made me sad.

I was still thinking about Leah a little later, when Diana and I were sitting in the parlor. My cousin worked on a needlepoint piece, while I finished the fringe on Edward's muffler. We flitted from one topic to another, until Diana told me about the man she's met, Captain Josiah Fitzjames. "He is older and a widower, so if we marry, I shall instantly become a stepmother to his two sons, Ian and William."

"Do you think he will ask for your hand?" I sensed her eagerness to become a wife. Diana and her sister, Mary, were two of the kindest women I'd ever met. Whereas Diana had a great affluence of life and was a natural leader, Mary was more docile and the perfect student. In my mind, they and their brother were my only living relatives, although that was not strictly true, as my Aunt Reed had left behind two daughters and a son. However, the Reeds were as different from the Rivers as chalk and cheese. Aunt Reed had petted and spoiled her brood, resulting in three nasty people, who were brutish in manners, ill-tempered, and uneducated. Although I'd heard very little about Eliza Reed, I had heard plenty about John Reed, because his reputation throughout London, as a scoundrel and dissolute gambler, was well-known. As for Georgiana Reed, I'd seen her a year ago, when Edward and I had attended the Opera with Lucy. Although Georgiana had once been considered a great beauty, I feel no compunction in saying her looks have gone to seed, the way a thistle turns from vibrant purple to dry, dead brown. Rumor was that she's since married a wealthy man, a reprobate whose character has been widely disparaged.

If the Reeds had ever been kind to me, I might find a way to put our past behind us. But they never regretted how they treated me, and they had been nothing but cruel, although admittedly they were only following the example their mother had set. When my status changed and word reached them, they offered no congratulations. In fact, upon meeting me at the Opera,

Georgiana had treated me as if I were a louse that had scaled her gown and grabbed onto her arm. Lucy had been appalled by her behavior, and she had encouraged me to severe any emotions that might naturally accompany the fact that Georgiana and I were blood kin. I needed no encouragement from Lucy or from Edward, who was equally infuriated by Georgiana's bad manners.

When it came to the entire Reed family, I regarded them the way one might the carcass of a bloated animal by the roadside. The stench could not be avoided, but further contact was inadvisable.

"I believe Josiah will ask for my hand, although not for a while." Diana's words returned me to the present moment. We were sitting on the end of the sofa, side by side. She grabbed both of my hands and turned an eager face to mine. "Josiah has made a few broad hints. We've discussed what a future together might hold. His sons seem resigned to admitting me into their lives, perhaps because I've never forced myself on them. They are both at boarding school, being fourteen and fifteen, respectively. I treat them like young men, because they are."

"Then I wish you well, and I shall do anything I can to help your cause," I said.

"Is it all you had hoped for? Married life?" Her eyes searched mine.

"All that and more," I said, wishing to convey the full measure of my happiness. "Knowing I am not alone in the world, having a friend who is always in my corner, and of course, he shares my burdens and multiplies my joys."

"I believe that's the best description I've ever heard of a blissful marriage," she admitted. "Certainly, when your husband reached out to me with his plan for a holiday surprise, I found a new reason for approving of your match. Clearly, Edward not only cares about you but dotes on you as well."

"That he does," I said. "Do you anticipate marrying soon?"

"No," she admitted with an expression of resignation. "He is serving the Crown and will be dispatched with his company the first of the year. We have agreed that a conversation about our future must wait, until his position is more secure."

Our tête-à-tête was so intimate, that I had not listened for an approaching carriage. Suddenly, a pounding at the front door interrupted my visit with Diana. I bounced to my feet, dragging my cousin along with me. "They have arrived! Come and meet Lucy and Adèle! I've written about them, and now you'll be able to judge for yourself whether my descriptions were fact or fiction."

Like two schoolgirls, we raced down the hallway and threw open the door.

There stood Lucy in all her glory! She wore a marvelous cape trimmed in what I took to be ermine. On her head was a matching fur cap and her hands were stuffed into a muff of the same. Those blonde curls of hers framed her heart-shaped face in a way that set off her cerulean eyes and her sweet smile.

"Sister!" I called to her, as I fell into her arms. I'd no sooner given her a hug, when Adèle pushed her way between us. "Mademoiselle!" the young girl shouted, hurling herself at me. I laughed, as I hugged the poppet. Adèle's cape was a copy of the one Lucy was wearing, and I swear the child had grown six inches.

"Welcome, welcome," I said, drawing Lucy and Adèle inside the Manor. "Come out of the cold!"

Mrs. Fairfax arrived in time to direct the coachman as to where to put the luggage, while Diana took it upon herself to welcome Mrs. Wallander and Evans. The nanny was a large woman with silver-grey eyes, dark grey hair, and cheekbones that could have been chiseled out of ice. She was tall, towering over me and my cousin by nearly a foot, which meant she and Edward were nearly the same height. One might designate the nanny as handsome rather than beautiful, but when she smiled, Mrs. Wallander was very attractive indeed.

This time, I remembered that my guests might need to freshen up, so I led everyone to their rooms. Of course, Adèle couldn't wait to see Ned, so she raced toward the nursery without any encouragement. Mrs. Wallander graciously followed along behind the little girl, hoping to get Evans acquainted with his new friend, Ned.

"This is lovely!" Lucy said, standing in the doorway of her room, as she clasped her hands in surprise. "The yellow is perfect. You know how much I adore it, Jane! You chose all of this yourself? Aren't you cunning?" With a sweeping motion of her cape, she twirled around in the middle of her room. "I am delighted."

I was ever so pleased that I'd made her happy. With one arm around my sister and the other around my cousin, I declared, "This has to be the best holiday gift I've ever had!"

CHAPTER 18

Cook served tea in the parlor. The tiny sandwiches were much admired and quickly devoured as were her cunning little cakes. Later, while the little boys and Adèle took naps, Diana decided to go to her room to write letters to her siblings. "I believe I shall have another cup of tea, and then I shall lie down, too," said Lucy. "The trip has tired me, and as this is Christmas Eve, I shall want to assist in your plans for decorating the Manor. We shall have much to do, and I am sure we will be up late."

"Yes," I agreed, as I poured the tea for my friend. "James and I went exploring on the property. We found juniper and spruce, as well as sprigs of holly and bits of mistletoe. The greenery awaits us in the cart, where it's covered by a bit of canvas. I hope you brought lots of ribbon?"

"I did indeed. Ribbon for decorating and for wrapping around gifts. In fact, I might have gone too far! I brought enough red ribbon to wrap around old London town twice over. You'll also find two boxes that are yours. One is from Hatchards, as per your instructions to them, and the other is filled with the gifts you asked me to purchase for you in London. I believe Edward instructed the coach driver to put them in a spare bedroom? He said something about one being used for storage? I overheard your husband admonishing Adèle that she was not to disturb the large item under the tarpaulin. Edward expressly said the same to the coachman."

"Yes," I said. "My husband has been very secretive about the bundle in that room. Right now, Edward's out at the barn, working with James. This might be the perfect time for me to wrap all of my gifts from London, since you and the others will be resting or busy. That way, I'll be free later, when we decorate the hall. Cook has prepared a wonderful feast for us to share this evening. She was much taken with the recipes and menus you suggested. Of course, she's also been preparing a cold collation for us to serve everyone who comes tomorrow."

Lucy yawned. "I am glad to hear that she received the recipes in the spirit which I intended. One never knows if a cook will respond happily or take offense."

"Cook is a treasure," I said, and I quickly explained that she had grown up on the Rochester estate. "In fact, I believe she and Edward played together when her father came to shoe horses."

"My," said Lucy, "I tend to forget how interconnected the families of landed gentry become with their tenants. I wonder if she has any amusing stories about young Edward? I bet he was ten times the scamp."

I imagined so, but they were still unknown to me. "For the most part, Cook's very circumspect," I admitted. "I haven't been able to encourage her to gossip about their youth."

"Then we shall have to ply her with strong liquor," said Lucy.

I could not help but laugh. In the months since I'd last seen her, Lucy had not changed a bit. I had missed her and her mischievous ways. For a girl who'd grown up on her own, caring for her brother and living on the streets, she'd developed an indomitable spirit that never failed to encourage me to see possibilities where obstacles loomed. This remark, this suggestion that we loosen Cook's tongue with liquor, was the sort of high jinks I would never have considered.

Until now.

With most of our household submitting to the sweet caress of slumber, I took my time unpacking the box from Hatchards. One by one, I examined the titles. The booksellers at Hatchards had done a marvelous job. Fortunately, there were more than enough suitable tomes for me to give as gifts. Armed with brown paper and generous lengths of red ribbon, I wrapped each book. When I finished, I wrapped the gifts that Lucy had procured for me. Belatedly, I realized the muffler and the drawing of Ned were both hidden in my lap desk. I would need to go downstairs to procure them. Suddenly, I yawned. For some inexplicable reason, I felt sleepy. Knowing that tonight would be a long evening, taking a nap seemed prudent. After all, everyone but Edward had taken to their beds. My husband barely needs any sleep at all, so he would be fine. But another yawn suggested that I needed a rest. First, I wound up the rest of the red ribbon and returned it to the box from whence it came. Then I stacked the wrapped books neatly back inside the Hatchards box and piled the other gifts nearby. Lastly, I tucked the ribbon boxes under one arm and I left the spare bedroom, taking care to close the door firmly behind me.

However, rather than simply walk away, I stood there and hesitated. I, too, was capable of surprises. Adèle has been known to be an ambitious snoop, especially when she thinks she's being left out. Knowing that presents were in this bedroom might prove an irresistible temptation to the girl. After turning the matter over in my head, I put down the boxes of ribbon. Standing on tiptoe, I ran my fingertips along the moulding around the doorframe. Once I seized upon a key, I used it to lock the room. Whilst pocketing the key and picking up the ribbon, I congratulated myself on thinking ahead. No one needed to go into that room but me. I had promised Edward not to peek under the tarpaulin, and I would keep my promise to my husband. After all, I was certain that his surprise for me would bring both of us great amusement. Ruining his secret would be a disappointment. Now that the door was safely locked, I'd removed all temptation. Neither Adèle nor I could satisfy our curiosity.

CHAPTER 19

A dreamless sleep refreshed me. I awakened to the sound of Adèle's happy chatter outside the master bedroom door. Truly, she was in her glory with two little boys as a rapt audience. Her high spirits were infectious. I sat up and stretched. A glance behind our heavy curtains assured me that the sun was going down and the long-awaited Christmas Eve had finally arrived. James would be on his way to help us decorate the Great Hall with greenery, and thanks to Lucy's benevolent largess with ribbon, the place would look very festive when we finished.

As I splashed water on my face, I heard the heavy front door creak open. Hurriedly, I toweled my skin dry. Surely the protesting hinges were announcing that James had arrived with twine and wire and a large ladder. After hurrying downstairs, I discovered I was right. He doffed his cap at me and went back to the cart to drag in the beautiful boughs we'd collected. I learned then that the enterprising young man had taken it upon himself to go out and collect even more greenery from local yews.

Lucy and Diana marveled at the Yule Log, which was of an impressive size. I pointed out how smaller chunks of aromatic woods had been laid in a crisscross pattern on the floor of the huge fireplace. The shorter logs would lift the Yule Log so it could be seen to best advantage. "Furthermore, Edward borrowed a trick from the French. James soaked the Yule Log in wine, so it will fill the room with a delicious scent."

James piled the greenery on the table in the middle of the hall. Diana and Lucy immediately took charge, discussing between them where the boughs should go. They were perfectly in tune with each other's wishes. It did my heart glad to see how well they worked together. In no time at all, they had wired pieces of spruce together and created a garland that would run the length of the musician's gallery banister. Meanwhile, Adèle was put to work producing bows and making them as consistent in size as possible. These she piled neatly in a basket. Once James had unloaded all of the greenery, he and Edward carried two wingback chairs from the study and the large parlor into the hall. These were trimmed with more greenery to serve as special seats for Mary and John.

Using wire and twine, Lucy fashioned a ball out of the mistletoe. She steadied the ladder and directed James in hanging it from the middle of the chandelier. A second ball, smaller than the first, was hung from the doorframe, so that anyone entering the Great Hall would be due a kiss.

My husband seemed as happy as I have ever seen him. Whilst James hung the second ball of mistletoe, Edward approached me with a solemn smile on his face, as he held his arm conspicuously tucked behind his back. "What are you hiding, sir?" I asked.

"Only this," and he raised over my head a sprig of mistletoe. After soundly kissing me (to my great embarrassment and joy), he tossed the sprig to Adèle. "Please add bows to all of the mistletoe bunches. James and I can position them throughout the entryway and the hallway. After all, what is Christmas without kisses?"

Whilst busily tying bunches of mistletoe together, Lucy hummed a carol, and Diana joined in. My lips twitched with amusement. "Too bad you do not own a harpsichord," said Lucy, "or a pianoforte. Then we could enjoy music while we work. I guess we must simply wait for the musicians to come and serenade us from the gallery."

I fought with myself as to whether to keep my secret. James caught my eye and raised his eyebrows to ask a question. He was wondering whether this was the time to share my surprise. And I decided it was. "James? Would you accompany me to the pantry?"

"Yes, missus, of course."

I led the way, with James tagging along behind. We walked down the hallway where Cook stood beside the door to the larder.

"I've kept it for ye, missus." She swung open the door and let us gaze inside. James and I studied the large rectangle with its brass wheels. It was still covered with a clean quilt, held snug with a length of string.

James put one hand on the object, turning to me for my directions.

"I think there's no need for it to linger here, when it could provide joy right now," I said, stroking the quilt that hid my gift. Cook came over to see what we were doing. "So ye are moving that thing out? Good! It's about time! I've been dancing around that big hunk of wood for days now."

Of course, her eyes sparkled with excitement, because she knew what was under wraps. Cook did not really mind the inconvenience, but she enjoyed fussing at me.

"Come along with us," I beckoned to her. "This gift wouldn't be as special, if you had not been so kind as to keep it hidden. I want you to see Edward's face, when he removes the covering. Besides, we'll need you to clear the way, as James and I wheel this into the Great Hall."

"I have a better idea. I'll go first to Eddie and bid him to close his eyes. How will that be?" Cook grinned widely.

I noticed she'd slipped back in time, as witnessed by her using her childhood nickname for my husband.

"Perfect!!" I exclaimed.

She was as good as her word, and what a sight to behold, as she marched into the Great Hall and demanded that "Eddie" not look until given her approval. Lucy smothered a laugh. "Eddie?" she repeated.

With obvious amusement, Diana watched the interplay between the two old friends. Adèle hopped up and down, chanting, "A present for Monsieur! Such fun!"

Together James and I pushed the bulky item out from the larder and began our travel down the hall. When we got to the entry of the Great Hall, the turn would be treacherous, as the item was top heavy. James instructed me to brace the top, while we attempted to force the base into a 90-degree shift of position. The piece tilted precariously to one side, but clever Diana recognized we needed assistance and rushed to our aid.

"When can I look?" Edward fumed, as he shifted his weight restlessly from one foot to the other. Thanks to the brass rollers on the bottom of the gift, James, and Diana, and I made light work of moving along the wooden plank flooring of the Great Hall. The *clickety clack* sound of the rolling wheels was odd, and Edward cocked his head to listen.

"Confound it, what have you got?" he bellowed. Cook reminded Edward not to peep, Adèle looked on in wonder, but at length, she'd puzzled out what sat beneath the quilt. Fortunately, Lucy clamped a hand over the girl's mouth in time to stop the little chit from spoiling Edward's surprise.

We did not bother to position the gift in its final spot. Instead, James and I stopped, once we'd rolled it in front of Edward. With a nod to me, James stepped aside.

"Edward? You can look now," I said.

When he opened his eyes, all he saw was a quilt-covered rectangle. However, I'd prepared for that. With a flourish, I gave the blanket a jerk and *voilà!*

"A piano!" Edward crowed.

"Yes, and it was made by Heinrich Engelhard Steinweg, a master piano maker over in Germany," I explained. "I had heard of his prowess, so I wrote to the man and ordered this especially for you."

My husband's voice was full of emotion. "It looks wonderful. Jane, would you play for us so we can hear how it sounds?"

"Yes, of course. James? Would you go and fetch the matching stool for me?" I asked. While the young man ran off, I proceeded to explain where we'd been hiding the beast. Edward chuckled and thanked Cook for putting up with my demands. Once James had fetched the seat, I sat down and played Piano Sonata No.18, Op. 44 by Dussek. The piano sounded glorious, with clarity in the top register and deep, sonorous lower notes. Truly, this was a magnificent instrument, although admittedly, I performed on it badly, as I was never a superb musician, and I hadn't played in years. When I finished, Diana kindly took my spot. She expertly produced a piece by Haydn that brought tears to all of our eyes.

"One good turn deserves another," said Edward. "Jane? I have a large gift for you, and I would like for you to see it now. That said, we must all troop upstairs. Shall we?"

I thought to stop him, since the rest of our gifts would be distributed on New Year's Day, but Edward's happy visage suggested this was very important to him, and therefore, I could not postpone his happiness. Instead of imposing my will on his, I took my husband by the hand, and we mounted the stairs together. When we got to the spare bedroom, the door was locked. I took the key from my pocket and gave it to my Master, my darling. As he turned the lock, I explained, "There are other gifts in this room, but they are to be opened on January 1. I need a promise from you, Adèle. No peeping!"

She complained, but a stern look from Edward quickly put an end to her lamentations.

Edward opened the door and walked in ahead of us. When he stood next to the large tarpaulin, he grabbed one corner of the covering with his hand. Waiting until we were all fanned out around him, with me standing squarely in front of the bundle, he repeated the flourish I had shown earlier. "Voilà!"

Most of the covering came free, but one edge of the tarpaulin was jammed between the lid and the body of the trunk. Edward gave a sharp yank and nothing happened, as the fabric seemed firmly caught.

"Perhaps I can help you, sir," James said. He and Cook both had followed us up the stairs, and now they waited near the door. Rather than call more attention to Edward's missing hand, the kind young Harrigan stepped forward and knelt in front of the trunk. The latch had fallen closed but was not caught. However, the fabric of the tarpaulin was jammed in the crevice between the lid and the trunk. James lifted the latch and pulled the fabric free.

In the center of the dome, next to the lock, were the gold initials JRE, the classic assemblage for Jane Eyre Rochester. My husband wrapped his arms around me, as I gazed at the piece in wonder. "It's marvelous," I stammered.

"Yes, and it's only a metaphor," he explained. "I want us to do the Grand Tour, Jane, you and I. With your love of beauty and your natural gift for languages, you are the perfect traveling companion for me. Besides, I know of no one who would more fully enjoy the beauty and wonder of the world than you. Think of the many sketches you could produce! I invite you to travel with me to all the capitals of Europe. Will you come with me, my love?"

Of course, I would. I would go anywhere with this man. Overcome with emotion by his invitation, I could only nod. After clearing my throat, I managed a weak, "Yes, of course I'll go with you."

"Open your new trunk, darling, and see how much room you'll have for all the gowns you're sure to buy," he pulled me into his arms and whispered to me. His lips were so close to my ear that his breath tickled. I thought about waiting, as it seemed unfair for me to enjoy such largess while others could only watch, but Lucy said, "Yes, Jane! Open it." Dear Diana picked up the chant as did Adèle, so I had no choice in the matter. Not really.

Lifting the brass lock buckle, I gave the lid a mighty tug.

The trunk would not open.

"That's odd," said James. "Perhaps the wood has swollen. Being new, that could have happened."

Edward agreed. "I commissioned the piece months ago. It was brought first to London so the initials could be added, and then the furniture carters brought it here. The various changes of humidity could have caused the wood to swell."

Open or shut, it did not matter. The trunk was a splendid piece of leatherwork, and the idea that it represented a Grand Tour took my breath away. Previously, I had only imagined seeing the Parthenon in Greece, the vineyards of Italy, and the Strait of Gibraltar, as well as so much more. My mind whirled with ideas and possibilities. So immersed was I, that I would have been content to simply admire the trunk in situ. Seeing the interior could wait, especially because the trunk was merely a representation of a larger gift, the Grand Tour. I was lost in thought, but the ever insistent Adèle joggled my elbow. "Mademoiselle, you must open it up! There might be more presents inside. We must see!"

James stepped closer and leaned in to assist

me in lifting the lock buckle. Gripping the buckle together, we gave it a good tug. The trunk lid resisted. Without a word, Edward positioned himself, so he could grip the handle on the center of the lid. Then the three of us would work together.

"On three," Edward Rochester said to James. "One, two, three!"

With a mighty heave, the trunk lid flew open.

"Eeekkkk!!" Diana shrieked.

Inside the trunk was a small figure. The curled up body of a young boy.

My heart stopped. *Was he dead or alive?*

CHAPTER 20

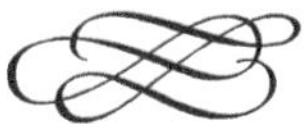

A moan assured us the child was, indeed, alive. The stench floating around him suggested he had not bathed in a long, long time. His skin was exceedingly pale against oily hair.

However, the child had been without food or water for most of the day and up until this late hour of the evening. Working as a team, the men lifted him out of the trunk, but the child could barely stand. He was streaked with dirt, the kind of dust common in the city. His hair reached his shoulders and separated into oily strands. His eyes flickered open only briefly and then shut. His skinny legs kept buckling out beneath him. James carried the stowaway to the nearby bed. To say the boy smelled badly was to offer a good shine on the mess. Clearly, the child hadn't made contact with a bar of soap in a long while.

Cook had been waiting in the hall to see my gift. Now she hurried downstairs to fetch a basin of water, while Lucy raced to her room to retrieve smelling salts. Diana disappeared and came back with a wet face flannel. Gently she bathed the boy's face and hands. By my quick calculations, he'd arrived in the trunk and been hiding up here for over three weeks. To stay alive, he had been slipping downstairs and raiding the Cook's close closet. Immediately I wondered, "How did this boy slip past Pilot?" The dog had not raised the alarm, nor had he seemed concerned that there was an intruder among us.

Why?

Mrs. Fairfax brought a glass of water and handed it to me. I pressed it to the boy's lips, but he didn't respond, so I dribbled a little onto his lips. He licked them eagerly.

Edward shook his head. "I think he needs something stronger. Adèle? Go and fetch a tot of brandy."

The girl was off like a flash. She knew that Edward kept a bottle of fine brandy in the bottom drawer of his desk.

"Poor little tyke," said Diana, as she worked the laces of his boots. Lucy peeled away from the boy a light jacket, threadbare at the cuffs and elbows. This revealed a thin shirt that hung limply on the boy. When Diana had wrestled the boots from his feet, I gasped. His blistered and dirty toes had been jammed inside oversized footwear. Crumpled newspaper filled the extra space, but the child wore no socks. Instead of soles, the bottoms of the boots were actually papers stuck together by layers of filth. Cook brought up a basin of warm water. "I wager ye that this is where all of that food's been disappearing to," she said. Edward dragged over a straight-backed chair to hold the basin. Diana wrung out the flannel and then dipped it into the water again. But when she wiped the face of the boy, the warm water removed very little of the smeared filth. "I think I need soap," she murmured, and Cook disappeared to fetch a bar.

Lucy waved the smelling salts under the boy's nose. He sat up with a jolt.

"Don't beat me!" he screamed, grabbing at Lucy's hand. "Don't send me to the poorhouse! Please! I was only hungry."

His green eyes were crusty with dirt and the remnants of infection. Edward put a staying hand on the boy's shoulder. "Son, you are safe here. No one will hurt you."

The child fainted dead away.

Adèle handed Edward the bottle of brandy and a glass jigger. After pouring a small amount into the glass, my husband used one finger and dripped a little onto the boy's lips. The fumes from the alcohol achieved the desired effect of reviving the child somewhat. When he licked his lips, his eyes went open wide. "Please, I was hungry," he moaned.

"James? Will you ride for the doctor?" Edward turned to the young man.

Lucy interrupted, "Mrs. Wallander is a nurse, and she's here already."

"Adèle? Please go and get Mrs. Wallander," I said. "I think we could use her assistance." My request served two purposes: we dearly needed medical aid, and I wasn't sure I wanted Adèle to see anymore. It was my impression that this boy was hanging onto life by a thread. Sending James for the doctor was a good idea in theory, but the physician might arrive too late.

Cook returned with a cake of soap. Diana rinsed out the face flannel. "Perhaps we might have a little privacy," she asked primly, as she set about bathing the child's scrawny frame. From the size of him, I judged the child to be no older than eight. Diana continued, "I think he'd do better with fewer people in the room."

Mrs. Wallander came rushing in. After taking one look at the boy, she put two fingers on his wrist, looked in his mouth, and peeled back his eyelids. Her face took on an expression of deep concentration, as she said, "He needs liquids and nourishment. I believe I have the skills needed to care for him, but if I could, I'd like a bowl of beef broth, please, and a fresh shirt for this lad. Miss Rivers is quite right—fewer people would be better."

Cook said, "I'll bring the broth right up to ye."

Lucy, Mrs. Fairfax, and I turned to go. Adèle had frozen near the door, unable to tear her eyes away from the spectacle on the bed. "Come along," I said, and I gently guided her into the hallway.

Edward and James both hesitated. I could imagine their thoughts. The child seemed disoriented and almost animalistic. Was he feverish? Delusional? We couldn't be sure that Diana and Mrs. Wallander would be safe with him. Not yet.

"Not to worry," said Mrs. Wallander. "I've taken care of men on the battlefield. This boy's no threat to me nor to Miss Rivers.

Amelia met us in the hall and promised to put Adèle to bed. Of course, the girl complained. In particular, she said, "But I did not get a present! And it is Christmas, or nearly so!"

I ducked back into the bedroom and grabbed one of the books I'd selected for Adèle. "Yes, *ma petite chou-fleur*. You have not been forgotten. Amelia? Please let her read for a little while."

"Yes, missus," Amelia said. "Adèle? Ned and Evans are fast asleep. You must be quiet, hear?" The nursemaid put a hand on the girl's shoulder and steered her away.

James and Edward came downstairs with us. They spoke to each other in low voices, going over plans for the next day. James would take the gig home. Tomorrow, he would come to Ferndean early, bringing Leah, Mary, and John. "If the boy needs anything, I can go back out. Matter of fact, I can ride for the doctor tonight if need be."

"I think Mrs. Wallander has the matter well in hand," said Edward. "Surely, she would have asked that we fetch the doctor, if she thought it necessary. She seems extraordinarily competent."

"One thing," said James. "The tarpaulin? If the boy was climbing in and out of the trunk, how'd ye keep the covering on it?"

I could answer that. "When he climbed back

in, all he had to do was hold onto one edge of the fabric as he closed the lid. That's why the tarpaulin was caught between the lid and the trunk. He was holding on from inside."

"But he climbed in and out," said James. "Didn't you notice anything?"

"No," I said. "Edward had warned me not to go into that bedroom or I'd ruin his surprise, so I didn't. No one did. The child was free to come and go at night, as long as he was quiet. Diana did hear noises in the hall, but we thought it was Pilot roaming around. The only time the boy had to fear being discovered was when we actually went into the room, so Edward could give me his gift."

I told the young man goodnight, and Edward walked James to the front door. Their voices echoed in the hall, but they were too muffled for me to make out what they were saying. I was in a melancholy mood as I dressed for bed. What had begun as a night of high expectations and great frivolity had changed into a scene from a bad dream. What if the boy died? Then this would be the saddest Christmas ever.

CHAPTER 21

I had a restless night, as the vision of that boy in the trunk came to me over and over. His plight brought back memories of the deprivation I had suffered at Lowood. As often as I reminded myself that I was safe and warm, now and forever, fear crept up on me and grasped me firmly in its rough hold.

Finally, I fell asleep and then I woke up late, far past my usual time for rising. In fact, it was closer to noon than to breakfast, when I hurried downstairs to the kitchen. There I found Mrs. Wallander waiting patiently, whilst Cook scrambled eggs in a pan. "How is he?" I asked anxiously. "The boy?" I added.

"Better. Your cousin is with him. He will be

fine in time," said the nanny. "Good food, warm clothes, and liquids will go a long way toward restoring him to the normal sort of vitality so common in a boy his age. Of course, it was not good for a child to spend so much time in dark confinement, although I suspect his actions were born of desperation. I am certain that he was starving, even before he jumped into that trunk. I hope you won't punish him." She stared at me, studying me.

"Of course not!" I responded.

"I do not think he meant you any harm, Mrs. Rochester. Despite his unorthodox hiding place, he has been mumbling that he tried not to soil anything." Again, she watched me carefully, as if hoping for a sign that I would be compassionate rather than judgmental.

But then I realized the woman did not know me. Not at all. She'd only heard of me through comments made by Lucy and Adèle. Now was her chance to see for herself what sort of person I was. Accordingly, my response to the plight of this orphan would etch my character in stone. It rather irked me to have to prove my merit.

"Someone, somewhere along the line did a good job of raising him. He has manners," Mrs. Wallander added.

"I care very little for his manners," I said. "I care for his health and well-being. He is only a child, Mrs. Wallander, and I do not begrudge him any attempt he made to save his own life. Rather, I think it speaks well of him. Obviously, the boy is resourceful. Furthermore, he managed for almost a month not to make any sort of mess, and for a boy that age, that's surprising. He did not do any damage to our home. Yes, he helped himself to food, but why would he not? We have plenty, and he had none. In short, if you think I'm going to turn him over to the authorities, you are wrong."

Mrs. Wallander took two steps back away from me. Her expression changed from disapproval to surprise. Behind the nanny's back, Cook gave me a wink.

"Then we are agreed," said the nanny. "The child was at the mercy of his situation and not a criminal at heart.

"Do you have a name for him?" I was tired of calling him "the child" or "the boy."

"Frankie, which I assume is short for Frances. His last name is Darnell."

"Did he share any information about his parents?"

The blue of her eyes darkened with my questions. "He is most certainly an orphan, missus.

Your cousin seems to have formed a bond with him, and he's talked to her…a little. Frankie is scared witless about going to the poorhouse. Over and over, he has begged us not to give him to the coppers."

I shook my head. "Poor child."

Cook plated the eggs and handed the plate to Mrs. Wallander. "More fool I am. I accused all and sundry of stealing from the kitchen, and it was that wee mite trying to keep himself fed."

"How could you know?" I put a hand on her arm. "None of us knew the boy was here, much less that he was hungry."

Returning my attention to Mrs. Wallander, I asked, "Do I need to bring up food for Diana?"

"No, she's already eaten, as have I," said Mrs. Wallander. With that, the nanny left us to carry the warm eggs upstairs.

Cook poured a cup of tea for me. Skillfully using a pair of tongs, she removed a piece of toast from the grate over the fire. After slathering it with butter, as I do, she pushed it my way. My habits were so firmly set that the good woman did not even ask what I might want to break my fast.

"Mrs. Wallander thinks I am someone who plots revenge on little boys," I said morosely. "You would think that I am personally responsible for filling up workhouses!"

Cook laughed. "She don't know ye, missus. Give her time. She's only feeling protective of the boy, as we all are."

As she put away the teapot, Cook continued, "Missus, don't ye fret too much over that boy upstairs. Ye've planned and planned for this big day, and ye have done your best to make it festive for the tenants. Shed loads of them are coming here to celebrate! Some ain't never been to Ferndean, as it wasn't open to them in the past. Most of them ain't never met ye, and they're looking forward to it. And they do not know what happened here last night, nor do they need to know, so ye cannot disappoint them!"

She was right. I pulled up a stool and ate the toast slowly, washing it down with the hot tea. "Yes, I must act the part of the hostess, but I feel despondent knowing..."

"Knowing that hunger exists in this world? Knowing that ye couldn't help that boy earlier? Well, he's here now. As for those going hungry, ye are helping to fill the bellies of your guests, aren't ye?" She frowned at me, standing with her fists resting on her hips.

Feeling the weight of her eyes on me, I

chewed more slowly. She was right. This was my chance to help the tenants by feeding them and assuring them that Edward and I cared about their welfare. Hadn't Edward recently toured their homes and noted that he'd fallen down in his duties? Wasn't this our chance to turn a page? Indeed, it was.

"Cook, you are both a sensible woman and a good one. Thank you for your wise counsel. I shall do my best to ensure that our guests enjoy themselves. I hope to get to know more of them." With a lump in my throat that I couldn't swallow down, in a moment of weakness, I added, "This is all new to me, Cook. I have never been part of a squire's family, much less the mistress of an estate, and I have much to learn."

Her eyes glistened with tears. "Does it matter how ye got here? I think not. Ye are here now. Ye are gifted with a kind heart, missus. That's more than most, I reckon. If your heart was hard and cold, nothing could touch it. Watching ye, I suspect ye can well imagine the trials your tenants face. There's those who would not understand and there is those who would not care. That ain't ye. Ye'll learn whatever it is that ye need to know. I know ye will."

I handed her my empty teacup and thanked

her again. Her words gave me much to think over.

I rapped lightly on the bedroom door, so as not to wake the child we'd found in the trunk. Diana heard immediately and opened up. Pilot came to the door, too. She pushed him away and back into the room, before she escorted me down the hall so we could talk.

She explained, "His name is Frankie, and he's eight years old. When his father died, he and his mother lost their place on a farm that the family had worked for generations. They went to London. His mother was hoping she could find work as a seamstress, but she took ill and died. He's been on his own for nigh unto a year. I suspect the authorities were chasing him for stealing an apple, when he spotted the open trunk and hopped in."

Seeing Pilot had reminded me of my earlier question. "How did he evade the dog? Pilot is neither so blind nor so deaf that he wouldn't notice a stranger in the house."

Diana chuckled. "Seems that this boy and that old dog came to an understanding. Frankie loves animals. When he did his late-night foraging, the boy shared tidbits with Pilot. As you can tell, the dog has befriended the boy. I suspect that Pilot did not see the child as a threat but rather as a friend."

I nodded. That made sense to me. I picked a stray thread off of Diana's dark skirt. "Have you been sewing?"

"Yes, indeed. Cook was more than willing to take charge of Frankie's clothes, promising to boil them or destroy them as she saw fit. But after one look at how threadbare they were, Lucy begged Cook for any castoffs she might have. I believe Cook keeps a bag handy, so she can tear old things into rags to use in the kitchen. Lucy has been modifying an old pair of Edward's pants, and I am working on undergarments and a shirt. Mrs. Wallander has volunteered to knit socks, and Mrs. Fairfax is working on a wool jumper."

"My! Such industry, and I slept through it." I thought back to when she'd undressed the boy. "What about boots? His were in miserable shape, as I recall."

Diana sighed. "As for those, we are perplexed about what to do. Perhaps a trip into town will be in order."

I agreed and added, "I can do that myself. I've

learned to drive the cart, using the donkey instead of a horse."

"Not today you aren't," Diana chided me. "Jane, you've obviously been working very hard in preparation for the holidays. The boy isn't going anywhere, and neither should you."

A knock at the front door interrupted us. I left my cousin and raced down the stairs. James stood on the stoop. "We came over early, because we thought you might need our help, getting everything ready." Dropping his voice, he added, "And Leah wanted to see the boy. I told her his shoes were rubbish. She found an old pair of my boots that might work for the child."

"How thoughtful of you both. Come on in. Let's get you out of the cold," I said. "John and Mary are with you?" I stood on tiptoe, craning my neck to look around him, so I could spot the gig.

"Aye, although I'm not sure that either know what's what." His face clouded with concern. "I'll go get them and Leah."

I called to Edward and he rushed out of his office. Heedless of the cold, he raced out to help James and Leah. When my husband came back, he was carrying Old John in his arms. The old man complained, muttering how he was perfectly capable of walking, but I knew it was pride talking. Leah and James had made a basket by linking their hands and arms together. Mary was carried thusly into the Great Hall. Very quickly, both of the older Harrigans were comfortably ensconced in the armchairs. Leah tucked heavy blankets around them, as they were both so feeble that we feared the cold would harm them. Edward set up a tea table between Mary and John, sending Mrs. Fairfax to alert Cook that the elderly couple was settled. The housekeeper carried in a heavily laden tea tray for our guests.

"Jane, shouldn't you go and change?" Edward asked me. He'd selected my claret-colored silk dress as his favorite and was eager for me to wear it this evening. "Lucy is upstairs getting ready. Mrs. Fairfax can help Leah and James feel at ease."

"Yes, of course," I said, although I did not want to leave the Great Hall. Not yet. I wished to commit every sensation to memory. The swags of greenery hung along the banister of the musicians' gallery, the deep green interrupted by bright red bows. Over the mantle was a wreath fashioned of yew intertwined with holly and topped with a big red bow. From the ceiling dangled balls of mistletoe. The long trestle table took up the middle of the room. We'd covered it with a long white damask cloth. Cook and Mrs. Fairfax had carried in enormous platters of sliced ham and sliced beef. A deep stoneware dish covered with a matching lid was filled with lamb stew, and the coriander, cloves, and fennel that spiced it scented the air. A large basket was lined with a tea towel on which had been piled small loaves of bread. Tubs of butter were set out at intervals, interrupted by boards covered with sliced cheeses. Miniature mince pies were stacked on a silver plate, while scones and small cakes decorated tiered cake platters. Mulled cider was in a large cauldron, and the cinnamon billowed out from it. Nearby was a large stoneware plate that supported a mountain of gingerbread. At intervals, large candlestands stood ready to illuminate the grand space. That, plus the Yule Log, would chase away the winter gloom.

Near the hearth sat John and Mary in their tall chairs, looking like visiting royalty. James had seen to their needs, and with full stomachs, they kept drifting off. Neither would be with us for long, and I was ever so happy that I'd sketched John's visage. Now I would need to do the same for Mary, so I could commit both retainers to paper and keep them evergreen in memory.

Edward took me by the hand. "This is a feast

for the senses, and I cannot thank you enough, dear wife, for all your hard work. You've turned this empty hall into a wonderland. Our guests will long remember this night." With a quick kiss, he pushed me toward the hallway. "Now, go and change."

CHAPTER 22

Lucy complimented me on my dress, before arranging my hair high on my head. She, of course, looked like a vision in a deep, midnight-blue gown trimmed in black lace.

"Before we go down, let's check on the boy," I said, grasping her hand.

"I have done, but I shall accompany you." Instead of tapping on the door, she turned the knob. Leah was sitting next to the bed, contentedly crocheting what looked like an undershirt. Our young guest was fast asleep. Putting a finger to her lips, Leah walked us back into the hall.

"He had a big bowl of beef broth and fell fast asleep," she reported.

"Is he doing better?" I asked. "Do we need to send for Mr. Carter? I'm not sure if the doctor will be able to attend the party tonight."

Leah chewed her bottom lip. "If the good doctor is here, you might send him up. Otherwise, I think that Frankie is on the mend. Now that he knows you won't call the coppers, he's ever so much more tranquil. Pilot is sleeping at the side of the bed, and the dog seems to comfort him immensely. Frankie told me that he missed his mother and his father, but most of all, he is sad because he loves animals, and therefore, Pilot is a sop to his misery."

"Let me get Jane downstairs so she can greet her guests, and then I shall come up and relieve you," Lucy spoke directly to Leah.

"I don't mind," Leah said, quickly. "I'm working on an undershirt for Frankie. As long as John and Mary are taken care of, I'm happy to spend time with the boy."

"Yes, but you need to make an appearance, too," I argued. "Elsewise, who will introduce me around?"

She laughed. She wore a lovely shawl over a simple black dress. The rose shades of the shawl brought out the pink in her complexion. I noticed that the stitches of the shawl were extremely delicate. "Did you make that?" I asked.

"Of course," she said.

"Come along, Jane," said Lucy, sternly. "Leah? If I do not take her down now, she will find a way to hide from all those people. See if she doesn't! I'll be back in a while to fetch you."

We all laughed, as my friends knew my proclivity for solitude. Leah seemed particularly amused, as Lucy could be very much the martinet when she wanted. Hand in hand, we walked down the stairs. I stepped into the Great Hall and froze. It seemed as if the entire village and every one of our tenants must have come!

"Come on," Lucy scolded me. "Don't be a silly old thing. Focus on the music or the food or the greenery. Anything but the people!"

Yet, I couldn't help but notice that a steady stream of guests flowed into the two-story hall. Once there, they would stop and gaze in wonder at their surroundings. The greenery was much admired, and the food was much praised. The musicians began by playing softly, so that our guests could chat among themselves. Cook, Mrs. Fairfax, and Amelia—freed from her childcare duties by Mrs. Wallander— carried platter after platter of delicacies to the long dining table. Our guests approved of all the comestibles, and they deeply appreciated the gifts of steamed pudding. At the center of all the activity was my husband, acting as host, and directing people to say hello to John and Mary, after their long abstinence from social affairs. Thanks to my husband's skillful maneuvering, many of our tenants went directly to say hello to the elderly Harrigans. When presented to John and Mary, our guests bowed and curtseyed to the elderly couple. Although by rights, such honors were due to my husband as their squire, and by marriage to me as his wife, I felt the gestures to be wholly correct. These two faithful retainers deserved the approval of the community, as their years of service were many and their fealty unmatched.

Lucy led me to the center of the throng. Being so at ease in social gatherings, she immediately introduced herself and me to anyone and everyone.

Edward, being so tall, spotted me very quickly in the crowd and excused himself so he could be by my side. "Jane, there are so many of our neighbors here. I want to introduce you around myself. Lucy? Are you coming?"

"Heavens, no. I'm busy meeting people myself." She made a tiny shooing motion with her fingers, while Edward led me to a distinguished looking man and his wife. The names and faces swirled around me, although I did my best to remember what I could. Most of our guests seemed genuinely interested in meeting me, although a couple of the wives regarded me coolly. Squire Hockney was one of the more effusive in his praise, as he noted that the Great Hall looked better than he could ever recall. "I once came here for a hunting party and nearly froze to death. I say, your father could be a tyrant. He was absolutely, positively convinced that misery was good for the soul. He and I never saw eye to eye about that," said the squire. Although age had spotted his complexion, his expressive eyes gave him a youthful vigor. The frank manner of his speech made me instantly comfortable with him. "I've heard that you are quite the artist, Mrs. Rochester. You know how tittle-tattle makes the rounds. I have invited a young portrait artist to come to my home and paint me. Perhaps you and young Rochester here will join us as well as my guests. I'd value your artistic opinion, Mrs. Rochester, on this artist's work. I'd hate to think I hired a poseur."

"You are very kind, sir," I said, conscious of

the blush working its way up my neck, "but I am not qualified to offer anything but the opinion of a novice."

"Even so, I would be deuced glad for you and young Rochester to come and be my guests at Tall Oaks. Oh, do say you will come for a long weekend! My daughter Melody will be home, and she will be so glad of young company. She finds me terribly boring, I'm afraid."

"Of course, we'll visit," said Edward, before I could demur.

Several other neighboring couples suggested we should get to know them better, and I could not help but think that alone made the evening a success. However, my primary goal had been to know our tenants better, so I asked Lucy to exchange places with Leah, so that I could draw upon her local knowledge. Leah was reluctant to leave Frankie. This I could tell, because she took her time about appearing in the Great Hall. James hovered over Mary and John, so I did not feel I could ask him for help. When Leah finally came down to the Great Hall, I took her by the hand. "You promised to introduce me. I am reliant on you," I said.

"Oh, Jane, forgive me. I was talking with

Frankie, and I didn't want to abandon him. He's such a sweet child." She allowed me to drag her into the midst of the crowded room. Any minute now, the musicians would begin playing, and their music was likely to make conversation impossible. Edward was signaling to James that the table needed to be moved to one side.

Leah quickly introduced me to Goodie Brown. Although tiny as a bird, the old goodwife fairly sparkled with vitality. There was something about her that impressed me immediately, and I could see that she was a wise counselor. She took my hands in hers and stared into my eyes. "The pain of the past is fire that you can use to temper the steel of your backbone now."

"I look forward to the day when we can get together and speak privately," I said, right before Leah led me away. The young Mrs. Harrigan proceeded to announce me to the Walkers, the Thomases, the Hughes, and the Clarkes. The women all stared at me curiously, and the men seemed incredibly dumbstruck. After a few awkward attempts at conversation, Leah again took my hand and escorted me to another area of the Great Hall. "What is wrong?" I whispered to Leah. "Why were all of them staring at me?"

She pulled me close to whisper in my ear. "They've heard so much about you, and they know you were once a governess. But they don't know you, not yet, and they wonder how it is that you enchanted the dour Mr. Rochester. He was known far and wide as a bit of a rake, you see, and a man not given to happiness. There was speculation he'd marry a wealthy heiress, and you ain't at all what they expected."

Yes, I did see. I felt disappointed, like I'd fallen in their esteem, and I believe it showed on my face.

"Not to worry," said Leah, giving me a quick hug. "The evening is a grand success. You've clearly gone to a lot of trouble, and yet you managed to include Old John and Mary, treating them like honored guests. So, the tenants don't know what to make of it or of you. They half-expected you to put on airs, but you aren't like that. So, they are confused. Really, they are. Once they get to know you, that'll change. Give them time, and they'll see you for the rare gem you are, Jane. If you don't mind, I'm going back up to sit with the little boy. I want to make sure that the garment I'm making for him fits."

A few of our guests brought us gifts, such as a haunch of venison, hanks of spun wool, and a pot of jellied squirrel. The foodstuffs were happily received by Cook, and the wool I kept for my further adventures with my crochet hook.

At the stroke of nine, the musicians struck up a lively tune. Edward appeared at my elbow, as if by magic. "We need to lead off the dancing," he said. "Everyone wants to gaze upon my wonderful wife."

"Oh, sir," I protested. "Must we?"

"Indeed, we must," he said smoothly, as he led me to the middle of the floor.

I dance rather poorly, but Edward is a strong partner, and the fact we were out on the floor encouraged other couples to join in. Soon we were surrounded by happy guests displaying a variety of abilities. I could not help but smile, because Edward was so thoroughly enjoying himself. I'd seen him before, when he'd invited other couples to Thornfield Hall, but that had been a somber affair, because he and I were not sure of our love. Here in the vast stone space, the Great Hall, surrounded by a surfeit of food, candle light, and music, we were at peace with one another, because we were secure in each other.

Lucy went from one dancing partner to another, charming everyone and ignoring nobody. Diana did her part, chatting to those who refused to take a turn on the dance floor. In truth, these two women were my ambassadors, spreading glad tidings throughout the crowd.

I had lost track of Mrs. Fairfax, but she arrived at my elbow and spoke in a low voice. "Jane, the rector and his wife are here."

"What?" I could hardly keep the astonishment out of my voice. "I did not invite them."

Mrs. Fairfax wrung her hands, whilst refusing to look me in the eyes. "I did. I rather thought they wouldn't attend, seeing as how the rector must conduct a midnight mass. By sending the invitation, I hoped to forestall any complaints against you."

I could only stare at her. Or rather I stared at the deep lace collar she had added to her best black silk as a nod to the season. I did not trust myself to engage her fully. Her conduct was beyond anything I could imagine! She had deliberately gone around me and around Edward as well. Although her reasoning was sensible, at least if she had told me, I should have been forewarned. Now I was caught on the hop, and yet I was forced to act the gracious hostess.

"We shall discuss this later," I said, willing myself to act with decorum. "Please go and explain to Edward what you have done, whilst I greet the Jones-Smythes."

I reminded myself, as I walked the length of the Great Hall, that they were on my turf now, under my roof, and in my home. Whatever pretenses they harbored, they were here as guests, and thus I expected them to act with civility. I was several strides from them, when Leah cut a path through the crowd and intercepted the rector and his wife. I could see the animated movements of Leah's hands as she talked to them. The interruption gave me time to study the couple. He was wearing his black cassock and dog collar, of course. She had on a ridiculous concoction trimmed with yard after yard of lace, dotted with ribbons, and glistened with faux gems. On her head was a tall bouquet of flowers and feathers. Heads turned to stare at her with slack-jawed wonder.

"There she is," the rector waved to me, just as Edward came striding our way. "I believe introductions are in order," he said, preening as Edward arrived. I did the dubious honor of introducing my husband to the Jones-Smythes, noting as I spoke that Mrs. Jones-Smythe had rather neatly managed to step in front of Leah Harrigan and block the woman out. I reached for

Leah's hand and pulled her close to me. Mrs. Jones-Smythe cocked a disapproving eyebrow at us.

"Mrs. Harrigan was relating a story," began the rector in sonorous tones, "regarding a young stowaway. A street urchin who took shelter in your new trunk, Mrs. Rochester."

"Yes. It seems the child jumped inside, not realizing how far he would travel," I said.

"He was running from the authorities?" the Reverend Jones-Smythe frowned as he spoke.

"He might well have been," Edward admitted. Meanwhile, Leah was growing paler and paler by the minute.

"The boy is a starving orphan," I explained. "He has admitted stealing an apple before leaping into the trunk."

"Then you must do your duty and turn him in to the authorities in London," said the rector with an unctuous smile.

"You cannot harbor a thief," added his wife. "What would people think? Besides, you must set an example. You and your wife. Theft is expressly forbidden by God's commandments, as you surely are aware."

Leah began to tremble, but I quickly took her hand and tucked it under my arm to give her strength. As I pulled her closer to me, she shook so hard that I worried for her health. I whispered to her, "That boy is not going to be turned in. Do not even think it!"

In sharp contrast to Leah's shivering, Edward's anger radiated from him, like the rays of the sun on a hot June day. "Mrs. Jones-Smythe, I believe you have forgotten yourself. Remember that Jesus himself said, 'Suffer little children to come unto me.' This boy is but a hungry child and an orphan. It is not his fault that his parents are dead. If he was in want of bread, perhaps that is our failure as a society to see to his needs."

The rector's mouth opened and shut, repeatedly. Before he could form a retort, Edward added, "I opened my home to you and to others tonight as a gesture of Christian charity. Now I must ask you both to leave. I am sure you can find your own way out."

Taking me by the arm, which also meant taking Leah, since I had a grip on her, Edward swiftly turned his back on the rector and his wife. As he often does when he is angry, Edward moved with alacrity.

"Blast that man," said Edward, when we found ourselves at the other end of the hall. "I shall see to it tomorrow that his living is withdrawn. A letter to the bishop will finish that vulture off."

Leah's eyes were wet with tears. "You won't send Frankie to the poorhouse, will you? Or give him to the police? He was only hungry!"

Edward reached for her hand. "Leah, I promise you that I shall do nothing of the sort. You have my word."

Lucy came up with a couple, who wanted an introduction. Her cheerful countenance reminded us this was a time for merry making, not stoking our anger, so Edward and I turned our attention back to our guests. But inside, I still harbored irritation at Mrs. Fairfax and fury at the Jones-Smythes. Try as I might, I could not banish their unchristian behavior from my mind.

During the evening, Adèle wandered in and out of the Great Hall, pirouetting and even offering to sing, when the musicians took a break. Her rendition of a French dance hall tune was much admired by our visitors, solely because they could not translate the Gallic lyrics into the bawdy English words.

"That girl," said Edward as his face turned red. "We'll have to talk with her about which songs she can share."

"Tomorrow," I said, reaching up to caress his face. "Tomorrow."

Close to ten o'clock, I noticed how Mary and John sagged in their armchairs. I looked around for Leah, and Lucy noticed my unspoken request. "She's upstairs with Frankie. The two are chatting," Lucy said. "She's very taken with the boy." Following my gaze to the elderly Harrigans, Lucy knew immediately what I was thinking. "Jane? I can go and fetch Leah. John and Mary are all done in, I believe."

While Lucy went up to get Leah, I made my way through the throng to find Edward. "I think John and Mary are exhausted," I said. He nodded and responded, "Yes, of course. That's not surprising. I shall go and get James. Perhaps I need to go with him. I don't know how he and Leah managed to get his grandparents into the gig, but as depleted as they are, I doubt they'll be able to do so again."

Adèle came skipping past, and I promptly sent her to ask Cook to heat bricks for the trip back to the Harrigans' cottage.

Leah arrived to help bundle up John and Mary, whilst James ran out into the cold and pulled the gig close to the Manor. Getting the old couple to their feet proved more difficult than I had reckoned.

"Edward, how will James and Leah manage moving them from the gig to the cottage?" I asked. Edward instantly saw what I meant.

"James? I shall go with you and Leah. I can bring the gig back after John and Mary are safely deposited," said Edward.

When James protested over the head of his grandfather, Edward grew testy. "I am not asking you, James. I am telling you," said Edward. "We really need a manservant," he said as he gave me a quick kiss before leaving. "After the holidays, that will be a priority."

Edward was back in less than a half an hour, which meant he was climbing down from the gig, when Mr. Carter arrived. The doctor apologized for being so late, but he explained, "Mrs. Winkle was giving birth to twins, and my presence at her bedside was a matter of life and death. I'm happy to report that mother and sons are fine, although she did give me a bit of a scare."

"Speaking of scares," Edward led the doctor out into the hallway. I followed, knowing that my husband was explaining about our young visitor, who was still recovering in the spare bedroom.

"Of course, I'll go up and see to him right

away," said Mr. Carter, and the physician mounted the stairs quickly, taking two at a time.

Goodie Brown sought me out again. Once again, I noticed that the goodwife was a tiny thing, only up to my shoulder, and probably half my weight. However, she had a spritely way about her. "Leah told me about the little boy ye found in the trunk. I'll bring by a tonic for the lad on the morrow. I'll be dropping by the Harrigans' cottage at first light with an early Christmas gift, a basket of dried herbs for John and Mary. Won't be a bother to put a bottle of tonic in there as well."

When I offered to pay the older woman, she frowned at me. "Edward Rochester is letting me live in that cottage of mine free of charge, and you are offering to pay me for herbs I gathered on his land? I daresay not."

"I meant no disrespect," I hastened to add.

"I know ye didn't, lass. None is taken."

Lucy escorted Adèle up to bed. My friend promised to turn the girl over to Mrs. Wallander, which meant that the French girl would be tucked away for the evening. Mr. Carter came downstairs shortly thereafter. "That boy has been living on crusts for at least a year and maybe more. His mother couldn't find work, so he and she made do by begging. Other than needing regular meals, generous applications of soap, and a clean bed, I think he will soon regain his health."

"Goodie Brown offered to drop off a tonic for him," I said.

"That would be helpful. She is a skillful herbalist. Probably do the boy all sorts of good." Mr. Carter's shoulders slumped. "Seeing a boy like that is a painful reminder of how cruel the world can be."

I agreed and suggested that the doctor help himself to the mulled cider and gingerbread, as that was all that was left. Cook had refilled the platters many times, but our guests had been very hungry, and they had appreciated her culinary skills. Once again, I was pleased that we'd planned for a generous Boxing Day.

Around midnight, guests began saying their goodbyes. Edward and I found ourselves stationed at the front door, accepting thanks and well-wishes. "The rector and his wife must have left early," I whispered.

"Thank the Lord for small favors," Edward returned. "I thought about turning them out immediately, but I remembered he would need to leave for midnight mass. That was all that stood between him and the sole of my boots."

Our neighbors and tenants were fulsome in their praise of the evening. Their kind words went a long way toward making me feel I had done a good turn. Squire Hockney was the last of our visitors. "Don't forget that you promised to come and stay for a long weekend," he waggled his fingers at me.

"Yes, when the artist is in residence," I agreed. We shook hands and said goodnight.

"That's the last of them," said Edward, closing the door behind the squire. "I'll stay up long enough to bank the fires. Why don't you go on up to bed?"

That freed me to go upstairs and change into my nightclothes.

First, I wanted to check on Frankie. Mrs. Wallander was dozing in a chair next to his bed, and my arrival aroused her. With assistance from light in the hallway, I bent down to examine the sleeping boy as she watched. His face seemed relaxed, and for once he was clean. "As you can see for yourself, all is well," Mrs. Wallander whispered. "Go on to bed, Mrs. Rochester."

I nodded and shut the door behind me.

After changing, I climbed into bed. Edward came up shortly thereafter. "Thank you, darling girl, for such a festive evening," he said, as he slid in beside me. Crawling closer to him, I rested my head on his chest and listened to the soothing beat of his heart. "Yes, sir. This was a long and happy Christmas. Whilst I was glad to see our guests coming, I am more than content that they are gone now. Aren't you?"

He chuckled. "Yes, I am."

CHAPTER 23

The next morning, I found Leah in our kitchen, drinking tea. Wet spots on her clothes suggested she had been outside in the snow recently, rather than a long while ago. She and Cook were chatting about the lamb stew from the night before. Leah had been much taken with the recipe. I hadn't eaten any, but our guests had pronounced it the best ever. Leah was perched on a stool, and at her feet was a bag that had been beautifully crocheted. The way the sack was weighed down suggested it held something heavy. Leah continued, "Goodie Brown is sitting with John and Mary, so I took the opportunity to bring over the tonics she made for Frankie."

"Thank you," I said. "Mr. Carter examined him last night, and the prognosis is good, but I fear the boy will need a good deal of nursing to gain back his strength. A year of living on the streets and going hungry is a long time in the life of a child."

Leah said, "Imagine, finding a boy hidden inside a trunk. That must have been a shock for all involved."

"Yes, it was," I admitted. "Food had been disappearing from Cook's kitchen, but we," and I stopped myself, rather than reveal the embarrassing fact that we'd blamed her husband, James Harrigan, for the losses. Behind Leah, Cook froze while mixing batter. Her arms were akimbo, and as I watched, her head drew up as her back stiffened. But Cook did not turn around. She had caught my hesitation and worried that I would share our accusations. Admittedly, they now seemed very churlish on our part. Recovering myself, I amended my remark to say, "We thought perhaps Pilot was helping himself at night. Little did we know that a starving boy was sneaking down the stairs and grabbing what he could."

"I hope I can help the lad," Leah said. "Goodie Brown has been teaching me what she knows of herbs and such. I am not a healer yet, and certainly not up to her high standards, but she and I discussed the matter this morning, and I know what to do. She dropped off these bottles of tonic at first light. If the lad has been living wild, in the streets of London, Lord only knows what pestilences he's brushed up against. Especially since he's gone without nourishing food. There's much his body has been fighting. I think these tinctures can help. With a bit of sugar added in, these will go down a treat." She opened her crocheted bag and pointed to three bottles inside.

Leah waited for me to finish my cup of tea, before we went upstairs. Mrs. Wallander had exchanged places with Diana, who greeted Leah warmly from the chair at Frankie's bedside. I could tell the two women—my cousin and James Harrigan's wife—had become immediate friends. A kindred spirit bound the women, a seriousness of purpose and the desire to heal and help. The two of them conferred about Frankie, agreeing that the boy suffered from various deficiencies and Leah's tonics could help.

I only had the chance glimpse of Frankie, because Leah reminded me that sugar would be useful to his acceptance of the tonics. I turned to retrace my steps and head back to the kitchen, but I nearly tripped over Pilot, who was resting at the foot of the bed. His head was partially hidden by the bedclothes, so I hadn't seen him.

When I returned with a ramekin of sugar, Leah sat next to the sleeping child, stroking his hair. To my surprise, Mephisto was there too. The black cat was curled next to the boy's head. I could hear Mephisto's purring from the other side of the bed.

"What ho?" I said. For as long as I've owned him, my cat has maintained a certain unapproachable nature. Yes, Mephisto has submitted to my caresses, but never has the puss curled up with me. Yet there the cat was, blinking at me as if to say, "Of course, I'm here watching over the boy."

Leah had taken on that dreamy look I'd seen on her face, when she'd spoken wistfully of a babe of her own. She removed a salve from her bag. Gently, she smoothed it onto Frankie's sores and bruises. These injuries mottled his face and arms. As she examined his skin more carefully, tears threatened to spill. But she was too strong to let her emotions overcome her good sense. Before they ran down her face, she paused and wiped her eyes with the cuff of her sleeve.

Diana had taken another chair, a straight-backed one, and she looked up from the book she was reading. But now and again, her head drooped. I could tell she was fighting sleep. Leah noticed me watching Diana, and she said, "Diana? Why don't you let me sit with him? You look as if you could use a bit of rest yourself. He's sleeping soundly, and I don't want to wake him."

"You are right," said Diana. "I am entirely spent. Nightmares kept him thrashing through the night. Best to let him sleep now that he's settled."

As she spoke, I could tell that Diana was beyond tired. "Mrs. Wallander and I swapped places shortly after two a.m. Frankie was prone to startling awake and crying out. The poor boy was worrying about his safety. He cried out for his Ma and his Pa, repeatedly. Then he begged me not to beat him. Poor, poor child. It nearly broke my heart," Diana said with a sigh.

"Diana? Go and have a lie down, please. It wouldn't do for you to fall ill." After she slowly got up and left the room, I gave the sugar and a spoon to Leah. I felt awkward and entirely extraneous. Leah took the ramekin and the cutlery from me. "I'll give the tonics to him, when he wakes up."

"Almost forgot," said my cousin. Diana had been waiting outside the door for me. Reaching into a pillowslip, she withdrew a pair of underclothes, a top and bottom that would fit the little boy perfectly. "Frankie's wearing a similar set. Cook gave me an old sheet and I revised it."

I hugged her. "You sewed all night?"

"Not all night. I came up after the party and slept for several hours. Then I took over for Mrs. Wallander. While I was in the room with Frankie, I dozed off and on. Poor wee mite. I couldn't have slept if I wanted to, not with his nightmares. I was far too concerned with keeping an eye on him. He's practically starving. Goodness knows how many nights he spent outside. You saw some of his open sores and bruises. He has chilblains on all his fingers and toes. Blisters all over his feet."

As if "feet" was a magic word, Mrs. Wallander stepped out of the nursery. "Here," she said, magically producing two pairs of thick socks.

"When? How?" I was astonished, turning them over in my hands. The workmanship was flawless and the size was perfect for the boy.

"I worked on them last night and this morning." The woman seemed nonchalant, as if she could knit a pair of socks in her sleep.

I said as much, and Mrs. Wallander gave Diana and me a lopsided smile. "Sure, and if you had grown up in Switzerland, you would have learned to do the same. Any Swiss child of ten could manage. Boy or girl. With our harsh weather, a lack of socks could prove fatal, and that's no exaggeration. I'll make him several more pairs today, see if I don't."

"Thank you very much," I said. "Someday, I hope to learn to knit. I'm doing my best to learn basic crocheting with Leah's help. My instructors tried to teach me to knit at school, but the skill didn't take."

With a nod of her head, Mrs. Wallander said, "Then you lacked proper instruction. If someone does not learn, I count it as a failure on the teacher's fault. If you want, I shall assist you in learning to knit. I've taught more folks than I can count."

"I might do that," I said, and I meant it. Her attitude was refreshing.

The rest of the day passed pleasantly. Mrs. Fairfax and I took turns reading out loud from the Bible, sharing the story of that first Christmas so long ago. The little boys played happily in the nursery. Diana had decided that she and Adèle would make a picture book to help Frankie learn

French. I drew whatever they required, starting with an apple, a tree, a cat, a dog, and a chicken and a nest of eggs. Diana had determined that she and Adèle could color in my sketches and work together to write short sentences that would be ideal for a beginner.

As always, I reflected on Diana's intrinsic talents as a teacher. She had an unparalleled ability to breakdown material and make it accessible to her students. Thanks to the project she had concocted with Adèle, the two were busy all day long. In the late afternoon, Lucy, Diana, and I played the pianoforte for Edward and Mrs. Fairfax. As we went into the dining room for our supper, Edward pulled me aside. "Hearing you play reminded me: Adèle needs to begin music lessons again."

"Yes," I agreed. "At the very least, she needs a new governess. More likely, she needs a governess and a music tutor."

"And we need a manservant," Edward grumbled.

"All of that can wait until after the holidays," I said, putting a staying hand on his arm.

Looking around our supper table filled my heart with gladness. Cook had truly prepared an expansive meal, but the real feast for my soul was the happy faces of friends and family. I'd decided I would not chastise Mrs. Fairfax for inviting the rector and his wife. As it happened, the visit by the Jones-Smythes had done more to tarnish their reputations than anything I could have shared with Edward. Now, my husband was happily disposed to send that couple packing!

More discussion about the Jones-Smythes could wait until after the holidays. Instead, we all raised our glasses high and toasted first each other, then Christmas, and the upcoming New Year. Cook proudly brought out the roasted goose. The crackling skin was lovely. The moist meat was pronounced, "Perfection!" by Lucy, who had consulted with Cook in the kitchen. Diana had contributed by helping Cook make a delicious soup with turnips, potatoes, and carrots. To complement the meal, we had a mince pie and a plum pudding.

Early on the morning of Boxing Day, we again opened the Great Hall to visitors, but this time we were welcoming only those who were our employees or tenants. They had lined up outside in the cold, before we even realized what was happening. When Edward threw open the front door, we were stunned by the number that awaited entrance. "Come in," said Edward. "No need to stand outside. There's room for all of you in the Great Hall, and it is warm in here." As a matter of fact, the Yule Log was still burning, making the hall a very comfortable room indeed.

Given the bitter weather, most of our visitors were bundled up securely in a variety of knitted shawls, wraps, and blankets. Unlike those who had come to the party on Christmas, these guests had not bothered to dress up. Perhaps that's why they looked genuinely needy. When Edward handed them their boxes, they took them with obvious gratitude. Their thankfulness caused my heart to ache. I could not help but think back to Edward's recent discovery that his renters were needy. He felt guilty, because he had neglected his responsibilities. Seeing the poor status of the gathered crowd reminded him that he really needed to do more for his tenants. I was also feeling a sense of rebuke, as I knew how it felt to be hungry and cold.

Seeing how thin our guests were and knowing how cold it was outside, I hurried to the kitchen. "Cook? We have a lot of cold and hungry guests.

Could you make more mulled cider and tea for our visitors?"

"Aye, of course, I can, missus." She'd also pulled a fresh tray of gingerbread out of the oven. Although it was meant to be our pudding after supper, I instructed her to feed it to our guests. I also went to the close closet and emptied it of all of the mince pies. These I carried into the Great Hall and served to our guests myself.

I was there, when Leah arrived. She had left her cloak in the kitchen to see if she could help out. "I was able to come, because Goodie Brown is sitting with John and Mary."

"How did you know we'd need you?" I wondered. Was it possible that everyone but us knew that our tenants were in need? That was shameful, but I quickly stopped myself. What others thought did not matter. What mattered was what we did next.

"After seeing the number of guests you had on Christmas, I thought you might be busy today. How can I help?" She worked beside me passing out food and pouring hot drinks, while Edward handed out boxes. For two hours, we were nearly run off our feet. Cook had to replenish the cider and tea many times over. In fact, we were serving our guests for so long that Lucy and Diana came looking for me. When they realized how many tenants Leah and I were serving in the Great Hall, they quickly donned aprons and did their part to assist.

Four hours later, the last of the renters had come and gone. My lower back was aching. Cook was a little irritated with me, because I'd cleaned out the larder once again, but her annoyance was more for show than serious. Edward, Leah, Lucy, Diana, and I finally wandered into the parlor. There we sank down into straight-backed chairs, while Mrs. Fairfax brought us a pot of tea.

"I blame myself," said Edward. "I thought I had entrusted the management of the estate to a capable man. I was wrong. He has let problems slide, and I have not managed him successfully. My tenants need more help, and I vow to all of you, right here and now, to give it to them."

"You have it within your power to make a change, dear husband," I said. "Today was a good start."

"If I may, Squire," Leah put forth gently. When Edward urged her to share, she said, "Remember at the party? On Christmas Night? Some of those same tenants came back today. I believe that folks are sharing what they learned. Now they believe you will be making changes. Overall, I think people are very pleased."

"I hope so," said Edward, "because I am totally to blame for letting things go so long without my supervision."

CHAPTER 24

Hourly, it seemed that Frankie was growing a little stronger. Most mornings, I bumped into Leah, either coming out of his room or going in. She was diligent about giving the child his tonics. Often, I heard her voice mingle with his as the two of them seemed to have become fast friends. Frankie wasn't much of a talker, and he still spent most of the day in bed, but in the afternoons, he and Adèle would play at card games. When she discovered he couldn't read, that little minx went from wanting to teach him French to demanding that I make the boy a picture book of the entire alphabet.

"I heard Adèle ordering you about," said Diana, as she tried not to laugh. "She can be quite the little tyrant. Now you have another task for that busy sketchbook of yours."

"I must admit that I can think of no better way to employ my skills," I said.

As time went on, Frankie was able to walk around a little more, typically with Pilot at his side. When the boy climbed into his bed, Mephisto always joined him. It was almost as if the dog and the cat were loaning the child their animal vitality, so he could get stronger.

"I have to wonder how he made it down here into the kitchen to steal food," said Cook, shaking her head when I stopped in to make myself a cup of tea. "He must have stopped and rested along the way up and down, because he wasn't fit to climb stairs when ye found him."

She was right. Of course, the desire to survive is powerful, and I had to assume it aided him, even when his strength was failing. Slowly, the boy was showing the results one might expect from a healthy diet. Goodie Brown's tonics seemed to improve his appetite and color. As for the bad dreams, I mentioned them to Edward. One night, Edward took me by the hand and walked me down the hall. "It's time we had a talk with the boy." We went into the bedroom, where I sat next to the bed and Edward stood at my side.

My husband said, "Frankie, no one will hurt you, lad. We shall see to it."

"But the coppers," the boy began.

"The coppers won't hurt you. I'm a squire. I can pay for anything you took."

"But I took your food, too," he said,

and big tears coursed down his face.

"If we'd have known you were hungry, we would have fed you," I said as I took his hand in mine. "I was hungry once, as a young girl. I know how that feels. You must trust us that you are safe now."

Later that evening, Mrs. Wallander told us that Frankie seemed to be more settled. "I think his fears dogged him. Now that you've put them to rest, he should be able to sleep through the night."

The last day of December was upon us, and Ferndean Manor was chockablock with secrets as everyone hastened to put final touches on their gifts.

Of course, Adèle was the only child who fully understood that Father Christmas was coming, and that he would both deliver presents and fill her stocking with sweets overnight. Ned and Evans were too young to guess at the frivolity the next day would bring. Frankie had no grand experiences with gift giving. As a consequence, Adèle was unable to sit still through afternoon tea, and her wild behavior convinced me that she should eat an early supper and go directly to the nursery.

But that willful French girl was having none of that. Instead, she slipped into Frankie's room. There she regaled the boy with stories of Christmases past. "Wait until you see what St. Nicholas brings you!" she said. Her eyes glowed with anticipation and her recitation of wonders seemed truly endless. Frankie was sure that she had lost her wits.

"Never. He never brung me more than an apple and an orange. Once't he left me a new jumper, but sweeties? I'd think I'd died and gone to heaven, if there is such a place," Frankie told her. "I'm sure that's all well and good for a fancy lady like yourself, but for someone like me, that ain't happening."

~

On New Year's Day, we were up early to see that everything was in order. Adèle must have heard us, because she was racing around upstairs shortly after we had closed the door to the parlor.

Lucy overheard the child making noise and cajoled her into coming into the newly decorated guest bedroom for a while. That did not last long, as shortly thereafter I stepped out of the parlor, and Adèle fairly threw herself at me.

"Ma cher mademoiselle," she whined. "Is it not time for presents? How much longer must I wait? I am *tant pis.* So sad! I have waited and waited all year for this."

Lucy called down from the second floor. "I tried to keep her occupied, Jane. But I fell back to sleep."

I took the little girl by the hand and led her up the stairs. When we reached Lucy's room, I told my friend, "Not to worry. I have her now. Adèle, you cannot roam the halls in your night slip. If you wake up Ned and Evans and Frankie, I shall be very cross with you! Go and get dressed. When you are presentable, come down for breakfast. Monsieur and I shall be waiting there for you. Only after you eat can you hope to open presents."

"What a high-strung little thing," said Mrs. Wallander, as the girl flounced into the nursery. "Mrs. Brayton explained how Adèle came to be a part of your household. I believe you will have your hands full as she gets older. She's a beauty, and she knows it."

I nodded. "Yes, I think we shall be busy with her. However, I am also sure that Lucy mentioned the girl has a big heart. There is not a malicious bone in her body. Her enthusiasm for life is infectious."

"Mrs. Brayton mentioned as much to me." Mrs. Wallander smiled. "There are those who think the only good children are obedient ones. Sheeplike. I tend to believe we were not put on this earth to emulate sheep. True, a willful child can be a challenge, but rough winds make for strong timber. Let her test herself on you and then go out into the world knowing she can handle whatever comes her way."

I nodded at her wisdom.

"I've detained you long enough, Mrs. Rochester. Thank you for having me as a guest in your home. So far, this holiday has been delightful, and I am sure today will be as well." With that, the nanny hurried back to the nursery.

"Good morning, again," I said to my husband, as I took my place alongside him at the dining room table. Lucy and Diana were sitting at the other end, talking quietly between themselves. "Adèle will be along directly."

"About that," said Lucy. "I tripped over her in the hallway. She was wearing a satin evening gown I had made my lady's maid make over for her to play in. As you might guess, it is wholly inappropriate for the breakfast table. So, I immediately sent her back to the nursery with a warning that she better not reappear unless dressed as a young lady of the manor should be."

Edward stifled a laugh. I couldn't help myself. "Lucy, did she take advantage of you in London? I hope she was not a terrible trial."

"Gracious, no. She was very amusing. Although I must admit, she nearly got the better of me several times. She's fallen in love with my brother, Bruce, and took to draping herself around his neck like an ermine stole. I told her such behavior was not permissible, and I threatened to take away her ribbons, her sweeties, and her doll babies." Lucy snapped her fingers. "Like that, she was willing to dance to my tune."

Diana smiled. "Have you considered when we will open our gifts? I cannot entirely blame the child. I, too, am nearly mad with curiosity."

"Actually, I had thought we would do it after a

leisurely breakfast," said Edward, folding his napkin and putting it on the table. "Note that I put particular stress on leisurely. But first I need a report. How does Frankie fare? And how are you feeling, Diana? Are you very tired after watching him all night?"

"I do believe he is doing better," Diana said. "His nightmares seem to have ended. I give much credit to Leah, as she has come over every day to dose him with Goodie Brown's tonics."

I agreed. "Leah has great faith in the old woman's powers of healing."

"Goodie Brown has lived on the estate since my grandfather's youth. She's known far and wide for her abilities. In fact, there was a time when she was accused of witchcraft thanks to her prodigious ability to heal the sick. I believe my father interceded on her behalf. She's neither wicked nor evil. Nor does she worship Satan. She's a good woman with a wealth of knowledge that she uses to help others. She also seems to have a sense of when and where she is needed, and thus, she turns up unexpectedly, when the time is right for her to make an appearance."

"Her visits to the Harrigans' cottage have certainly been advantageous. They allow Leah to leave John and Mary at home, so she can bring healing tonics to Frankie," I said.

Diana and Lucy exchanged furtive looks. "Jane?" Lucy said in a voice that suggested I needed to listen carefully.

Diana spoke up. "We have to tell you that Leah has been doing more than you suspect. She's been coming over before first light and setting the fires."

"What?" Edward's eyebrows shot up. "That's a job for a man! James does it!"

"Yes," said Lucy calmly, "but Leah is so determined to watch over Frankie that she begged James to let her take his place. Whilst it is true that Goodie Brown has helped with John and Mary, I believe the old woman has visited them only once or twice."

Diana continued the explanation, "Leah cajoled James into letting her take his place. He's staying home with his elderly grandparents, so that she can spend time with Frankie."

Lucy added, "Not to worry. Cook always has a cup of hot tea for her, first thing. Leah reminded me she's accustomed to hauling wood for the hearth at their cottage. Really, Edward, you should not be so surprised."

"The point is," continued Diana, "Leah has

grown very attached to the boy. I suspect that she and James are going to ask if they can take him into their home."

I felt my heart take wings. "Truly, that would be the best for all involved. Leah has been longing for a child of her own. James wants one, too. Frankie's appearance might just be a Christmas miracle."

"Isn't that wonderful?" said Lucy.

"And isn't that the way the Lord works?" said Diana, with an expression of pure wonder on her face. "That boy came here, escaping trouble, and with faith that the trunk would provide his salvation. He arrived sick and dirty and plagued with bad dreams. But for all of that, he is a gift, isn't he?"

"I cannot help but think of the rector and his wife. Do you know she encouraged Edward to turn Frankie over to the police? She pointed out that he was breaking a commandment." I could hear my voice quiver with indignation.

"And, so, she broke the most important commandment of all," said Edward, taking my hand. "Love thy neighbor as thyself. If ever a child needed love, it was Frankie. If ever a couple needed a child, it is James and Leah."

Lucy set her napkin down beside her plate.

"Proving for once and for all that the best gifts aren't the ones we hope to receive, but those that Heaven decides to bestow on us."

"Speaking of gifts," said Diana, "I am excited about opening some. Is that entirely too juvenile of me?"

"Not at all," said Edward. "Today's a day for children, no matter how young or old. I would never deprive you, Cousin Diana. Would you like to take tea or coffee into the parlor?"

"Allow me to give the first present." Lucy reached over to the chair next to her. She pulled up an oddly-shaped lump wrapped in brown paper. "This is for you two, Edward and Jane."

Edward gestured for me to take possession of the gift. I did and quickly unwrapped what looked to be a glass contraption with various chambers. "I am afraid you have the better of me, Lucy. I don't know what this is."

"It brews coffee. What you are looking at is an invention by a Frenchman named Jacques-Augustin Gandais. There are two chambers, connected by a tube. You set the pot on the stove with water in the bottom chamber and the ground coffee in the top. When the water boils, it shoots up through the tube and sprays on the coffee, before dripping down into the bottom chamber. Really, it makes a marvelous brew. Try it with cream and sugar. Oh, and do be advised, if you were sleepy before, you shan't be after you sip this."

As if on cue to represent her nationality, Adèle flounced down into a chair. I was gratified to see that she wore a neat white blouse, trimmed in ruffled lace and tucked into a velvet skirt. Around her waist was a satin belt that, sadly, had not been tied correctly. "Come here, *mon petit chouchou,*" I said to her. "Turn around." I tied the satin into a fluffy bow. "There you go. Now you must eat a little something. A piece of toast and a cup of hot chocolate will do nicely, and then we'll go and open presents."

"I shall be right back," said Lucy.

While we persuaded Adèle to eat her breakfast, a wonderful aroma drifted into the dining room. At length, Lucy returned with a pot in her hand. Cook trailed along behind her, carrying a tray full of teacups and saucers. "I never," said Cook. "What a contraption!"

Lucy pursed her lips with concentration as she poured a cup for Diana. "Be sure to add sugar and cream. I know you like sweets, my friend."

"My," said Diana, sampling the beverage after stirring in the condiments, "this is good."

"I'll send you a pot like this and a bag or two of coffee," said Lucy to my cousin, as she poured a cup for me. "Consider it a late Christmas gift, Diana."

"Thank you kindly," said Diane, as she savored another sip.

"And me!" said Adèle. "I want a cup, too!"

"All right, *pauvre petite*," said Lucy, dispensing a half a cup for the little girl, before turning and filling a cup for Edward.

"How is that boy? The dirty one?" Adèle asked, while masticating a piece of toast.

Sometimes I despaired of the child. She knew very well that he was no longer dirty, and of course she knew his name.

"Really, Adèle," I scolded her. "Do not be unkind. You know better."

"I don't want to share my presents with him," she said with a big pout.

"Ladies do not talk with food in their mouths," said Lucy, giving the child a tap on the shoulder.

"And ladies do not make unkind remarks about other people," I added.

"It's not unkind. It's true!" Adèle protested.

"And why do you think he was dirty?" asked Edward. "Because he wanted to be? Because he had a nice home and a warm bath but couldn't be bothered to clean himself? Is that also why he was hungry?"

Tears welled up in Adèle's eyes. "I am sorry. You are right. He is a *pauvre petit.* He isn't hungry anymore, is he? I hope not. I should like to play with him." Then slyly, "And if Père Noël has brought me any sweeties, I might share them with him. I might."

Clearly, we were torturing the poor girl. Once Adèle finished her toast and most of her hot chocolate plus two more sips of coffee, we moved on into the parlor. The stack of gifts piled up near the hearth seemed to have grown overnight. Diana hesitated before sitting down. "Just allow me a moment to run upstairs and make sure Leah is all right."

"Please tell Mrs. Fairfax that we're ready to open gifts," said Edward. "She's free to join us, whenever she pleases."

"Of course, Diana. Do go check on Leah," I said. "We can wait that long. Can't we, Adèle?"

The girl mumbled a French curse under her breath, but the rest of us pretended not to hear her.

True to her word, Diana was upstairs and back down in a flash. "Frankie is awake and chatting with Leah. They are like old friends!"

With a sigh of relief, I asked Edward to pass around the Christmas gifts.

Of course, Adèle ripped through the paper like a woodpecker demolishes an old tree. She laid claim to a remarkable collection of new hair ribbons, a rabbit muff, a new silk scarf in a pastel pink, several books, a new French doll with eyes that opened and closed, dresses for the doll, a trunk for the doll's wardrobe, and a large bag of sweeties. Mrs. Wallander had also knitted several pairs of tights that would be welcome during cold weather, but Adèle failed to see their purpose.

She would, I thought to myself. Once there's snow on the ground and she wants to go outside and play!

The *coup de grâce* was a red sledge, with gleaming metal runners that Edward had ordered for her. "There's a marvelous hill on the way to the Harrigans' cottage," he explained. "When the snow freezes, I'll show you how to go coasting down it. You'll never believe how much fun it is. Of course, it's much, much more fun if you share with a friend. Like with Frankie."

Adèle was not entirely convinced this would be enjoyable, but she wisely thanked Monsieur and immediately stuffed her mouth with sweet-ies, while disrobing her new doll.

Diana and Lucy were charmed by the books I'd chosen for them. They even promised to swap them after reading, so they could double their fun. Edward was pleased with his new muffler. He modeled it for us, and everyone remarked on how nicely it had turned out. Most of all, he loved the portrait I'd done of Ned. His voice grew husky as he admired it. "I shall have this framed and keep it in my study. Thank you, little Janet."

"There is more," I said, and I carried over the biggest box. Edward was thrilled with his new boots. Mrs. Fairfax joined us after a suitable interval. I wasn't sure why she had hesitated, and so I whispered, "Why did you not come right away?"

"This is for family," she said.

I felt instantly ashamed. Of all the people in that room, I knew what it was like to be alone in the world. Certainly, the housekeeper could annoy me. Admittedly, she stepped on my toes. But where would she be if not here? Out somewhere in the cold? I could feel pity for the boy upstairs, but not for the woman who had introduced me to my husband?

I could do better and I would. "This is for you," I said. Since she had admired my pearl pin many times, I'd found a similar one, when I was shopping in Millcote. Her breath caught in her throat, as she opened the velveteen jewelry case.

"I am so very pleased," she said. "I never thought to own anything so grand."

"This is also for you," I said. I handed her the gift I'd wrapped in brown paper, the bilberry jam. Mrs. Fairfax received it with an equal portion of delight.

"My favorite! How did you ever?"

I only smiled.

"Jane? You are very naughty. You have opened nothing!" said Edward. He got up and opened a desk drawer. From that, he lifted a large package and carried it to me. I opened the gift to find a soft leather bag cinched closed with drawstrings. Inside was a new set of paints, two new sketchbooks, and a selection of charcoals and pencils. I could not have been more delighted. Now I could discard that tattered muslin sack.

"Jane? I have something for you, too," said Mrs. Fairfax. She opened a bottom door to a bookshelf and withdrew a paper wrapped gift. Inside was a lovely trug, a wooden basket perfect for gathering any variety of natural objects.

Lucy gave me two new dresses, both of the latest fashion and far grander than anything I currently owned. Diana hesitated before handing me a slender package. Inside was a lovely scarf in a pattern such as I have never seen before. Stormy colors of grey, dark blue, and turquoise swirled around elements of yellow-orange and red. "St. John sent his love. This came from a native craftsperson he met on a south sea island. He wanted you to know that it reminded him of you. In particular, he wanted you to know that fabric is silk, and therefore, deceptively strong, while soft and pliable."

Edward took the scarf from my hands. "St. John knows you well," he said, before gently looping the fabric around my neck.

Diana also had two more parcels, one was a book in German and another was a more simple book in Italian. "It's time for you to learn Italian," she said primly. The teacher in her was forever searching for her next student. She continued, "The German book is from Mary. The Italian primer is from me."

CHAPTER 25

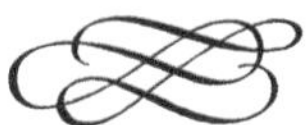

It was eleven o'clock and we were still enjoying our presents in the parlor, when James Harrigan rapped on the front door. The formality of his choice of entrance was not lost on Edward or me. Mrs. Fairfax answered the summons. When we heard the young man's voice, Edward sent me an even look. I knew exactly what he was thinking, as Mrs. Fairfax escorted James into the parlor.

Holding his cap in his hands, James stood at attention. "Squire? Missus? Leah and I were hoping to speak with you, if you can spare a minute."

"Yes, of course," said Edward. "Come in and sit down, James."

Mrs. Fairfax stood on the parlor's threshold. "I'll go get you some refreshments."

"I'll run upstairs and get Leah," said Diana, rising from her chair. "Lucy? Would you and Adèle care to come with me? Adèle, I think you agreed to share your sweets with Frankie, didn't you? I believe there's a gift for him in my room. Shall we give it to him?"

Reluctantly, Adèle stood up. She held her sweeties in a white-knuckle grip "I will not give him *all* the sweeties. Just a few."

"Come along," said Diana, but Adèle danced away from her.

Lucy grabbed Adèle by the hand not holding the sweeties. "Little miss, I would hate to have to take every one of your sweeties away from you, but I shall, if you won't share."

"All right," Adèle snarled, as she stomped out of the room.

"James, please sit down," I said, as I gestured to one of the vacant armchairs. "How are your grandparents?"

"I can't lie, Missus, Squire, not to ye. They seem to have given up on life. They rallied for your party. It was such a gay occasion, how could they not? But I'm thinking they are tired. Like two old clocks winding down, ye see?"

"Edward and I did not realize that Leah was taking your place in the mornings," I said. Their choice of subterfuge was disappointing. I thought that Leah and I were building trust. I wish she would have told me what she was doing!

"Here's hoping ye aren't angry with us," said James, shuffling his feet as he sat in the chair. His hands crumpled and uncrumpled his hat. "We didn't mean no harm by it. She wanted to be with the boy, and there weren't no other way. Not when my grandparents needed someone to stay with them."

Mrs. Fairfax brought in a tea tray and put it on the side table. She'd wisely included slices of ham, bread, cheese, pickles, and a variety of sweet biscuits.

"Please help yourself, James," I said.

Edward added, "We insist. I shall go see to Leah."

Even after Edward left, James didn't move, so I got up and prepared a plate for him. "Here," I said, handing the dish to our guest, along with cutlery and a cloth napkin. "How do you take your tea?"

"With milk, please," he said timidly. I suddenly realized he would never have served himself. He was too shy and too overcome by being here with us in the Manor. I understood his reticence. I could remember when I first arrived at Thornfield Hall, and the place seemed like a palace to me. Edward Rochester had been immensely intimidating. How far we'd come!

Edward held the parlor door open, and Leah walked through. "Leah? Please let me make a plate for you," I said, as she took the armchair next to her husband's. My strategy of fixing a plate seemed to be working for James, as he'd nearly finished all of his food. As I filled a plate with food for Leah, Edward sat down and regarded the young couple thoughtfully.

I knew Leah took her tea with milk and sugar, so after I prepared her plate, I poured a cup for her. "Thank you very much," she said.

"You must be hungry, Leah, as I know you've been up since dawn," said Edward. "We only just realized you were coming over and setting the fires. I wish we'd known!"

"Please, Squire. I hope you are not angry with me." Leah nearly dropped her teacup.

"I am not angry. I only wish I'd known. If so, I could have helped you. That wood can be heavy and hard to carry," said Edward.

"That was my job to do, Squire," said James, "and I didn't mean to shirk it. Leah does such like at the cottage, so apart from having to walk a ways in the cold, it were not so very different than her usual chores."

"You see, sir, we couldn't leave John and Mary alone. Goodie Brown is willing to come, but some days she can't and some she can. Like now. She's there helping out special," and then Leah hesitated, "because we were hoping to talk to ye. Not planning to take much of your time."

She paused and stared at James, as if urging him to speak. But her husband coughed and seemed unable to find the right words. I could almost feel his misery. I felt certain I knew why they were here. They wanted to add Frankie to their family. However, a proposal to take the boy home would be an admission that they had given up on having a child of their own. Could James bring himself to say that? Would such an admission be a slight to his wife?

Leah could not wait any longer for her husband to say his piece. "Squire Rochester? We'd like to take Frankie home with us and raise him as our own."

A silence filled the room. Leah had spoken, but James had not. Did her request accurately represent what James wanted? Edward and I looked to the man for a sign.

"I'd raise him proper like a son," said James, in a voice that was strong and confident. "I'd do my best for him."

My heart caught in my throat. This was such a powerful oath for James to make. It made clear his good intentions. There was only one question left to be answered.

Edward spoke softly, "Then I think we need to talk to Frankie and see whether that would sit well with him or not."

EPILOGUE

January proved a perfect month for having houseguests. Diana and Lucy were gracious visitors, who filled the manor with music and laughter. They got into the habit of taking their breakfast in their rooms, so that Edward and I could have a little time to ourselves in the morning.

The morning of January 20th, we woke up to a deep snowfall. A weak sun glinted off the smooth surface of the soft snow. The air smelt crisp and chilly. At the breakfast table, Edward blinked in the harsh light as he pulled out a chair for me. Before I could get comfortable, Cook came in and held up a staying hand. "Not yet," she said. "Ye can't eat your breakfast yet. I have something I want to show ye both."

Edward shrugged in acquiesce and helped me out of my seat. We followed Cook into the parlor. The stout woman marched over to the crate next to the hearth. With a flourish, she pulled back one of the pieces of blanket that made up Mephisto's bedding.

A litter of four kittens was revealed. Mephisto blinked up at us, as if to say, "This is my Christmas gift to you. It's a little late, but…"

"Oh, my," I said, sinking to my knees so I could admire Mephisto's babies. The four little shapes that were all different in their coloring. There was a calico, a grey and white, a yellow tabby, and a pure black cat like its mother. The tiny babies squirmed around, jockeying to get close to their mother, so they could nurse.

"And all along, I thought the cat was a tom!" I said.

"Nay," said Cook. "I knew all along Mephisto was a girl cat, but it wasn't my place to question ye. I figuring ye had your reasons for naming the cat as ye did and pretending she was a he. She's been fair ready to pop with her babies for some days now. She must have had them last night. Our Mephisto is a proud mother."

I could not help but laugh. Edward shook his head. "That beats all."

Once again, we entered the dining room, expecting to eat our breakfast. In fact, we had just sat down, when James drove up in the donkey cart. As we watched from the window, the young Harrigan lifted first Leah and then Frankie down from the passenger seat.

"Cook? Please send our visitors on in to join us," said Edward.

"As ye wish," the good lady responded. "I'll bring in extra tea and more sliced ham."

"Good morning," said Edward, rising to his feet as the Harrigans walked in.

"We did not mean to interrupt," said James. "We'll go and—"

"Nonsense," said Edward. "I've asked Cook to bring more food."

I got up to give Leah a hug and guide her to a seat. Then I leaned down to speak to the little boy. "Frankie," I said, "please come and sit by me. I'm glad to see you."

Once our guests were made comfortable, I got up to serve Frankie. The child seemed to have grown in the past month, or perhaps he'd simply begun to hold his head up high. I knew from previous conversations with Leah that he was always hungry.

"How are John and Mary?" Edward asked. After I put food in front of Frankie, I fixed a plate for Leah and one for James. Edward poured our guests cups of tea.

"Mary and John are happy to have a child to love," said Leah. "I do believe they're better now than they've been in a long time."

James agreed, "Frankie keeps them busy at the cottage. He talks to John. He plays cards with Mary—"

"He helps me with the chickens, the ducks, and the geese," inserted Leah.

"I get the eggs," said Frankie. "You have to be careful that you don't hurt the birds when you take them, but I am. Very careful. And they know I'll feed them after."

"He also helps me when I cook," said Leah. "I plan to teach him to spin wool."

"I might learn to knit," said Frankie, with a serious expression on his face. "Then we would never need socks."

We all laughed at that.

"Frankie was hoping that Adèle might want to go sledging," said John. "I built a sledge for Frankie, and I know Adèle has hers. The snow is fresh and soft."

"Why don't you run upstairs and ask Adèle if she would like to go sledging with you?" I asked the boy, after noticing he'd cleaned his plate.

Frankie turned a sweet face to James and Leah. "May I be excused?"

"Yes, you may," said Leah, trying to hide a smile.

As his footsteps faded in the hallway, I said, "He looks completely different. That child is growing, and his cheeks have color!"

"Did you know the boy can read?" asked James, with a tinge of pride about him. "Aye, he can. Seems his mother was an educated woman. He can do simple sums, too. Ye should hear him read to Grandpapa. It definitely keeps the old man's attention."

"Frankie pretended not to know how to read at first," explained Leah, "because he was afraid. He thought you might send him back to London. He worried that if you knew he could read, you might sell him into an apprenticeship."

"Poor lamb," I said. It was doubtful that we'd ever know the half of Frankie's worries.

"We should like to repay you for the food Frankie took," said Leah. "He wasn't happy to be thieving, but he didn't know what else to do."

Edward quickly waved away her offer. "That

has long been settled. It's not up for discussion. I am delighted with how this has turned out, as I can see you are getting along splendidly."

"He is our son," said Leah. "He's begun calling me Mama and he calls James Papa."

"But that is not what we came to tell you," interjected James. "We wanted you to know that Frankie is very good with animals. In fact, he drove the donkey cart today. Growing up on a farm, he's more comfortable with them than with people. So, there's no reason for you to sell Mesrour. Not unless you want to. Frankie is learning to drive the goats and cows out to pasture. As you heard, he's good with the ducks, geese, and chickens. With the boy's help, I should be able to exercise your stallion, Sir. Of course," and James reddened, "if you want to sell your horse, that's certainly your business, but…"

"That's splendid news," said Edward. "I still think we should hire a manservant to help around the Manor, but from what you've told me, I agree. There's no reason to find a new home for Mesrour. Speaking of animals, we had a surprise this morning. Come and see."

Edward led us into the parlor. Leah and I walked arm in arm, whilst James tagged along behind. "Mephisto is the proud mother of four kittens," said my husband, tugging back the blanket to reveal the squirming babies. "Of course, it is too soon to give them away, but when they are ready, do you think Frankie would like one?"

"He would be delighted," said Leah.

James smiled. "Squire? You keep enlarging my family, and I can't thank you enough."

Thus, it happened that we saw proof that James and Leah Harrigan had bonded with their new son, Frankie. Their visit that day erased any lingering worries we might have had. It was clear that the boy had fit into their lives like a foot slips into a well-worn shoe. In fact, the child was supplying them with as much or more than they were giving him. Frankie had brought a new zest for life to John and Mary. He'd freed up time for both James and Leah. And of course, he filled a hole in their lives, as they had wanted a child to love for so very long.

Later that evening, I found Edward standing in front of the window in his study. He was staring out at the winter landscape, a stark picture in tones of black, grey, and white. The trees were skeletal hands appealing to a dark and gloomy sky. A full moon provided enough light to render distinctive the drifts of snow that surrounded Ferndean Manor. The air was scented with the wet smell of snow.

Edward did not hear me approach. "Sir?" When I slipped my arm around my husband's waist, he pulled me closer to him. After planting a kiss on the top of my head, Edward spoke slowly, "How wondrous life can be. One good deed—my purchase of a trunk for my darling—begat an opportunity for a boy to escape life in a debtors' prison. Furthermore, thanks to the fortuitous timing of his adventure, this manor was able to provide him with the sort of care he needed to be brought back to good health and ultimately to deposit him in the bosom of a loving family."

"And so," I continued, "the greatest gift of all is the simplest: it is love."

~The End~

~

How the Georgians Celebrated Christmas

The holiday, as we know it, has changed a great deal, since the 1800s. For the sake of this story, I've encouraged Jane and Edward to open a few gifts early, but otherwise I've tried to follow my research.

Christmas Eve – Putting up greenery before Christmas Eve is to invite bad luck, so this task was saved until December 24th. Although we've all been told that Prince Albert (Queen Victoria's husband) started the tradition of decorated Christmas trees, it was actually Queen Charlotte (the wife of George III), who first introduced a Christmas tree at a party. A yew tree was decorated with fruits, sweets, toys, and small candles.

Christmas Day – This was the day for people to feast, and of course, you couldn't have a proper sit-down Georgian feast unless you are being waited on by servants! So, it was considered a normal workday for servants.

St. Stephen's Day (Boxing Day) – If Christmas falls on a Friday or a Saturday, Boxing Day would be celebrated on the following Monday, because Boxing Day is always on a weekday. This was the time when wealthy landowners "boxed up" leftovers and gave gifts to their servants. The box would be sealed, and inside there would certainly be money, and sometimes gifts of useful items, such as fabric for making clothes and/or tools.

New Year's Day (January 1) – This was the day for opening gifts, although there are some indications that people were beginning to do gift giving on Christmas Day.

THE JANE EYRE CHRONICLES

Death of a Schoolgirl: Book #1 in The Jane Eyre Chronicles

Death of a Dowager: Book #2 in The Jane Eyre Chronicles

Christmas at Ferndean Manor: Book #3 in The Jane Eyre Chronicles (2021)

Death of a Gentleman: Book #4 in The Jane Eyre Chronicles (Coming Soon)

The Jane Eyre Chronicles Series
https://amzn.to/39IliwT

A SPECIAL GIFT FOR YOU

I am deeply appreciative of all my readers, and so I have a special gift for you. It's a full-length digital book called ***Bad, Memory, Album.*** Just go here and tell me where to send your digital book https://dl.bookfunnel.com/jwu6iipe1g.

All best always,

Joanna

For any book to succeed, reviews are essential. If you enjoyed this book please leave a review on Amazon. A sentence or two can make all the difference! Please leave a review of ***Christmas at Ferndean Manor***

About the author...
Joanna Campbell Slan

Joanna is a *New York Times* and a *USA Today* bestselling author who has written more than 40 books, including both fiction and non-fiction works. She was one of the early Chicken Soup for the Soul authors, and her stories appear in five of those *New York Times* bestselling books. Her first non-fiction book, ***Using Stories and Humor: Grab Your Audience*** (Simon & Schuster/Pearson), was endorsed by Toastmasters International, and lauded by Benjamin Netanyahu's speechwriter. She's the author of four mystery series. Her first novel—***Paper, Scissors, Death: Book #1 in the Kiki Lowenstein Mystery Series***—was shortlisted for the Agatha Award. Her first historical mystery —***Death of a Schoolgirl: Book #1 in the Jane Eyre Chronicles***—won the Daphne du Maurier Award of Excellence. Her contemporary series set in Florida continues this year with ***Ruff Justice Book #5 in the Cara Mia Delgatto Mystery Series.*** Her fantasy thriller series starts with ***Sherlock Holmes and the Giant Sumatran Rat***.

In addition to writing fiction, Joanna edits the

Happy Homicides Anthologies and has begun the Dollhouse Décor & More series of "how to" books for dollhouse miniaturists.

Joanna independently published ***I'm Too Blessed to be Depressed*** back in 2004 when she was working as a motivational speaker. She sold more than 34,000 copies of that title. Since then she's gone on to independently publish a full-color book, ***The Best of British Scrapbooking,*** numerous digital books, and coloring books. Her book ***Scrapbook Storytelling*** sold 120,000 copies.

She's been an Amazon Bestselling Author too many times to count and has been included in the ranks of Amazon's Top 100 Mystery Authors.

A former talk show host and sought-after motivational speaker, Joanna has spoken to small and large (1000+) groups on four continents. *Sharing Ideas Magazines* named her "one of the top 25 speakers in the world."

When she isn't banging away at the keyboard, Joanna keeps busy walking her Havanese puppy Jax. An award-winning miniaturist, Joanna builds dollhouses, dolls, and furniture from scratch. She's also an accredited teacher of Zentangle®. Her husband, David, owns Steinway Piano Gallery-DC and five other Steinway piano showrooms.

Contact Joanna at JCSlan@JoannaSlan.com.

Follow her on social media by going here
https://www.linktr.ee/JCSlan

www.ingramcontent.com/pod-product-compliance
Lightning Source LLC
Chambersburg PA
CBHW060816310726
48980CB00002B/308

* 9 7 8 0 9 6 6 4 7 0 7 6 5 *